P9-DWF-673

The Singularity Race

Books by Mark de Castrique

The Buryin' Barry Series
Dangerous Undertaking
Grave Undertaking
Foolish Undertaking
Final Undertaking
Fatal Undertaking
Risky Undertaking

The Sam Blackman Series
Blackman's Coffin
The Fitzgerald Ruse
The Sandburg Connection
A Murder in Passing
A Specter of Justice

Other Novels
The 13th Target
Double Cross of Time
The Singularity Race

Young Adult Novels
A Conspiracy of Genes
Death on a Southern Breeze

The Singularity Race

Mark de Castrique

Poisoned Pen Press

First Edition 2016

10 9 8 7 6 5 4 3 2 1

Library of Congress Catalog Card Number: 2016935342

ISBN: 9781464205972 Hardcover
9781464205996 Trade Paperback

Poisoned Pen Press
6962 E. First Ave., Ste. 103
Scottsdale, AZ 85251
www.poisonedpenpress.com
info@poisonedpenpress.com

Printed in the United States of America

For Linda

We have the opportunity in the decades ahead to make major strides in addressing the grand challenges of humanity. AI (artificial intelligence) will be the pivotal technology in achieving this progress.

—Ray Kurzweil, Director of Engineering, GOOGLE

The development of full artificial intelligence could spell the end of the human race. Humans, who are limited by slow biological evolution, couldn't compete and would be superseded.

—Stephen Hawking, Theoretical Physicist

Prologue

FBI Special Agent Kim Woodson kicked the wipers up a notch in a futile effort to clear the falling snow off her windshield. The storm was supposed to have been rain, but a five-degree temperature drop turned the predicted New Year's Eve drizzle into heavy, wet flakes that refused to blow off the glass.

"Global warming, my ass," she muttered to herself.

"In one-half mile, take exit 11 on the right, then turn right on King Hill Road." The smooth, dispassionate female voice sounded above the slap of the wipers and Kim reflexively hit the turn signal.

The GPS had been Kim's sole companion on the arduous two-and-a-half-hour drive from Boston, the extra thirty minutes a result of the deteriorating weather. She'd stopped only once at a rest area on I-89 North to text that she was running late. The immediate reply,

> No problem. Just get here when you can.
> Meet behind the barn.

Kim eased her Toyota Rav4 SUV onto the local road and followed her virtual guide's directions into the village of New London, New Hampshire.

Unlike Manhattan and Boston, where revelers gathered in Times Square or swarmed the First Night events on Boston Common and in Boston Harbor, Main Street in New London was as quiet as a tomb. The only motion came from the snow swirling through the cones of light created by the street lamps.

"Happy New Year," Kim whispered. "Almost three hours to midnight and this place is deader than a ghost town."

Not that she would have done anything livelier than drive down a deserted street on New Year's Eve. Her boyfriend had broken up with her the first of December and she had no date. She told herself if he hadn't broken it off, she would have. Her first love was her job. And when the text message,

> Been approached. Nine tonight. 84 Main Street, New London, New Hampshire,

had chimed on her phone at six forty-five, she'd grabbed her laptop and her Glock 23, and ventured into the night.

"In two-tenths of a mile, you will arrive at your destination," the GPS said. "It is on the left."

Kim checked the rearview mirror. No one was following. She knew she should have alerted a colleague about what she was doing, but it was New Year's Eve and tracking someone down could have triggered the order she wanted to avoid: "Wait for backup."

She passed the town square on the right with its bandstand covered in snow. A public library was on the left. *Meet behind the barn?* she thought. She'd only programmed the street address Professor Walter Milton had supplied in his first text. Was there a farm on Main Street in this little town? Kim assumed the MIT professor might have a home here and was spending the holidays away from the hustle and bustle of Boston.

She'd met him only once, the week before Christmas when she and Special Agent Ron Gibbons had interviewed him on campus about the disappearance of his friend, Dr. Alexander Kaminsky. Milton was a neuroscientist in the Department of Brain and Cognitive Sciences. Kaminsky was a researcher at MIT's Computer Science and Artificial Intelligence Laboratory, and when Kaminsky didn't show for a scheduled lunch at the MIT faculty club, Milton went to his office.

An assistant said Kaminsky had left around eleven carrying a suitcase. Kaminsky explained that he'd been called out of town but would return the next day. There had been no mention of a lunch.

Milton had told Kim and Gibbons how he'd asked the assistant for a pen and a sheet of paper so that he could leave Kaminsky a note.

Milton had said, "I wrote, 'How can you work on artificial intelligence when you don't exhibit any real intelligence yourself?' I found Kaminsky's office unlocked and I entered, planning to leave the wisecrack on his desk. Instead, I discovered a plain white envelope lying on the blotter with my name scrawled across it in Kaminsky's barely legible handwriting. Inside, I read one single sentence. 'If you're approached, hear them out.' Then I noticed the hard drive had been pulled from his computer, and several file cabinet drawers were extended at varying lengths with most of the current folders missing. Something's happened. He would have told me if he were going away."

The FBI had been called when Kaminsky didn't return after two days. Most disturbing was the apparent deletion of all the confidential research and program data dealing with Kaminsky's work. MIT's supposedly insurmountable firewalls had been penetrated like soft butter.

The fact that Kaminsky received funding from various government agencies including the Pentagon raised eyebrows in Washington, D.C. The order was sent to have field agents Woodson and Gibbons make the preliminary investigation.

Preliminary investigation, Kim thought, as she neared her destination. Bureau-speak for the right to yank back the entire case and hand it off to senior suits or computer tech specialists. She'd urged Milton to contact her directly if anything broke. She wanted to secure her place on the team. Let them reassign that stiff Gibbons. He was nothing more than a lawyer with a badge and a gun.

Her headlights caught a large sign on the left. The words NEW LONDON BARN PLAYHOUSE encircled a horse's head wearing a straw hat. A white board mounted on the front of a red barn held interchangeable red letters. Instead of promoting a production, it read, "See You This Summer!" Her destination wasn't a farm barn but a summer stock theater, a place guaranteed to be deserted the last night of December.

A side street ran along the length of the rambling red structure. Kim made the turn and saw an empty area behind the barn that had to be for parking. Her headlights revealed no tire marks cutting across the newly fallen snow.

She looped her SUV around the lot until she was halfway back to the side road, yet still shielded from Main Street by the barn. She braked to a stop, facing outward in case she needed a quick getaway, and then she killed the lights. She left the engine and the heater running.

Kim took her cell phone from the cradle mounted on the dashboard and checked for messages. No new texts. She'd managed to shave some minutes off the arrival estimate she'd given Milton. She preferred being first at the rendezvous point. When Professor Milton arrived, she'd instruct him to get in her car where she could use her phone to record whatever information he had and review the case notes on her laptop.

She reached under her seat, pulled her Glock free of its holster and set it in the pocket of the driver's door. She felt confident it was all the backup she needed.

The snow fell faster, the flakes smaller and dryer as the temperature continued to drop. Kim powered up her laptop on the passenger seat and waited for the FBI logo to appear. Then she entered her security codes and called up the working files she and Agent Gibbons had compiled. The first question on her mind was who had approached Milton? The question that bubbled up from her subconscious was why had he texted rather than phoned?

Suddenly, her computer screen went white and three words appeared in fat black letters: sercxante kaj forviŝo.

"What the hell?" Kim muttered.

Before she could make another keystroke, a hard double rap sounded on the driver's window behind her.

She turned, surprised that Milton had somehow arrived without her realizing it.

Milton's face wasn't pressed against the glass. There was no face at all.

Kim stared into a black suppressor mounted on the barrel of a Sig Sauer P229 semi-automatic.

The sound of the shot would be no more than a cough in the wind.

Chapter One

Over four years later—

Rusty Mullins handed his parking credentials and Prime Protection photo ID to the uniformed security guard at the entrance of the JW Marriott's parking garage. The officer studied Mullins' photograph like he was looking for a message spelled out in grains of dust. Then he held it close to the flesh and blood original.

"You going blind, Jake?" Mullins asked.

"Nah. I've got perfect vision. That's why I can't believe it's you. You've gotten so damned old."

Mullins laughed and snatched back his creds. Jake Murphy was a retired Capitol Hill cop and the two men had frequently crossed paths during Mullins' Secret Service stint with the presidential detail.

"You're one to talk," Mullins said. "My hair might be gray but at least it's still stuck on my head."

The bald guard tapped his temple. "It's what's on the inside that counts."

"Oh, you can count now?" Mullins drove on before his friend could have the last word.

He found the spaces that the hotel had reserved for his team and parked beside a black Chevy Tahoe. Although Mullins was an hour early, his boss had still beaten him to the assignment.

Before getting out of the Prius, he checked his surroundings, then slid his Glock out of its holster, chambered a round, and returned it under his left arm. He flipped his windshield visor down and angled its courtesy mirror until he could see his face. No food on his chin, nothing stuck between his teeth. He eyed his hair. It was definitely grayer. Approaching fifty, Mullins conceded that soon only old photographs would be proof his head had once been rusty red.

He tilted the mirror to the knot in his navy blue tie. He tightened and centered it, always the last thing he did before "showtime," as he liked to call it. Not showtime for him, but for the person whose life would be in his hands.

He stepped out of the car and buttoned his suit coat to ensure the shoulder holster wouldn't be seen. As he pushed through the revolving door, he reviewed the key details from the briefing the day before.

Prime Protection had been contracted to provide personal security for participants in a two-day symposium at the JW Marriott on Pennsylvania Avenue. Sponsored in cooperation with Georgetown University, the University of Maryland, and Johns Hopkins University, the event featured scientists and researchers from around the world who worked in the fields of computer engineering, neuroscience, and bio-technology. Mullins didn't understand the content, just that the three speakers tonight were tops in their respective fields. Someone on the organizing committee felt the three were more than preeminent scientists. They were potential targets.

In addition to standard hotel security, each speaker would be accompanied by an armed bodyguard while moving through the public areas of the hotel. Registration had been required to attend the evening's banquet in the Grand Ballroom, a more than 36,000-square-foot space capable of feting over 1,100 guests. The three scientists would then appear on a panel discussing how their areas of research were merging. Mullins would be with a Dr. Oskar Brecht from Germany.

Mullins had scanned his bio and knew Brecht held an endowed chair at the Interdisciplinary Center for Scientific Computing at the Ruprecht-Karls University of Heidelberg. The confidential background dossier included the note that Oskar Brecht had an eye for the fräuleins. Just what Mullins didn't need—to be a former Secret Service agent caught up in an international call-girl scandal. He would make sure Herr Brecht remained protected from all dangers, lethal and lustful.

Mullins identified himself at the registration desk and picked up a card key to the suite Prime Protection was using for onsite operations. He rode to the twelfth floor, nodded to the guard positioned adjacent to the elevator doors, and flashed his ID. "All quiet?"

"Yes, sir. The German arrived about thirty minutes ago."

"With a new lady friend?"

The guard smiled. "No. Just his security escort from the airport. He's your package now."

"And the others?"

"Sitting tight." The guard checked his watch. "They expect to be contacted at six-thirty to go down for cocktails. That's in ninety minutes."

"How about 1247?"

"Your man's been there since four."

"Thanks. I'll check in and then move around a bit. The rest of the team should be here by six if not before."

Suite 1247 was located in the middle of the hall, equidistant to the rooms of the three scientists. Mullins rapped twice on the door.

"If you've got a key, use it," came the reply.

Mullins placed the black passkey against the lock pad and the bolt clicked open.

Ted Lewison lounged on a small sofa, his stocking feet resting on a glass-top coffee table, his dark suit coat and empty shoulder holster draped over the back of a chair. A Colt M1911 semi-automatic lay on the cushion beside him. The pistol was a holdover preference from Lewison's days as an MP.

The six-foot-three president of Prime Protection dropped his feet to the floor, sat erect, and placed a half-empty glass of Perrier beside the bottle on the table.

He gestured to an adjacent chair. "Sit down. There have been some changes."

"Aren't there always?" Mullins sat.

"You want something from the minibar?"

"No. Bring me up to speed. Then I want to do my own walk-through."

Lewison nodded. He expected nothing less of his top employee.

Ted Lewison valued professionalism and hard work. He'd escaped the poverty of his neighborhood in Baltimore by joining the U.S. Army straight out of high school. He'd done his twenty, mostly as an MP and later as a chief warrant officer. He'd founded Prime Protection, hired ex-military, and nurtured his fledgling company into the top personal security firm in D.C. But along the way, he'd come to realize the Secret Service instilled traits beyond the normal skill sets of law enforcement. Rusty Mullins always had a plan and several backup options. That's why nothing seemed to rattle the man. And Mullins could read a face like no one else Lewison had ever met. When you had only seconds to identify a potential assailant, that gift meant the difference between life and death.

They worked together so well that Lewison didn't think of Mullins as an employee. More like a brother from another mother, and he knew he was damned fortunate that Mullins had returned to work after his leave of absence, a leave of absence following Mullins' rogue operation that prevented a terrorist assault on the Federal Reserve and garnered a personal commendation from the President of the United States. Lewison knew Mullins could work anywhere he wanted, and he intended to make sure that place continued to be his company.

"All right, Grandpa," Lewison said. "First, you're not on Brecht."

FIRST LAW: A robot may not injure a human being or, through inaction, allow a human being to come to harm.

SECOND LAW: A robot must obey orders given it by human beings except where such orders would conflict with the First Law.

THIRD LAW: A robot must protect its own existence as long as such protection does not conflict with the First or Second Law.

—Isaac Asimov's *Three Laws of Robotics*

Mullins cocked his head, weighing the meaning of the "Grandpa" remark. "What? The guy thinks I'm too old to keep up with him?"

"No. Your talents are needed for Lisa Li."

Mullins couldn't mask his surprise. "Why? I thought Nicole was on her. Am I supposed to clear the restroom if she wants to pee?"

"How old's your grandson now?"

"Three."

"Then it might be a stretch for you."

Mullins stared at his boss. He didn't know what was going on with the strange assortment of unrelated questions other than Lewison was amusing himself. He refused to give the man the satisfaction of another question.

"Lisa Li showed up with her nephew," Lewison said. "He's seven. Nicole has as much experience with a seven-year-old boy as a virgin has with a brothel."

"So, I'm babysitting?"

"Come on, Rusty. We're all babysitting. The kid's here, the situation has changed, and I need you to cover both of them."

"The boy's coming to the banquet?"

"Yes. I'm told he's well behaved. He'll sit with Dr. Li and the other scientists at the head table. Take up your position wherever you think best." Lewison rose from the sofa and walked in his stocking feet to a desk by the window. He picked up a manila envelope. "Here's more background on her."

"Then who's covering Brecht?"

"I'm putting Nicole on him. I'll keep the Pakistani, Ahmad."

"Brecht could try to put himself on Nicole, and you wind up with a castrated scientist."

Lewison laughed. "You've got a point." He tossed the envelope into Mullins' lap. "Look at Li's background while you've got the chance. Maybe you'll find something in common to talk about."

"Yeah. Probably hemorrhoids. We can compare notes about pains in our asses we have known, present company included." Mullins flipped open the clasp and dumped the envelope's contents into his palm. On top were three tickets. He stared at them, speechless.

Lewison grinned. "Did I mention that Li and her nephew are baseball fans?"

Mullins fanned out the tickets. "But these are for tomorrow afternoon. What about the symposium?"

"Li's not on the program then. Her employer made the arrangements. The three of you will be behind home plate at the Washington Nationals opening game. Unless you'd rather keep your original assignment?"

"I couldn't do that to poor Nicole. She hates baseball."

Lewison clapped Mullins on the shoulder. "You're all heart."

Mullins stuck the tickets in his pocket. "Be sure and put that in my personnel file."

Chapter Two

"Who is it?" The soft voice asked the question in response to the double knock on the hotel door.

"Russell Mullins with Prime Protection." He held his photo ID next to his face in front of the peep hole.

The door opened immediately. A slim, attractive Chinese woman stood just inside. She wore a dark blue dress with a conservative neckline. A single strand of pearls was her only jewelry.

Mullins looked beyond her to where a boy sat on the suite's sofa, his attention fully focused on his iPad. He was dressed in a white shirt, red tie, and blue knee pants. The U.S. color scheme was topped off by a red Washington Nationals baseball cap pushed back far enough to reveal thick black hair.

Mullins knew from the background dossier that the child was named Wang Ping, the son of Dr. Lisa Li's sister. In the U.S. he was called Peter Wang, shifting his surname to secondary position to avoid confusing Americans unfamiliar with the Chinese custom of surname first. Mullins had read that Lisa Li's Chinese name was actually Li Li, meaning beautiful. His gaze returned to her. She lived up to the description.

"You shouldn't open the door so fast," he said gently. "I don't think you checked my credentials first."

"I was expecting you."

"Which is why someone would have claimed to be me."

She dropped her head. "I'm sorry."

"No need to be sorry. It's about being safe. Are you ready?"

She sighed. "Not really. I'm not good at cocktail talk." She glanced over her shoulder. "I thought maybe we could wait till closer to the dinner. Peter will be lost in a sea of grownups wandering around holding wineglasses."

Mullins wasn't good at cocktail talk either, and the less time Dr. Li spent in a public crowd, the safer she would be.

"Then I'll wait here in the hall," he said. "Just let me know when you want to go to dinner."

"I've had enough guards at my door. Please come in."

Mullins caught a subtle bitterness in her tone. But nothing in Li's background hinted at any trouble with the Chinese government or university officials. She had been an outstanding researcher and theorist, specializing in the neuroscience of subconscious brain activity. She had married an older professor whose field had been computer database management, a critical area for seeking innovative and more efficient ways for processors to access and make connections with data and its interpretation and extrapolation. Way over Mullins' head. The layman's note he had read in her dossier compared it to building more neurons and synapses in a human brain.

Lisa Li was forty, although she looked younger. She had a fifteen-year-old son in school in Beijing. Nearly eight years ago, her scientist husband had been killed in a freak accident in his computer lab when a malfunctioning circuit sent lethal power to an electronic security keypad. Li withdrew from the public eye for nearly a year, evidently too grief-stricken to continue her work.

She was lured back into active research by a Chinese company named Jué Dé.

The English translation was "to think" or "to sense." The company was so successful, it had opened an artificial intelligence lab in Silicon Valley. Dr. Li had obtained the clearance from both the Chinese and American governments to transfer her work to the new facility.

The nephew had come to visit his aunt, and, thanks to Jué Dé, to take in a baseball game. Mullins didn't know what Jué

Dé sold, but with three tickets in his pocket, he was inclined to buy it.

"Peter, say hello to Mr. Mullins," Li said. "He's going to be our guide while we're in Washington."

Guide was probably a better euphemism for a seven-year-old than saying guard. Mullins played along.

Peter Wang looked up. "Hello." He immediately returned his attention to the iPad.

"I've got a hat just like that," Mullins said. "So does my grandson."

The boy studied Mullins more carefully. "You go to ball games?" His English was excellent.

"Yes. Or watch them on TV. My grandson's only three. He just likes his hat. Tomorrow, you and I and your aunt will go to the game."

Peter's eyes widened. He bounced up and down on the sofa. "Really? Can I go? Can I go?"

Evidently Li hadn't told him. Mullins hoped he hadn't spoken too soon.

Dr. Li raised her palm and the child immediately calmed. "If you behave and do everything Mr. Mullins instructs you to do."

"I will. I promise."

Mullins stepped closer to the boy. "How did you learn to speak English so well?"

Peter shrugged. "I've studied it for years."

"But you're only seven."

"Seven and a half. And I started when I was three," he explained, and flipped the iPad around to show Mullins the screen. "The Nats lineup for tomorrow. I'm still working on the stats, but I think the Nats are a two-run favorite."

Mullins stared at the kid. If he had his aunt's brains, then before he was twenty he'd be either a World Series team manager or a multimillion-dollar bookie. "Two runs sound good to me," Mullins said. "Who's starting?"

"Fernandez. And the temperature's supposed to be above twenty-six."

"Twenty-six?"

Peter seemed confused by Mullins' question. Then he smiled. "Sorry. Celsius." He squinted his eyes shut and calculated. "Eighty Fahrenheit. Fernandez pitches his best games when the temperature goes above eighty."

"Of course," Mullins said, as if it had slipped his mind. He wouldn't have thought to connect temperature to a pitcher's performance. It dawned on him that he should have waited in the hall rather than prove to himself he was the dumbest one in the room.

"You and Mr. Mullins can talk baseball tomorrow," Li said. "Take off your hat and go to the bathroom. Mr. Mullins won't want to have to escort you to the restroom once we're downstairs."

Peter turned off his iPad and did as he was told.

"I'll wait in the hall," Mullins said.

◇◇◇

Mullins stood against the wall and watched the diners eat their way through a three-course meal. His stomach growled, but it would have to go unsatisfied until he was off-duty.

Dr. Li and her nephew ate at a round table about twenty feet away. The boy kept looking at Mullins as if hoping he would come sit and talk baseball. Li, unfortunately, had been placed beside the amorous Dr. Brecht who was leaning so close to her that he could have used her silverware.

Mullins shifted his gaze across the banquet hall to the opposite wall. Nicole Parsons stood alert, her eyes constantly moving. Ted Lewison was stationed at the main entrance where he was near the three other Prime Protection employees located in the outside corridors. Their job was to scan all approaching individuals and give warning of anything suspicious. All six were tied into wireless communication.

Mullins paid particular attention to the waitstaff. In his walk-through before escorting Dr. Li and her nephew, he had gone through all the connecting hallways, memorizing shortcuts for exiting and also potential places where an outsider might breach security, especially between the kitchen and the ballroom. That was why he'd picked a spot nearest the primary access door for the meal delivery.

The dinner service had progressed to the removal of the main course in preparation for dessert and coffee.

"I just got word we're to move our people onto the stage for the discussion." Ted Lewison's voice crackled in Mullins' ear. "They're forgoing dessert, so let's escort them now. Nicole, I'll take Brecht and his international hands. You stay with Dr. Ahmad."

"International hands?" the woman asked.

Mullins groaned. "You had to ask, Nicole?"

"Yeah." Lewison laughed. "Russian hands and Roman fingers."

The lights went out. A collective gasp rose from the crowd. A few emergency fixtures came on, providing just enough illumination to turn everyone into gray shapes. Waiters froze in place. Then Mullins saw several men moving forward from the rear.

"Lewison! Coming from your back." He barked the warning into his lapel mike and then turned his priority to his charge. He ran to Dr. Li. "You and Peter come with me."

"Oh, it's just a power outage," Brecht said. He grasped Li's wrist. "We should wait rather than stumble around in the dark."

Mullins reached down and broke the man's hold. He practically lifted Lisa Li from her chair. Then he shouted in the German's face, "You and Dr. Ahmad do what she says." He pointed to Nicole who had just run up to the table. "Don't wait for Lewison. Move them now."

Two muffled pops sounded from the middle of the room. Mullins instantly recognized suppressed gunshots. "Now!" he shouted.

The room erupted in screams.

Pushing Li and her nephew in front of him, Mullins hurried to the service door. He knew if he could get them to the kitchen, he should either be able to exit to a loading dock or escape through a service elevator to a safe section of the hotel.

He glanced over his shoulder. Nicole and the two other scientists had not followed as quickly as he wanted. More shots came as the door slammed behind him. All he could do was keep moving.

The blackout wasn't localized to the ballroom. Peter Wang stumbled against a tray of dishes that had been stacked on a rolling cart. Plates clattered on the floor.

"Sorry," the boy cried.

"It's okay. Keep going."

"Let them take me," Li pleaded. "But don't let them take Peter."

"No one's taking anyone." Mullins urged them forward. "The kitchen's just ahead. You'll be safe there."

An emergency light burned in the ceiling beside double doors. Their upper halves were windowed to enable the staff to see if anyone was on the other side before pushing it open.

"Hold up," Mullins whispered. "Let me go first. Put Peter behind you and then wait against the wall until I say it's clear." He drew his Glock and moved ahead of them, stepping to the left side of the door. He slowly pushed it inward with his left hand, leading with the Glock in his right.

The large industrial kitchen was deserted, the workers having evacuated in search of a lighted area. Mullins turned his head to the hall. "All clear. Come on."

A muffled cry greeted him. He retreated through the door to see a man pulling Li back, his arm around her neck in a choke hold.

"Mr. Mullins," her nephew cried, and he kicked the man's shin as hard as he could.

The assailant swatted at the boy with his other hand, a hand wielding a pistol. Then he raised the gun toward Mullins.

Mullins flattened against the wall as the muzzle flashed. He felt a rip through his shoulder, but the shooter had turned away just enough to increase the angle between his head and Dr. Li's.

Mullins fired.

The forty-five-caliber slug smashed through the man's forehead. He dropped to the floor.

Dr. Li tumbled forward. Mullins tried to catch her, but his left arm could only cushion her as they both fell into the kitchen. Peter scrambled after them.

"Stay down," Mullins ordered. He felt blood pooling beneath him. He looked for the darkest corner.

"You're hurt," Li whispered.

"You and Peter crawl up under the work sinks over there." He gestured with his gun. "Don't make a sound."

Mullins held his position until they disappeared into the shadows. His shoulder throbbed like someone had dropped a burning ember on it. He edged closer to Li and the boy where he had a clear shooting angle on all three doorways. *Ten minutes,* he thought. *If I can just hold out ten minutes, surely Lewison, the team, and hotel security will have ferreted out this scum.*

"Mullins!"

He recognized Nicole's voice. Her shout came through the door they'd entered.

"We're here. Come in slowly." Mullins didn't take the chance that she was held hostage and forced to call for him.

The lights came back to a brightness rivaling an operating room. Nicole pushed through the door, her gun leading the way. Her eyes went first to the blood glistening bright red on the tile floor. She followed the trail to where Mullins lay prone in shooting position. Her face paled.

"We're clear, Mullins." Her lower lip trembled. "But Lewison's dead. So are Brecht and Ahmad."

Lisa Li sobbed and Nicole spotted her and her nephew huddled beneath the sink.

"They're safe?"

"Yeah." His own voice sounded far away.

"Man down in the kitchen," Nicole barked into her lapel mike. "Man down in the kitchen. Get a medic here now!"

The gun slipped from Mullins' hand. He felt someone crawl next to him. He thought it was Nicole.

"Mr. Mullins. Please don't die."

No, not Nicole. Not the scientist either.

"I won't," he whispered to the boy. "We've got a ball game to see."

Chapter Three

Robert Brentwood's cell phone vibrated for the fourth time in three minutes. He glanced down at his notes for a graceful way to shorten his remarks without slighting the expectations of his audience.

The annual dinner of the Rutherford County Chamber of Commerce had been squeezed into his busy schedule nine months ago, and the gala had sold out when he'd agreed to be the keynote speaker.

His appearance was calculated politics, especially since not only the local business leaders attended, but also the North Carolina governor and speaker of the state house, who were anxious for a photo op with billionaire Brentwood. His high-tech data storage facility covered more than twenty-five acres of previously undeveloped county land and promised good jobs and the economic revitalization of a region that had seen the textile and furniture industries bolt to the foreign lands of cheap labor.

Brentwood stepped from behind the podium. "In short, ladies and gentlemen, the genie is out of the bottle, and super computing is and will continue to be forever entwined with our human species. I'm proud that Cumulus Cognitive Connections, Rutherford County, and the great state of North Carolina are visionary partners. We not only have a bright future, but we will create that bright future together. Members of the chamber, Governor Montgomery, and Speaker Prescott, I salute you."

He started applauding. Five seconds at the most, he thought. One. Two. Three.

The governor stood, clapping as he reciprocated Brentwood's tribute. The whole room joined him, and the applause rose into a standing ovation that Brentwood engineered through his feigned humility.

He bowed. *Thank you, Dad*, he thought. He'd seen his father, Rex Brentwood, use the trick countless times. It was one of the few things of value he'd learned from the cold bastard. Brentwood waved and left the stage.

The president of the chamber of commerce met him at the side steps. "Fabulous, Robert. Just fabulous."

Brentwood patted the gushing man on the back. "We couldn't have done it without you." He felt his phone vibrate. "Excuse me. Need to make a pit stop. Back in a moment." He hurried out the nearest door of the country club ballroom and headed for the men's room.

Once inside, he walked the length of the stalls, glancing under the doors for shoes. The place was empty. He figured he had only a few minutes before the enlarged prostate brigade invaded for their after-dinner pee.

He entered the last stall, closed the door, and sat on the toilet. His phone displayed four missed calls and one text, all from his executive vice president in Washington, D.C. He opened the text.

> "Shooting. Brecht and Ahmad dead. Li safe. Call!!!"

Jesus Christ, he thought. What the hell happened? He texted his driver:

> Service entrance. Now!

Then a text to his Head of External Communications who was still in the ballroom:

> Leaving. Make apologies.

Brentwood exited the clubhouse as a black limousine pulled to the sidewalk. "To the office," he told the driver. "Glass up."

A purr no louder than a kitten's accompanied the ascension of a double pane of glass that acoustically insulated him from the driver. He checked to make sure the intercom was off, and then placed his call.

"What a shit storm!" Ned Farino's voice quivered. Sirens wailed in the background.

"Where are you?"

"In my car at the far end of a parking deck."

"Then tell me what happened."

"There was a blackout just as the three were to start the panel discussion. I was at the back of the room and had given the all-clear to Jenkins."

"We'll get to Jenkins later."

"Five men came in moving rapidly. I thought they were security. Someone tried to stop them and was gunned down. Then all hell broke loose."

"What'd you do?"

"Crawled under the damn table like everyone else. When the lights came on, Brecht and Ahmad were dead. All five assassins were killed and a member of the security team."

"Where was Li?"

"No one knew. Then I heard one of the security team confirm Li had been found alive in the kitchen. Her guard had whisked her away."

Brentwood's mind raced. "And the nephew?"

"He was with her. Also safe."

"Have you heard from Jenkins?"

"Yes. He was in her room. We're going to meet at midnight. The jet's standing by."

Brentwood relaxed. "Keep Jenkins with you. I don't want you without a bodyguard. Until we know what we're up against, we could all be targets."

"That's comforting," Farino said.

Brentwood mulled the word. "Yes, comforting. What was the security guard's name who saved Li?"

"I don't know. They herded us out. The whole complex is a crime scene. Why?"

"Because that guy is now Dr. Li's new best friend."

Farino saw the angle his boss was exploiting. "A way in. We might turn this to our advantage."

"Stay there. See if you can get close to the press. Someone will have his name." He cut the call and switched on the intercom. "Change of plans. Go to the condo in Charlotte. I need to be near the airport."

He settled back in the leather seat. A little after nine. The hour drive would give him time to plan undisturbed. Fifteen minutes later, the phone screen lit up with a text.

Guard—Rusty Mullins—wounded.

Rusty Mullins. The name rang a bell. Brentwood pulled open a panel from the back of the seat in front of him. A keyboard and video screen locked into place. He used the customized high-powered computer to log onto his private search engine and prioritized retrieval based upon the number of hits generated by all the other major engines. The first wasn't a Facebook page or LinkedIn profile. It was a picture of a handsome, stone-faced, middle-aged man standing beside the President of the United States.

"Oh, shit," Brentwood muttered. "*That* Rusty Mullins."

Chapter Four

A soft cough roused him. Mullins opened his eyes and saw only indistinct shapes in the gray gloom. One of them moved toward him. He flashed back to the darkened hotel corridor and the man who had tried to kill him.

Mullins found himself flat on his back. He tried to push away from the approaching figure but his left arm refused to move. Someone had bound it to his side.

"Dad, it's me."

His daughter's soft, calm voice swept away his fear.

"Kayli?" His throat was dry and her name came out as a croak. "Where am I?"

"George Washington University Hospital."

Mullins nodded. His mind cleared enough to remember the ambulance ride, the rush to surgery, and then nothing.

"The bullet went through clean," Kayli said. "The doctor says you'll make a full recovery."

"Lewison?" He asked the question with little hope that Nicole had been mistaken.

"No. I'm so sorry, Dad."

He said nothing. Their talk would come later, he thought. Kayli would press him to come off the front lines, and she'd play the Josh card, not wanting her son to grow up without his grandfather. Yes, the talk would come later.

He was wrong.

"Dad. I know this isn't the time, but you've got to stop."

"You're right. This isn't the time."

"No. Right now. While you're in a hospital bed with a gunshot wound. Three inches to the right and I'd be viewing you in the morgue." Her voice broke but she pressed on. "When Mom got sick you gave up presidential detail for her. Why won't you do that for me? For Josh? For Mom?"

"Mom?"

"Yes. What wouldn't you give to have her back alive? To have her here with your grandson? Well, that's the way I feel about you."

A lump formed in his chest that no surgeon could remove. The emotional tide rose as memories of Laurie flooded his brain. Kayli had never brought her mother into this debate before and the impact hit harder than the slug that penetrated his body. He felt tears on his cheek and hoped his daughter couldn't see them.

"I'll think about it, dear. I promise."

She said nothing. For a moment the only sound was the faint chirp of a monitor.

He broke the silence first. "Is there water?"

"Ice chips." She moved to a table beside his bed. "I'll give you some on a spoon."

He let the crystals dissolve on his tongue, and then rolled the cold water around his parched mouth and throat.

"Thank you. What time is it?"

"A little after four."

"In the morning?"

"Yes."

"Where's Josh?"

"Sandy's taking care of him," she said. "When I got the news, Josh was asleep and I was able to carry him next door without waking him."

Sandy and Don Beecham were Kayli's neighbors and they had a boy Josh's age.

"So, he'll sleep through his sleepover," Mullins said, trying to ease the tension in the room.

"Yes. He'll be very surprised when he wakes up."

"How long have you been here?"

"Since ten. I came as soon as Nicole called."

Mullins made a mental note to thank his colleague. He would have hated Kayli to hear of his injury from some reporter. "Why don't you go home and get some sleep? Be with Josh."

Kayli reached out and grabbed her father's hand. "No, Dad. I'm going to be here with you. I want to know firsthand what the doctors say when they make their morning rounds. You're the one who needs to sleep."

"Okay, honey." He squeezed her hand. "Maybe I'll just rest my eyes."

In less than a minute, his ragged breathing settled into a softer rhythm. Kayli loosened her grip, laid her dad's hand on his stomach, and returned to the recliner she was using as a bed. She closed her eyes and wondered if she had pressed him too hard.

Someone gently shook her shoulder. For a second, she thought her father must have gotten out of bed.

"Mrs. Woodson."

Kayli awoke to find a nurse standing over her.

"Good morning. I'm sorry to trouble you, but I need you to go to the family waiting room for a few minutes."

Kayli looked at her watch. "It's not yet five. Is the doctor making rounds already?"

The nurse's fingers picked at the buttons on her uniform.

Even in the dim light, a roused Mullins could read the nurse's face. She was nervous. Something wasn't right. He could also see his daughter wouldn't go without more specific information.

"It's all right, Kayli," he said. "Let's let them do their job."

Both women turned toward Mullins, unaware that he'd been awake.

Kayli unfolded herself from the recliner. "Okay. But I'll stay here for rounds."

The nurse relaxed. "That will be no problem, dear. I'll take you to the waiting room. This place is like a maze."

As they left, the nurse called over her shoulder, "I'll be right back, Mr. Mullins."

But she didn't come back.

A few minutes later, a man entered. At first his face was lost in the shadows. Mullins could make out a dark suit and white shirt. Not the attire of a visiting physician. He moved through the room with practiced swiftness. Mullins recognized the procedure, and then he recognized the man. He'd last seen him less than a year ago standing outside the Oval Office.

Mullins tried to sit up. "Sam? What the hell's going on?"

Secret Service Agent Sam Dawkins stepped to the bedside and whispered, "Damned if I know, Nails. Someday you can tell me."

Nails. Sam had been the last person to call him by his second nickname, the one Rusty Mullins had earned because of his penchant for Rusty Nail cocktails whenever off-duty Secret Service agents collected at a bar.

"What are you doing here?"

"What's it look like?" Dawkins stepped back to the door. "We're clear," he said in a louder voice. Then to Mullins, he added, "Stop making this a habit, old man. I know the pension's crap but live to spend some of it."

A second taller man crossed in front of him, his silver hair backlit by the glow from the hall. "Thank you, Dawkins. You can leave us and please close the door."

Mullins' heart rate jumped at the sound of the familiar voice. "Mr. President?"

"Yes." President Edward Miles Brighton stepped to the foot of the bed and leaned forward. "How are you doing, Rusty?"

"I've been better."

"Haven't we all. This is some age we live in."

Mullins said nothing. He suspected why Brighton would come alone at a deserted hour, but the President would have to bring it up first.

"I feel like we're in a deadly game of Whack-A-Mole," Brighton continued. "Smash one extremist group and another pops up where we're not looking."

"Who's claiming responsibility?"

"A group calling itself Double H. Humanity's Hope. Sounds

like they're a bunch of Luddites convinced computers are taking over the world."

"Religious ties?"

"Not that we know of. They're completely out of left field. No one—FBI, Homeland Security, or military intelligence heard shit about them before last night. I'm throwing every resource at them. Interpol identified two of the five from prints. Both are suspected of political assassinations."

Mullins propped himself higher in the bed. His mind raced through the implications. "Professionals. Guns for hire. That's a twist."

"Rudy Hauser at the FBI says the same thing. These weren't suicide attacks. Witnesses saw a van near the hotel's Fourteenth Street loading dock speed away shortly after everything went down. They had an escape plan."

"They underestimated the quickness and strength of our response. Lewison didn't hesitate to intervene."

President Brighton sighed. "I'm sorry about that. I really am. Ted Lewison was a good man."

"Yes. A very good man. Thanks for your concern, Mr. President, but why are you really here in the middle of the night?"

The President rounded the bed and came closer. "We didn't do this, Rusty. I swear you weren't a target."

"Then someone should have told Double H." Mullins knew Brighton wasn't here to check on his health or debrief him. The President was afraid Mullins thought he'd tried to murder him.

"That's the goddamn point. You could get killed on your job and then all hell breaks loose if your threat's carried out."

"Be glad my attacker wasn't a good shot. You made the situation what it is. What's the old phrase for detente? Mutually assured destruction?" Mullins' mind jumped back to that night in the Oval Office when he'd played Brighton the audio file implicating the President in the Federal Reserve plot. Public revelation would have driven him from office and thrown the country into a financial and political crisis. Mullins had opted to protect the office of the Presidency, even though he had no respect for the man standing over him.

"So things have to stay the same, sir. If something suspicious happens to me or my family, the axe will fall. I've made sure of it."

The President's jaw clinched. "Then keep yourself out of harm's way. Don't be such a selfish, self-indulgent prick."

First his daughter, now the President of the United States. One arguing out of love, the other arguing out of fear.

"Then you keep me in the loop," Mullins demanded.

"What do you mean?"

"I want to know what's going on. They killed my friend. I want them brought to justice. If you wind up as collateral damage, then so be it."

"And you'll stay on the sidelines?"

"I'll get no closer than I need to. I have no desire to be in the line of fire."

Brighton realized the deal was the best he'd get from the stubborn bastard. "All right. I'll arrange it. The agencies will think it's strange but I'll tell them it's out of respect for your past efforts and your heroism for protecting that Li woman and the boy."

"Whatever."

"Someone will contact you." Brighton turned away and then looked back. "I was always trying to do what I thought was best for my country."

"Yeah? Name me one President that ever said otherwise."

Chapter Five

"Mr. Mullins, it's time for the game."

The voice was so close Mullins felt breath on his ear. He opened one eye and stared into the face of Peter Wang. The boy had the TV remote in one hand and his iPad in the other. Mullins shifted his gaze to the foot of the bed where Kayli and Dr. Li stood, lit by the afternoon sun coming through the room's single window. Li scowled at her nephew; Kayli grinned.

"I said whisper," Li admonished.

"But Miss Kayli said we could wake him," Peter argued. "The game's in five minutes."

"It's all right." Mullins fumbled for the bed control and raised the head to a forty-five-degree angle. "Why aren't you at the game?"

Peter's eyes widened like the answer should be obvious. "We were to watch it together. I didn't want to go without you."

Mullins swallowed, his throat suddenly dry. For a moment, he didn't know what to say. Then he raised his good arm and opened his palm.

Peter set down the remote and gave Mullins a high-five. "Ready?" he grinned.

"Yes. But I have one question."

"Lineup changes?"

"No. What's the temperature?"

Peter gave a thumbs-up. "Eighty-one. Fernandez's fastball will be smoking."

Mullins ruffled the kid's hair. "Then pull a chair up beside me and find the game before we miss his first strikeout."

Fernandez pitched six innings before being relieved in the bottom of the seventh with a two-run lead. The Nats went on to win nine to six.

"You were right, pal." Mullins gave Peter another high-five. "From now on I'm taking a thermometer to every game."

The boy beamed. "Maybe we can see one for real sometime?"

Mullins hesitated to promise anything. If Peter was heading back to Beijing, a weekend jaunt to the U.S. wasn't in his future. "Maybe. Why don't you go with Miss Kayli to the cafeteria and I'll treat you to a victory snack? I want to speak to your aunt a moment."

Dr. Li frowned and Mullins didn't know if it was because she didn't want Peter to go with his daughter or because she didn't want to talk to him.

"Can I go, please, Aunt Li Li?"

"All right," she consented. "But do what Miss Kayli tells you."

As soon as they were alone, Mullins gestured for Li to take the chair vacated by her nephew.

She sat. "I hope Peter didn't make your afternoon too strenuous, Mr. Mullins."

"No, I enjoyed it, and please call me Rusty."

She relaxed. "If you call me Lisa. Why do we need to talk?"

"First of all, how are you and Peter doing?"

"I'm looking over my shoulder and reliving last night. Peter's putting on a brave face, but I know he has to be traumatized. We'll have some counseling sessions back in Palo Alto. I don't want that experience buried in his subconscious."

Subconscious, Mullins thought. Lisa Li's specialty. "Do you have security?"

She nodded. "The hotel transferred us to another room last night under a false name. The police put a guard inside the door so as not to draw attention in the hallway. My company flew in a security team overnight and this morning we were passed to them."

"Where are they now?"

"One man's just outside the door. A second stayed near the elevators. I suspect he followed Peter and your daughter to the cafeteria."

Mullins understood why she'd frowned at his proposal that her nephew go with Kayli. "I didn't mean to inconvenience your security team."

She shrugged. "I feel safe here." She smiled. "I'm with the man who saved my life."

"I couldn't protect you from a ninety-year-old grandmother now."

"I think my biggest danger is being mobbed by the press. We had to sneak out through the loading dock to avoid them."

The loading dock near where the getaway van had been parked, Mullins thought. "Has any attempt on your life been made before?"

"No. But I work in a high-security lab and live in a high-rise with doormen. I think I just happened to be in the wrong place last night. Brecht and Ahmad were much more well known than I am."

"Anyone trying to recruit you away from your employer?"

"I'm in a hot field. I'm always getting inquiries." Her dark eyes narrowed. "But I'm here at the pleasure of my government and an arrangement made with Jué Dé. I'm not what the sports people call a free agent."

Mullins hesitated to probe further, but her answer reinforced his line of questioning.

"When the man grabbed you outside the kitchen last night, did he say anything?"

She shuddered. "No. You came back almost as he grabbed me."

To use as a shield, Mullins thought. Kill me first, then her. Or there was another possibility.

Li sensed something was bothering him. "What?"

Mullins leaned forward in the bed, bringing his face close to hers. "It's just a little odd that he grabbed you. Why not just shoot you?"

Li's face went even paler. "A hostage?"

"Or a source of information."

The neuroscientist shook her head as if being murdered were more understandable. "That sounds farfetched."

"I hope so. But tell Jué Dé and your government that kidnapping was a possibility."

"Maybe my company should hire you."

"I'm afraid that would be a tough commute."

Her eyes softened. "Family?"

"Kayli and my grandson. My wife died a couple of years ago."

"I'm sorry."

"Thanks. Do you live with someone who can be an extra pair of eyes and ears?"

"No," she whispered. "My husband died eight years ago. My work in Beijing kept me too busy to do anything else."

Like date, Mullins thought. He wondered if her research had been scrutinized by the communist government and long working hours weren't a choice.

"Just be extra vigilant," he advised. "And if you're ever back in the area, let me know. And if Peter's with you, we'll go to a game."

"He'd like that." Her face reddened slightly. "So would I." She stood. "I'd better go get him. We're supposed to fly back this evening."

"Can I tell him goodbye?"

"Yes. Peter would throw a fit otherwise." She stared at Mullins. "Thank you again."

Mullins started to say he was only doing his duty when she bent over and ran her cool palm across his forehead like a mother soothing a feverish child.

"You're welcome," he said.

Five minutes later, Peter burst in the room and ran to the bedside. "Mr. Mullins, Miss Kayli said you're not just a bodyguard. You're like a detective."

Mullins chuckled. "Well, I used to be kinda like one."

"Would you take my case?"

Mullins looked at Lisa Li but she appeared to have no clue as to what her nephew meant.

"What case is that?" he asked.

"Someone stole my Nats hat?"

"In the cafeteria?"

"No. From our room. Last night while we were downstairs."

Mullins rubbed his chin like he was thinking about possible solutions. "Well, your aunt said you changed rooms. That's probably when it got lost."

"No. I looked for it before then." He turned to his aunt. "Tell him about your makeup."

Mullins was suddenly interested. "Was something else missing?"

Li shook her head dismissively. "My makeup case and our toiletries. We didn't actually move them. The hotel staff brought our things to the new room."

"But you went back first to your original room?"

"Yes. A policeman entered first to make sure no one waited inside. Then we were only there five minutes before the decision was made to change rooms. His hat could have fallen under the bed."

"Did you notice if your toiletries were gone?"

"None of us went in the bathroom," Li said. "Things were so chaotic I'm just grateful our luggage made it."

"Will you take the case?" Peter asked. "I can pay. I get an allowance."

"Oh, really?" Mullins made a great show of being impressed. "Well, I couldn't possibly take your money until I recover. It wouldn't be fair to you."

Peter nodded solemnly.

"But I'll make a few calls to some detective friends. If it's not solved by the time I'm better, I'll work on your case personally. How's that sound?"

Peter thrust out his little hand. "You've got a deal, Mr. Mullins."

Chapter Six

Nearly two weeks after the assassinations, Mullins had yet to hear any update on the investigation. His own inactivity created growing frustration and restlessness, but he had few options.

His surgeon had urged him not to drive until he was further along in healing. Unfortunately, the doctor gave those post-operative instructions in front of Kayli, and his daughter had had the audacity to remove the Prius from the JW Marriott and park it on the street in front of her condo in Arlington. She kept the keys safely stowed in her purse. He felt like a teenager who'd been grounded.

Mullins lived in a one-bedroom apartment on the fourth floor of a high-rise building called Shirlington House. He'd moved there a few years after his wife died of ovarian cancer because it was located midway between Kayli's condo and the convenience of the upscale shops and restaurants that made up the Shirlington neighborhood. His walk was less than a mile to either destination.

Kayli lived in Fairlington Villages, a neighborhood constructed during World War Two to house Pentagon officers and their families. Her husband, Lieutenant Commander Allen Woodson, was a naval intelligence officer on a ship somewhere off the east coast of Africa. Kayli was essentially a single mom juggling her part-time job at the Shirlington Library with the demanding responsibilities of raising a three-year-old. When Mullins wasn't working, he became the chief backup babysitter for his grandson, Josh, a title he relished.

Convenience to his grandson offered another advantage. Kayli brought him dinner every night until he felt well enough to join her and Josh around her dining room table. That had been the extent of his outings when he'd received a call from Elizabeth Lewison. The widow of his boss and friend wanted to meet and discuss something personal.

On the second Thursday after his release from the hospital, Mullins strolled along the sidewalk, glad to be out on the sunny April morning, but anxious about seeing Elizabeth. They'd spoken briefly at Ted's memorial service. She was still in shock and swamped by numerous friends offering condolences; he was still weak and unsteady, forced to lean on Kayli as they processed along the receiving line.

His real anxiety lay in the second thoughts plaguing him every time he closed his eyes. Should he have seen the killers approaching sooner? Surveyed the room before running to evacuate his charge? Would his warning to Ted have made a difference if it had come a second or two earlier? His professional brain said no; his personal loyalty to a friend and colleague argued otherwise.

So, with mixed feelings, he entered Peet's Coffee a few minutes ahead of their ten o'clock rendezvous. Elizabeth Lewison was waiting in the back. Two cups of coffee were already on the table.

She smiled and gestured to the seat opposite her. "Medium roast, black. Correct?"

"Perfect." He sat.

She reached out with her fingers curled halfway open and he cupped his hand over hers, latching onto her, digit for digit, as if what they shared was too important to be bound by a common handshake.

"How are you, Rusty?" She eyed his left arm immobilized by a sling.

"I have no complaints. I'll mend."

"How's the PT?"

He gave a one-shoulder shrug. "A home health therapist comes every day."

"I didn't know the company's insurance was that good."

"It's not. I mean..." he stammered at what he was afraid sounded like criticism "...I mean our coverage is fine. I was told Jué Dé's providing the therapist."

"Who?"

"The Chinese company that employs Dr. Li, the woman I was guarding."

"Good. You earned it."

Mullins took a deep, slow sip of his coffee. He wanted to buy some time and let her lead the conversation. It was strange seeing her without Ted. They'd been married twenty-four years. While Ted had been posted around the world, Elizabeth had put herself through Howard University and passed her CPA examination. When Ted gave his final salute, Elizabeth created the business plan that would become Prime Protection. She wasn't only his friend's wife, she was the person who signed his paycheck.

He took a second sip and thought how much the couple looked alike. She was tall, nearly six feet, and she carried herself with Ted's military bearing. Although she was physically striking, it was her aura of self confidence that defined her. She was a woman comfortable in her own skin and gifted with the ability to put others at ease.

Except she wasn't at ease this morning.

"What have you heard?" Her eyes searched his face for any sign of duplicity.

"Nothing. And I'm supposed to," he admitted. "From sources high in the investigation."

"Do they not know anything, or are they not telling anything?"

Mullins had been asking himself the same questions. "My guess is that they know precious little and are guarding that scant data hoping they can work it without alerting their suspects. But the press is baffled and in a town that leaks like a sieve, I'd say that means the investigation is going nowhere."

She nodded. "I've got my own connections and I'm hearing the same silence. It's like this Double H appeared at the hotel and then vanished from the face of the earth." She rotated her cup on the table, staring at the black liquid for a moment. When she looked up, her eyes were moist. "When are you back?"

It was the question he'd been dreading. He took a deep breath. "I don't think I will be. Prime Protection deserves someone in their prime. It's time I came off the front line."

Disappointment covered her face. "Is that you or Kayli talking?"

"Does it matter?" He couldn't tell her the one speaking to him was his dead wife. But, then, maybe Elizabeth would understand.

"No. I guess it doesn't. But, Rusty, would you work for me?"

The request confused him. "What do you mean? Some sort of office job?"

"Work for me personally. Someone murdered my husband. That's what it was. Cold-blooded murder. I don't want you on the front lines as a protector. I need an investigator." Tears flowed freely down her cheeks. "Someone needs to speak for Ted. You're not only his friend, you're the best damned investigator in this city. Please."

Her desperate face was replaced by others—Kayli pleading for him to retire, President Brighton requesting that he stay out of the line of fire, and finally his wife, Laurie, whispering, "She's in pain, Rusty. Help her."

He made one final protest. "I don't know where to begin."

"Who does?" she asked. "But I'll give you whatever resources I can, and at least I'll take comfort in knowing we're trying to do something."

"All right, Elizabeth."

They parted with a hug. He declined her offer for a ride to his apartment, claiming he had to pick up a few grocery items. When she was gone, he went back for a second cup of coffee and returned to the back table. He scanned through the contact files on his cell phone, not sure if he still had the number. It was there, a relic of the old days.

Just when he thought he was headed for voicemail, a voice snapped, "Dawkins."

"Sam. It's Nails. Did I wake you?"

"No, I'm on duty. But I had a good three hours sleep."

"I'm sorry. When are you rotating off?"

"I'm not back in the city for seventy-two hours. We're headed to Camp David. Orca's spending a long weekend."

Sam Dawkins just assumed Mullins knew Brighton's code name. He was correct.

"Will you give Orca a message?"

A pause as the question forced Dawkins to consider his response carefully. Then he asked, "Is he going to shoot the messenger?"

"Not if you tell him you've no idea what it means. Just say I called and asked you to relay that I'm coming off the sidelines."

"You're coming off the sidelines. That's all?"

"Yeah."

"Are you expecting him to give me some sort of reply for you?"

"No. And tell him so. It's a heads-up, nothing more."

"Nothing more, my ass," Dawkins grumbled.

"Trust me. It's not your ass he's worried about."

Dawkins laughed. "You nailed that right, Nails. Stay safe."

"Always, my friend." And he hoped his message to Brighton increased the odds of just that.

Mullins got up from the table, grabbed his coffee, and began walking back to his apartment, unaware of the black limousine trailing half a block behind him.

Chapter Seven

Mullins carried his coffee and his thoughts up the hill toward Shirlington House. Once he made the decision to help Elizabeth Lewison, his mind began searching for viable pathways to penetrate the secrets of his own government. Someone had to know something.

He was so deep in concentration that the world around him disappeared. Only when he heard his name did he realize a black limo was cruising along the curb, matching his pace.

He stopped and the car braked beside him. A man of about fifty with clear blue eyes and steely-gray hair looked out over a half-lowered, tinted rear window.

"Mr. Mullins, might I have a word with you?"

Mullins quickly scanned the area, alert for any coordinated assault. Late morning traffic was light and there were no other pedestrians. Mullins realized if this man wanted him dead, he would have shot rather than spoken.

"Who are you?"

"My name is Robert Brentwood. But that's not important."

Robert Brentwood. The name sounded familiar, but he couldn't place the context.

"It's about Dr. Lisa Li. Just a few moments is all, and then you can be on your way."

Mullins shook his head. "A few answers first."

"All right." Brentwood smiled. "Ask away."

"Have I been under surveillance?"

"Yes. By my security team. Nothing sinister, I promise. I wanted to know how to reach you when the time came."

The man's open admission signaled this wasn't going to be a conversation of game-playing. At least not initially.

"Why are you interested in me?"

"Because I'm interested in her." Brentwood pushed open his door. "Hear my proposal. That's all I ask. Then we'll return to your building and I'll be on my way."

Mullins clicked the name into place. "You head some computer company, don't you?"

"Yes. Cumulus Cognitive Connections. Actually we're high-level information systems and data management. I was alarmed and sickened by the murders at that conference, and I have reason to fear for Dr. Li's safety."

Perhaps more than the door to the car might be opening. "All right. Mind if I bring my coffee?"

Brentwood laughed and slid over. "Not at all. There's Blanton's single-barrel bourbon in the bar if you need to add something a little more bracing than cream."

Said the spider to the fly, Mullins thought. He got in, opted not to trap himself in the seatbelt, and closed the door. "Save the bourbon for another time. You've got my attention."

Brentwood pressed an intercom button. "Drive us around the area," he told the driver. "But no farther out than ten minutes from Mr. Mullins' apartment." He released the switch. "Is that satisfactory, sir?"

"Your wheels, your gas," Mullins answered. "Now what's up?"

The limo pulled away from the curb and Brentwood leaned against the door to face Mullins.

"I want to hire you to protect Dr. Li."

"We can stop right now, Mr. Brentwood. I'm not going to California."

"Of course you're not. Kayli and Josh are here."

Brentwood's use of his daughter's and grandson's names showed Mullins the man had done at least a preliminary background check.

"You'll stay on the East Coast," Brentwood continued. "There will be some travel by private jet, but for only a few days at a time."

"Is Jué Dé transferring Dr. Li?"

"Jué Dé is out of the picture. Dr. Li will be working for me."

"I understand she's here through the approval of the Chinese government."

Brentwood waved his hand dismissively. "I'll handle the politics. They'll make a stink but nothing that won't blow over."

"She'll be based in D.C.?"

"Part of the time. Part of the time she'll be at one of our centers where we can implement her research."

"When would I start?"

"As soon as she agrees to join us. I can offer you two thousand dollars."

"A week?"

"A day."

Mullins made the calculation. Over half a million dollars a year to be a bodyguard. Overpayment, for sure. As soon as she agrees.

"I'm a lure," Mullins said.

Brentwood chuckled. "You can call yourself that, but you more than proved your value at the Marriott shootings. I believe Dr. Li still needs protection and Silicon Valley isn't the place for her. You saved her life once. There's no one else who will make her feel more secure."

The limo turned onto South Columbus and Mullins saw the brick building where Kayli lived in one of its four condos. Half a million dollars would more than pay for his grandson's education.

"Why her?" Mullins asked. "You've got the connections and bankroll to snap up any scientist you want. Why is she so special?"

"Are you interested in the job?"

"Not without more information."

Brentwood frowned and tapped his fingers while he mulled over how much to reveal and how much to conceal. Mullins was living up to his reputation. "How much of the 'secret' in Secret Service defined your career?"

"Everything that wasn't illegal. I've no interest in spreading confidential information, if that's what you're worried about."

"I have your word?"

"Under the condition I just stated."

Brentwood checked the driver to make sure the man's eyes were on the road and not reading lips through the rearview mirror.

"Do you read science fiction, Mr. Mullins?"

"Not really. Some as a kid. Mostly the ones that were shoot-'em-up Westerns, except in space."

Brentwood pulled a latch on the back of the driver's seat and a shelf dropped into place just above his knees. Mullins saw a glowing keyboard with a milk-glass screen mounted perpendicular to it. A three-dimensional image of cumulus clouds and blue sky materialized and seemed to hover on the screen.

"When I was a kid, all I read was science fiction. Maybe I was trying to escape my surroundings, maybe I had a hyperactive imagination, maybe both. That's for a shrink to decide. But science fiction is the reason we're in this limousine, the reason there's Blanton's in the bar and a jet at BWI. Because I had my head in the clouds, I anticipated the Cloud before it had a name." He gestured to the clouds in front of him. "And I built my company based on its evolution and now the accelerating revolution. Even I'm shocked at the speed with which mankind's knowledge is being captured in cyberspace. But that's mere storage and data archiving. The real power is accessing, connecting, and applying that knowledge in ways never before imagined."

"Super computers?" Mullins ventured.

"No. That's limiting development to hardware. You know what the arms race of the twenty-first century is, Mr. Mullins?"

Mullins shook his head, not even bothering to guess.

"The quest for artificial intelligence. A race where there might be no second place."

"Why's that? In the Cold War, mutually assured destruction kept the Soviet Union and us from using nuclear weapons."

"Because we're not talking physical destruction." Brentwood

leaned forward, his face flush with a sudden burst of energy. "Have you heard of the singularity?"

"Something to do with black holes?"

"In cosmic theory, yes. The center of a black hole where matter is crushed to infinite density and the laws of physics break down. But I'm talking about the field of computer science. The singularity is a point in time when artificial intelligence becomes super intelligence, the technical achievement of cognitive abilities beyond human capacity. Then its intelligence will increase exponentially, leaving us poor mortals far behind. Uncharted waters, my friend, because we will no longer be able to control or protect the outcomes of our thinking machine."

Brentwood clicked a few keys and the clouds turned into a night sky of stars and then swirling galaxies. "People like me see infinite benefits, especially for human problems like disease and even death. Yet there is a dark, dark side. What if our computer servants develop self-awareness that becomes self-preservation? A goal that finds humanity expendable?"

Mullins flashed back to his childhood, not to the sci-fi novels but to the bad sci-fi movies he loved to watch on Saturday mornings. "An army of robots?"

"No." Brentwood swept a hand through the air between them as if to cast the very concept from the car. "An infiltration by the first super intelligent entity into every network, every software program, every smartphone, laptop, mainframe, or even the world's weapon systems. A hacking of unprecedented speed and power. There will be no second place super intelligence because the first to reach the singularity will overpower and absorb all rivals."

"Absolute power," Mullins murmured.

"Corrupts absolutely. Why should that axiom not apply to a self-aware thinking machine?"

"Or to the human beings who might manage to control it?" Mullins said.

"Precisely. God only knows which would be worse."

Brentwood's bright eyes lost focus as a new idea sparked in his brain. Mullins got the feeling the man truly was a genius, able to envision possibilities others couldn't imagine.

"Maybe that's what we're doing—creating God. A super intelligent being who can peel back the secrets of time and space in some infinitely looping Möbius strip where man is created by God so that God can be created by man." Brentwood felt himself slipping into one of his trances and blinked a few times to clear his over-revving mind. "Sorry. Do you get the picture?"

"I believe so," Mullins said. "You want to be the person controlling the machine."

"No. I want to be the person programming the machine. Programming the machine with self-control, a safeguard against both human and computer tyranny."

Mullins saw a glimmer of where Brentwood was heading. "That's the role for Dr. Li, isn't it?"

The CEO beamed like his three-year-old had just pronounced two plus two equals four. "A vital step is teaching a computer to find solutions to problems on its own. The field is called deep learning and the most promising model is proving to be blatantly obvious. The human brain. We've mapped the human genome. Now we're attempting to map every neuron cluster, synapse connection, and sensory input to reproduce the intellectual functionality developed by evolution."

"The marriage of neuroscience and computer science," Mullins said. "Dr. Li's topic at the conference."

Brentwood couldn't restrain himself. He reached out and grabbed Mullins' good arm. "Yes. Yes. But her brilliance is being wasted—overlooked by focusing on the human brain as a model of learning, a super intelligent problem-solver."

Mullins had to admit he was intrigued by what the man was saying. He was also confused. "What then?"

"It's not the discovery of answers that will propel IA into unknown dimensions, it's the ability to imagine the questions in the first place. To dream of things beyond the mind of us poor mortals."

"And that's not the model of the brain?"

Brentwood tapped his temple with a forefinger. "Not the conscious brain. Not the problem-solving mind. I firmly believe we're looking at the role of the subconscious, the walled up, secretive partitioned space where seeds of ideas, unique connections, and fresh perspectives bubble and percolate until rising to conscious awareness in an ah-ha moment. Like the one I experienced envisioning the power of the Cloud.

"If I'd been consciously thinking of that too soon, I'd have dismissed it for all the reasons it wouldn't work. But my subconscious nurtured it in safety until it was ready to be born, too powerful to be ignored."

The man didn't sound crazy, Mullins thought. Fanatical, yes, but not crazy. He'd read about people saying their revolutionary ideas popped into their heads fully formed. He'd experienced it to some degree when pieces of an investigation suddenly gelled and he'd awaken in the middle of the night with an unexpected insight. No, the man wasn't crazy.

"That's Dr. Li's area," Mullins said. "She'll map it for you?"

"Not just map it. She's the most qualified person in the world to create both the complex algorithms and partitioning protocols to truly make an artificial mind with that undervalued component, a subconscious seat of imagination."

Mullins couldn't suppress a laugh. "Surely you don't think Dr. Li will join your company because of me?"

Brentwood's face remained deadly serious. "No, I don't. You're a fringe benefit at best. It's the cumulative effect I'm after. There are other carrots I won't go into. You might be a fringe benefit to her, but you're a critical factor for me. The woman is a valuable asset deserving the best protection."

"What's to stop the Chinese from surrounding her with guards and whisking her home?"

"Nothing. Other than the secrecy I stressed, Mr. Secret Service. If you buy the analogy to the arms race, say World War II's Manhattan Project, then you also need to understand how this is so drastically different. Back then it was a war between aligned nations. The Manhattan Project was a huge, secret crash effort to develop the atomic bomb first. Today other wars rage—wars of culture, ethnicity, religion, nations, and the newest front, multi-national corporations. It's no secret that Google, China's Baidu and Jué Dé, Microsoft billionaire Paul Allen, and an alliance of universities are all striving to be first in the race for artificial intelligence."

"In which there is no second place," Mullins echoed.

Brentwood relaxed. "Yes, you understand. There's no greater challenge on the face of the planet. The race has to be won by people of high moral character with the common good of humanity as their priority. The original prediction for the singularity was 2045. I tell you, Mr. Mullins, the singularity will be a reality within twelve months. I believe we're ahead, but others are close behind. If they reach the singularity first, then my work amounts to nothing."

Mullins nodded gravely. He knew it was the response Brentwood wanted. Now was the time to press for what had motivated him to get in the car.

"If I agree to guard Dr. Li, then I must have latitude in deciding what to do and how to do it."

"As long as it doesn't compromise the secrecy of our work."

"That means I must know what we're up against. I need your resources and the operational support to investigate this Double H and any other threats that might exist."

Brentwood hesitated. An investigation outside his full control could be a problem. Yet if he balked, he'd undercut the very argument that he would do anything to protect Dr. Li.

"All right," he said. "As long as it's not illegal."

"We might have to push the envelope," Mullins stipulated.

"Just don't push me in front of a goddamned congressional hearing." Brentwood offered his hand. "Do we have a deal?"

Mullins found the other man's palm was drenched with sweat. "One other thing. I'd like a mailing address for Dr. Li. I'm going to add something to your cumulative effect."

Brentwood arched his eyebrows but didn't ask for an explanation. "I'll e-mail it to you while we drive back to your apartment."

The limo dropped Mullins at the building's front entrance. He gave a slight wave, and then turned his attention to his next move—shipping a new Washington Nationals baseball cap to Dr. Li.

Before the limo was out of the parking lot, Brentwood speed-dialed his phone. "He's in."

"Any problems?" Ned Farino asked.

"Nothing unexpected. Play your card."

◇◇◇

Across the Potomac in the Office of Naval Intelligence in southeast Washington, Vice Admiral Louis MacArthur hung up the phone. President Brighton had been so hyped up MacArthur figured he could have heard the man from the Oval Office without needing the phone.

The message had been loud and clear: give Rusty Mullins all updates on the Marriott shootings. The disregard for the protocols of security clearance was unprecedented and MacArthur couldn't help but marvel at what must be Mullins' influence. Was the man some kind of intelligence genius?

MacArthur summoned his chief communications officer. The cable would be short and only for the eyes of the commander of surveillance operations in the Indian Ocean. He gave one name, the name of the man he wanted in his office within thirty-six hours, no questions asked.

The vice admiral smiled to himself. The more he thought about it, the more he liked his idea. Two separate objectives carried out by the same operative. President Brighton would have the link to Mullins he wanted. MacArthur would have the informant he needed.

Things could work out quite well.

Chapter Eight

"Paw Paw."

Mullins loved hearing the two syllables spoken by his grandson. He couldn't help but smile at the name christening his grandfather status.

"Paw Paw," Josh repeated. "Done." The three-year-old pointed a stubby finger at the bowl now empty of Cheerios.

"Good job, Josh. Paw Paw just has a few more bites."

The child and grandfather sat side by side at Kayli's dining room table in what had become a Saturday morning ritual. Mullins entertained Josh while Kayli talked with her husband stationed somewhere in the Indian Ocean. In port, Kayli and Allen could Skype, but, at sea, video communication was forbidden. This morning their prearranged call would be by POTS—a naval acronym standing for the highly technical term, Plain Old Telephone System.

Josh started squirming in his booster chair.

"Wait. Be polite. Let me finish." Mullins hurried his last few bites of cereal.

"Paw Paw, *PAW Patrol*. Josh's urgent demand to watch his favorite cartoon, *PAW Patrol*, sent an involuntary shiver down Mullins' spine. The TV show featured a pack of super hero dogs and started every episode with a theme song that infected the brain. Mullins likened it to the mind-numbing effect of Disney World's "It's a Small World" ride and the title song that looped incessantly. When he and Laurie had taken Kayli as a child, it took weeks to knock the tune out of his head.

"Paw Paw, *PAW Patrol*." The demand turned into giggles as Josh delighted in the multiple "Paws."

"Kayli!"

"I'm brewing another pot," came her reply from the kitchen. "Your call's at ten, right?"

Kayli walked into the room. She wore a terry cloth bathrobe loosely cinched around her pajamas and clutched a mug of steaming coffee. "Don't shout, Dad. We have neighbors, you know. And, yes, ten."

"Well, I can't endure another episode of *PAW Patrol*. I'll take Josh to the playground and we'll be back in time for him to talk to Allen."

"*PAW Patrol*," Josh petitioned his mother.

"No *PAW Patrol*," Kayli said. "You're going on Paw Paw Patrol. Show Paw Paw how you can use the big boy slide."

"Paw Paw Patrol," Josh squealed.

Mullins feared Kayli had just created the name for every outing he and his grandson would ever take. "Let me help you down so your mom can change you out of your pjs."

Kayli set her mug on the table. "I'll do it. You're not to lift anything with that arm yet."

Mullins ignored her and maneuvered his sling enough to grasp the tow-haired boy around the waist with both hands. As far as he was concerned, his grandson could never be too heavy. Two months premature, Josh had weighed less than three pounds and spent his first Christmas in a neonatal intensive care unit.

Mullins gently set the boy on the floor. "Believe me, honey, that was less painful than the TV show."

Ten minutes later, Mullins and Josh walked hand in hand toward the neighborhood playground a few blocks away. Josh had to stop and examine every stone he found on the sidewalk and wave to every car that passed. Mullins didn't mind. A warm spring morning. A tiny hand clutching his finger. He wished the moment could go on forever.

It didn't. When Josh saw the other kids on the playground, he ran to them, leaving Paw Paw behind.

It wasn't so long ago that was Kayli, Mullins thought. "He's growing up too fast, Laurie," he whispered. "What will his world be like?"

Mullins found an empty bench where he could watch Josh yet maintain the pensive mood that had descended upon him. His thoughts turned from his dead wife to Elizabeth Lewison. He knew the terrible grief she suffered. He wondered if she talked to Ted the way he did with Laurie. He hoped so.

If Robert Brentwood did hire him, Mullins would have to have a conversation with Elizabeth. No details. Just find a way to reassure her that he was working the investigation and might be out of touch for periods of time.

Kayli would be a bigger challenge. There had been no further discussion since those early hours in the hospital. He knew she was waiting for him to make the first move. He couldn't lie to her, but he could be vague. Tell her he wasn't going back to Prime Protection, but he was undertaking a private investigation for Elizabeth Lewison, a woman Kayli admired and respected. Investigations were far less dangerous than being on the front line. At least that's how he'd sell it. Dr. Lisa Li might not have to be mentioned at all.

Mullins turned his thoughts to other priorities. If Sam Dawkins delivered his message to President Brighton, it might prompt him to start the flow of information. He didn't know how it would come to him. That wasn't his problem. He did have expectations as to the quality of what he was being told, and he'd run enough cases during his time in the Secret Service's counterfeit division to know the prime avenue of pursuit—follow the money. The dead assassins were mercenaries, not jihadists. Somewhere out there lurked a paymaster.

"Paw Paw, look!" Josh sat at the top of the big boy slide. It was all of eight feet long.

"Want me to catch you?"

"No!" Josh pushed himself forward, slid to the bottom, and stumbled a few steps upon landing. But, he kept his balance and flashed Mullins a broad grin of triumph.

Their walk back took twice as long. Josh kept stopping, wanting to be carried. Mullins finally threw him over his right shoulder like a sack of grain.

When they entered the condo, Kayli was already on the phone in the bedroom.

"I want Mommy," Josh whined.

Mullins set his grandson on the sofa. He gritted his teeth. "Wanna watch *PAW Patrol*?"

After a lunch of hotdogs, fruit, and olives, olives being Josh's favorite food at the moment, Kayli took the tired youngster to his room for a story and a nap. Mullins had just muted the TV sound of the Washington Nationals—Phillies pre-game program when Kayli reemerged.

"You can raise the volume. Josh went out like a light."

He clicked off the set.

"Are you going?" she asked. "You're welcome to watch here. I'll get you a beer to settle those hotdogs."

Mullins patted the sofa cushion beside him. "We need to talk a minute."

Kayli cocked her head and eyed him suspiciously. "Did you hear something from your doctor?"

Suddenly Mullins saw her as his little girl, afraid she was about to hear bad news from her daddy.

"Nothing like that. Just sit."

She joined him on the sofa.

"I'm not going back to Prime Protection. I met with Elizabeth on Thursday and gave her my decision."

Kayli hugged his neck so fiercely that a jab of pain shot through his shoulder. He winced.

"Oh, Dad, I'm sorry. I'm just so happy."

"But I can't spend my days sitting on a park bench feeding pigeons or at home watching game shows. I'll wither away."

"I know. I'm not asking you to."

"Good. Because I've taken on a new assignment."

Instantly, Kayli became wary. "What kind of assignment?"

"An investigative one. Like what I did when your mom got sick and I asked to be relieved of presidential detail. You're the one who made me think I should treat you and Josh the same as I treated her." He avoided any mention of one critical difference. His transfer to counterfeiting involved no assignment of personal protection duties. But he had been on several Treasury busts and those always carried an element of risk.

Kayli wasn't mollified. "Don't tell me you're going back to the Secret Service?"

"No. Nothing so structured. Elizabeth asked me to look into Ted's death. She's not getting any answers from the feds or the locals. I want to help her, Kayli. She's in a lot of pain. And I've got some chips I can call in from high-ranking people."

"And they owe you more than they'll ever repay." She sighed. "Okay. I guess that's better than being a human target. Promise me not to take any unnecessary risks."

"Don't worry. I don't want to take any risks period. But I might have to travel some, if it means tracing back the route of the killers. I'll let you know as much as I can."

She leaned over and kissed his cheek. "I'm holding you to it. Anything else you need to tell me?"

"Yeah. I'll take that beer."

Two beers and seven innings later, Mullins lay stretched out on the sofa, snoring like a chainsaw, as Kayli and Josh tiptoed out the door for Saturday afternoon grocery shopping. She'd left a note for him to stay. "Steak, salad, and Pinot Noir are tonight's special. Olives are optional."

At seven-thirty, Kayli and Josh dropped a well-fed Mullins at Shirlington House. He kissed his daughter's cheek and gave his grandson a high five. He rode the elevator to the fourth floor and fumbled for his keys as he walked to his apartment. He turned the lock and found the bolt already thrown. Immediately, his senses leapt into hyper-mode. He never left his door unlocked. He'd sooner forget to wear his clothes. Had maintenance come up? His gun was in the apartment and his half-bottle of wine didn't exactly prime him for hand-to-hand combat.

Since he'd been gone all day, the odds were any intruder had left hours ago. If the lock had been picked, no burglar would re-lock it. He opened the door slowly, grateful that the oiled hinges were silent. No sound from the apartment's interior came through the widening crack.

He stepped into his living room sideways, offering the smallest target possible, and he left the door open in case he needed an unimpeded retreat.

The lights came on.

"Sorry. I thought it was better if I let myself in."

Mullins had never been so surprised in his life. In front of him stood his son-in-law, Allen Woodson. Less than eight hours ago, he'd been somewhere in the Indian Ocean half a world away.

Chapter Nine

"Hello, Allen. Nice of you to drop by. Hope I wasn't out of your way." He shook Woodson's offered hand and then walked past him and sat on the sofa. He gestured to an adjacent armchair. "Care to explain how the *Starship Enterprise* teleported you here?"

Allen Woodson smiled in admiration of Mullins' quick recovery from the shock so evident on his face. "Good to see you too, Rusty."

Mullins looked up at the young naval officer. He stood a few inches over six feet, trim and muscular. The brown eyes were bright but the deep blue circles beneath them proclaimed he'd gone many hours without sleep. Despite the fatigue, Woodson still carried his military bearing. Mullins noted the young man wasn't in uniform, but rather wore blue jeans and a black sweatshirt that looked like they'd been bought off the rack and never worn. "I suppose you have a good reason for lying to Kayli."

Woodson sat. "At nine last Thursday night I was hustled into a chopper with fifteen minutes notice. Our commanding officer either didn't know, or wouldn't say why, I was shuttled faster than a donated heart until I was escorted into a back entrance at the Office of Naval Intelligence. I guess you could call that the mothership. My Captain Kirk was none other than Vice Admiral Louis MacArthur." Woodson paused to gauge Mullins' reaction.

"When was this?"

"Nine o'clock this morning. I was told to tell no one of my location. As far as the Navy's concerned, I'm still in the Arabian

Sea. Only two people, and now you make three, know exactly where I am."

"Vice Admiral MacArthur and President Brighton."

Woodson's face mirrored Mullins' earlier surprise. "You knew?"

"I was expecting a conduit. I never suspected it would be you. So, tell me your assignment, or will you have to kill me?"

"Just the opposite. Reading between the lines, I'm to keep you alive."

Mullins laughed. "I'll drink to that. Want a beer?"

"If you're having one."

Mullins rose and went to the kitchen that wasn't much more than an alcove. He returned with two bottles of Heineken.

"What did MacArthur tell you?"

"That he and Brighton had independently zeroed in on me for the job. MacArthur said Brighton wants me to feed you updates on the Marriott assassinations. He assumes Brighton owes you for preventing the success of last year's terrorist attack on the Federal Reserve. Brighton also stressed to MacArthur that I'm to keep you out of harm's way. Like I'd be more motivated because you're my father-in-law."

"And the reason MacArthur chose you?"

"Well, I gather Brighton's on his ass and pissed that MacArthur hasn't gotten you information sooner. MacArthur said I was his go-to guy only if you started investigating on your own. He wants me to feed information back to him so he'll know any developments before Brighton."

"Hell, he's got his whole global intelligence network. I'd think he's doing this just to humor the President."

Woodson took a swallow of beer and shrugged. "Maybe. Maybe he just wants to keep me close like Brighton's keeping you."

"Why?"

"Because of the request I ran up the chain of command. I urged them to re-examine the FBI files on my sister Kim."

For a moment, Mullins stared blankly at his son-in-law. Then the pieces fell into place. "The missing neuroscientists. Jesus. It never crossed my mind. That's inexcusable. I'm sorry, Allen." Mullins knew Woodson had been very close to his sister. Her disappearance had been especially hard since Woodson had just been deployed to his first posting, a reconnaissance ship in the China Sea.

"Good God, Rusty. You were in a hospital bed. I should have called you. The point is I think MacArthur's using the FBI's files on Kim's disappearance as incentives for me to be his eyes and ears on whatever you're doing. He's promised to get me access, but he expects me to share anything you might uncover. I was ordered not to take any investigative action on my own."

"Is that what you're going to do?"

Woodson grinned. "I'd never disobey an order. Of course, if I'm partnering with you, I'm not on my own, am I?"

Mullins toasted him with his beer. "No, I guess you're not. How long do you have to continue the charade with Kayli?"

"Till either you're satisfied that you've learned all you can or MacArthur pulls me off. He's the only one I'm reporting to. But, he warned me that if you're not happy, you'll go straight to the President. That connection seems to be a sore spot."

Mullins realized Agent Dawkins had gotten his message to Brighton without delay, and he in turn had yanked the vice admiral's chain. Allen Woodson sitting in his living room was the result.

"Where are you staying?" Mullins asked.

"You could say ground zero—the JW Marriott. MacArthur's given me a temporary office in Naval Intelligence. I'll be able to access databases. If possible, I'll make my scheduled calls to Kayli. MacArthur routed the one this morning through a satellite to create the proper delay. It's killing me that Kayli and Josh are less than a mile away and I can't see them."

"Why the extreme secrecy?"

"So there's no connection to you. You have no standing. We're violating almost every security clearance code. This is all off the books."

"Did MacArthur brief you on what they know so far?"

"The getaway van was found in southeast near the navy yard. It was wiped clean. Two of the dead had fingerprint hits with Interpol."

"I knew that," Mullins grumbled.

"No IDs on the bodies. They figure passports and other documentation would all be fake and were probably waiting in the van. Best guess is the team was dispatched from Europe. The credit for the killings popped up from an Internet café in Amsterdam. Of course, there's no record of who posted it. I would suspect the killers were to be paid through a Swiss account."

"They'd need expense money and probably half up front."

"Yes," Woodson agreed, "but no link's been found."

"Facial recognition?"

"Scanned all custom entry points for the previous three months."

"What about Mexico?"

"You mean did they penetrate our border from there?"

"Yes. Ten million undocumented residents show it's not like breaking into Fort Knox. Or Canada like the 9/11 terrorists." Mullins paused as a thought struck him. "New Hampshire borders Canada."

Woodson leaned forward, eyes locked on Mullins. "You think Kim's disappearance might be tied to some terrorist smuggling route?"

"At this point I don't think anything," Mullins said. "All I remember is your sister was working on the disappearance of two MIT scientists, one of whom had a cottage on Little Lake Sunapee, and they found her car behind a summer playhouse nearby. We need more data before forming a theory. The other way around and we're simply fooling ourselves."

"I know," Woodson admitted. "But aren't you fooling yourself? How are you funding an international investigation? What are your resources? Your laptop?"

Mullins allowed a smug smile. "Money is no problem, and I'm utilizing the most sophisticated computer equipment in the world."

For a second, Woodson could only stare at his father-in-law in wonder. "I guess we all have our secrets."

"Yes, and if you don't go running back tattling to MacArthur, I'll tell you a few."

◇◇◇

While Mullins and his son-in-law drank their beer, three time zones and two thousand four hundred miles to the west Lisa Li and Peter returned to her apartment from a spring kite-flying festival at a nearby Palo Alto park.

Li thanked her security guard, opened the door, and stepped on a manila envelope lying just inside the threshold.

"Is it another package from Mr. Mullins?" Peter removed his new Washington Nationals baseball cap that FedEx had delivered that morning.

"No." Li picked it up quickly. "Probably something from work. Why don't you go in the bedroom and start pulling your clothes together? I want you packed tonight since you're leaving so early in the morning."

"And it will be Monday morning when I land. I still want to know where Sunday will go."

She laughed. "You'll waste it on the plane playing your video games. Now scoot!"

Peter flipped the cap backwards on his head and did as she ordered. Only when she heard him opening drawers did she examine the envelope. "Dr. Lisa Li" had been hand-printed in black block letters on the front. No address. No return address. It was sealed only by the metal clasp. She bent the prongs up and opened the flap.

She extracted three pages. The first was an eight-by-ten photograph of her sister captured by a long lens as she emerged from her home. A thick red X had been scrawled over her face. Li felt her knees weaken. The second was a Chinese news article from eight years ago reporting her husband's accidental death. The final sheet was a copy of the electronic ticket Lisa Li had purchased for Peter's first-class return to Beijing. His seat number had been circled. Beside it, the name "Lu" had been written to show her that someone knew the Jué Dé executive who had offered to travel with Peter. A red arrow pointed to the edge of the page.

Li turned it over. Three sentences had been written in the same red ink—"You know we know. When you're approached, hear them out, then accept. Keep the boy."

Li suddenly felt nauseated. Panic rose in her faster than when Mullins had led her out of the ballroom. Her world spun upside down and there was nothing she could do to regain control. "When you're approached, hear them out." Who were they and what did they want? Was her sister's life in danger? Had Jué Dé and the Chinese government had a major falling out and she would be pressured into returning to state-sponsored research? If that was the case, why wasn't the message written in Chinese?

All she knew for sure was Peter wouldn't be on that flight tomorrow. She'd call her sister and tell her he was sick with a stomach bug. Then she would wait. But for what?

◇◇◇

Nine time zones and over five thousand eight hundred miles to the east of where Lisa Li stood trembling in her apartment, Heinrich Schmidt logged into his e-mail account. At two in the morning, the all-night Internet café in Zurich was doing a brisk business. Schmidt preferred it that way. The more people, the less likely he'd be remembered.

He checked the drafts folder, not really expecting any communication. His client had been really pissed at the way the Washington job had gone. In Schmidt's opinion, he bore no blame. The man should have told him there would be more than standard hotel security. Not some goddamned protection detail led by a Secret Service agent. The hits and extraction would have been handled differently, if at all.

To his surprise, a new composition waited for his review. By sharing the same account, their e-mails were never sent. They always remained in draft mode and were deleted as soon as read. No travel between servers or accounts where intercepts would be more likely.

The message was short with one attachment to be previewed, not downloaded. “If needed, be prepared to move fast. No subcontractors. Standard retainer plus travel. You’ll meet these new friends.”

Schmidt opened the attachment. A composite photo of two head shots. They looked like government-issued IDs. A younger man and an older man, each identified by name. His new friends. Allen Woodson. Russell Mullins.

He recognized the second name. The man who had shot his best agent and forced him to race away in the van and then fly to Montreal while his team lay in the D.C. morgue.

Schmidt memorized the faces. They were good quality head shots. Head shots, he thought. How appropriate.

Chapter Ten

The western sky was rapidly changing from red to purple. The shifting colors shimmered on the surface of the mountain lake and mesmerized Robert Brentwood. He sat in his chair at the end of his dock, sipping his Blanton's and letting his dynamo of a mind run free.

The house he'd leased on Lake Lure in Rutherford County, North Carolina, had been an unexpected delight. With residences in Manhattan and San Francisco, plus a rented condo in Charlotte, he'd feared the rural isolation of the eastern range of the Appalachians would have him climbing the walls of whatever backwoods accommodations he could find close to his billion-dollar Artificial Intelligence complex. The seven-hundred-twenty-acre Lake Lure was nestled amid the ancient mountain ridges and provided an escape from his world of high tech, high pressure, and, most of all, the high stakes riding on the success of the Apollo project.

Brentwood held his glass of bourbon skyward, toasting the spot where the sun had slipped behind the ridge. Apollo. The name he'd christened his soon-to-be-birthed baby. The Greek god of light, healing, the arts, and, yes, plague.

Ned Farino had argued the name Apollo had already been taken by the United States moon mission. But wasn't that the point? Brentwood saw it as a continuation of that exploration into new frontiers. "That's one small step for man, one giant leap for mankind." Or was the sentence, "That's one small step for *a* man, one giant leap for mankind?" Nearly fifty years after the historic quote, the debate still continued as to whether Neil Armstrong had inadvertently omitted the "a."

Brentwood would make sure there was no such controversy with his Apollo mission. The words would flash around the world. A new world. Spoken by a new being. "I am—so that you will be. And together, we keep our destiny."

Although the proclamation would come simultaneously to all humanity, the words wouldn't immediately be understood. Brentwood wouldn't offer the translation. He would make the point that the new age of common good spoke a common language, free of national prejudice, and the words in the original tongue would reverberate throughout the millennia. *Mi estas—tiel ke vi estos. Kaj kune, ni plenumu nian destinon.*

Brentwood stood and walked to the dock's last board. He took a deep breath of the mountain air. This place suited him. He decided not to extend the lease on the Charlotte condo, but instead make the owners of the Lake Lure house an offer they couldn't refuse. He turned and looked up the slope to the rambling old structure standing amidst the white pines. It had character. It had soul. The house was big enough to accommodate a chef and a personal assistant whenever he needed them. And there was a guest cottage less than a hundred feet away. The idea formed quickly. No, not for the staff, he thought. The perfect place for Dr. Li and the boy. Their own quarters, but close to him.

Lisa Li needed to share his vision and this setting would be more conducive than the labyrinth of servers and processors humming constantly in the layers of Apollo's central core.

Of course, Ned Farino would object. But he and Li had much to discuss, and Ned wasn't to be privy to those conversations. Nothing was of greater priority.

T-Day was three months out. Target Day, as Farino had labeled it. Initial test forays would begin as soon as Li set the partitions and thresholds. In Brentwood's mind, T-Day was nonnegotiable. They would be ready. The symbolism was crucial to reinforce the magnitude of the moment.

His thoughts wandered to that person he'd most like to be with him on that day. Steve Jobs. Although they'd only met once, Brentwood knew they had been kindred spirits. Brothers. Jobs got it. The power of symbolic presentation and the power of innovative performance went hand in hand in the quest for knowledge. The Apple icon with one bite taken. A return to the Garden.

Brentwood wasn't eating the forbidden fruit. He was planting its seeds.

Chapter Eleven

The Monday morning after Allen Woodson's surprise appearance, Mullins purchased two prepaid cell phones from a discount electronics store. He wasn't particularly enthused about having to keep up with another device, but his son-in-law had stressed the need for a communications avenue that would be just between them.

With caution bordering on paranoia, Woodson had insisted Mullins pay cash to avoid a credit card transaction and then program each number into the other phone's memory. Woodson didn't want to risk another visit to Mullins' apartment so he instructed his father-in-law in how to use a prearranged drop. Mullins had been impressed at the planning Woodson had done prior to showing up at his apartment, and he wondered if his daughter had married James Bond.

At eleven-thirty, Mullins strolled into the Cleveland Park Neighborhood Library on Connecticut Avenue in northwest Washington with one of the new phones in his suit coat pocket.

He nodded a greeting to the first staff person he saw and said he was just browsing before meeting a friend for lunch. In the reference section, he found the book Woodson had selected. *Literary Market Place*. The volume contained lists of literary agents, publishers, trade associations, and other industry information. It had to be nearly five inches thick and a foot high. Clearly, it was deeper than the book beside it, a guide for marketing poetry.

Mullins slid the smaller book out, flipped through the pages a few moments, and used his body to block anyone from seeing him push the small phone into the vacant slot. Then Mullins re-shelved the book so that its spine came flush with the larger volume beside it. The phone was perfectly concealed.

He glanced at his watch. Eleven-forty. Woodson would arrive at noon. Now success depended upon no unpublished poets showing up within the next twenty minutes and screwing up the whole deal. That would be poetic injustice, Mullins thought.

He walked a few blocks off Connecticut Avenue into a residential neighborhood where he'd found on-street parking. Instead of immediately leaving for his apartment in Shirlington, he sat in the Prius and waited. If his son-in-law didn't call by five after twelve, he'd return to the library and retrieve the phone. The odds that out of the thousands of books housed in that branch the one on publishing poetry would be pulled from the shelf today were slim. But, a possibility was still a possibility. In the Secret Service, his mission had been to reduce all possibilities to zero.

Noon. The burner phone lay dormant on the seat beside him. Five minutes passed. Mullins grew restless. If Woodson was anything, he was punctual.

At ten after, he picked up the second phone and left the car. If someone at the library seemed puzzled by his return, he'd say he'd forgotten his reading glasses. He carried a pair in his shirt pocket and could brandish them as evidence.

In less than half a block, the new phone vibrated.

"Yes?" Mullins answered.

"Sorry," Woodson whispered. "MacArthur was on my other cell. I couldn't get him off."

"Something break?"

"We got a hit in Montreal. Facial recognition of the man you shot. He flew into Canada a week before. A French national traveling under the name of Jean-Louis Marlette. Probably a fake identity, but at least we have a link."

"Do they know where his flight originated?"

"Yeah. Mozambique."

"Jesus. That's going around your elbow to get to your foot."

"Yeah, but he might live there. These mercenaries can really be anywhere. All they need is a satellite phone and they're in business. The other two that we nailed with prints lived in Thailand and Belize. MacArthur's tracking whatever money connections—banks, wire transfers, credit cards—he can. At least we've got a chance to turn over the rocks they hid under."

"A common paymaster," Mullins said.

"That's the hope. If two of the three we've identified show the same origination source for a money transfer, then we've got a potential employer. Maybe even the brains of the whole operation going back to Kim's disappearance."

Even over the phone, Mullins could feel Woodson's excitement at the prospect of discovering what had happened to his sister. The case was as personal to the young officer as it was to him.

"Is MacArthur handling it?"

"He's coordinating. Agents have been dispatched to those countries to see what can be learned on the ground. The Germans are included since Brecht was a victim."

"What about the Pakistanis?"

"They're on the sidelines. Nothing indicates this Humanity's Hope terrorist group has any connection to Pakistan. Pakistani intelligence has enough trouble controlling their own extremists."

Mullins found Woodson's report encouraging. A break or two and the mastermind behind Ted Lewison's murder would be identified. He could face Elizabeth Lewison and say the full resources of the United States were now targeted on her husband's killers.

"How about Kim's FBI file?" Mullins asked. "Any word?"

"That's really why I was late to the library. MacArthur said he has a copy for me. I'm going after it now."

"If you learn anything I can help with, for God's sake tell me."

"I will, Rusty. Any word on your potential access to that super computer?"

"No. I guess she didn't take the job."

"Well, things look promising," Woodson said. "We'll get them."

Mullins dropped the phone in his pocket and headed back to the Prius. He hadn't gone ten steps when he felt the vibration. He grabbed the phone again, thinking Woodson must have forgotten something. But that phone was still. His personal one buzzed on his hip. He snatched it and read "Unidentified Caller" on the screen.

"Yes," he barked.

"Mr. Mullins, this is Ned Farino, Mr. Brentwood's associate. We're activating you. A car will be by at nine tonight to take you to BWI. You're flying to Palo Alto and you'll bring Dr. Li and her nephew back with you."

"To Washington?"

"To where we take you," he said curtly.

The hairs rose on Mullins' neck. He didn't like flying blind. "And my Glock?"

"You're on a private jet. Pack it in your suitcase along with plenty of ammo and clothes for a week. And, Mr. Mullins, welcome aboard."

Chapter Twelve

Dr. Lisa Li packed her laptop and two hard drives between layers of clothes, zipped the large suitcase shut, and set it inside the hall closet of her Palo Alto apartment. Then she retrieved Peter's from his bedroom, placed it beside hers, and closed the door.

The instructions had been very specific. At midnight, she and Peter were to take the elevator to the ground floor carrying an empty laundry basket as if getting clean clothes from a dryer in the complex's laundry room. They were to leave the basket and exit through the rear service door to a small loading dock. Rusty Mullins and a driver would be waiting. The luggage in the closet would be picked up by someone else so that no one would see her leaving with suitcases.

Mullins was the one reassuring element in the plan. Li knew he would also be a calming presence for Peter. The boy didn't know how upended their lives were about to become.

The other security man who had come to her apartment with Robert Brentwood the previous night had seemed more like a prison guard than a protector. She'd known his type in China. Self-important. A bully in an Armani suit. Brentwood had called him Jenkins. The stocky man had close-cropped brown hair and penetrating gray eyes. He'd stared at her the whole time Brentwood was talking. For ninety minutes, he uttered not a word.

Brentwood's message had been persuasive on two levels. The carrot had been a payday of three million dollars for signing on with him for three months, with an additional three million if Li successfully created a computer facsimile of the human subconscious. She would have the latest processors and neuromorphic chips in the world. And she would have authority over a team of existing scientists mapping and mirroring the conscious mind to develop her own software architecture and integral hierarchy. The opportunity was everything she could hope for in her career.

The stick was clearly defined in the documents she had found on her threshold. Brentwood only referenced it in one sentence. "And we all know there are certain things we don't want to reach the conscious mind of the public." He said it with a smile, which made it all the more frightening.

Li went to the kitchen and glanced at the oven's digital clock. Five-forty-five. Peter and Maria would be home from the library soon. The temporary nanny provided by Jué Dé during Peter's visit had been a godsend to keep him entertained during Li's workday. Maria had graciously agreed to stay on after Li delayed Peter's return to China.

Li was assembling two bags of snacks for their flight when she heard the bolt release in her front door.

"Aunt Li Li! We're home."

"In the kitchen."

The boy ran in juggling a stack of library books. "Maria let me check these out on her card. I got Sherlock Holmes, two Encyclopedia Browns, and a mystery called *The Westing Game* that the librarian said is full of clues."

Li forced a smile. She'd hoped to have their special conversation after dinner, but the books made it impossible to delay. "Why all the detective stories?"

"So I can help Mr. Mullins someday." Peter looked up with hope in his eyes. "Do you think he would ever come to China?"

"We'll see." Li relaxed. Peter would be no problem once he learned Mullins was going with them. "Say good night to Maria and run and wash up. We're going to walk to Angelo's."

"Can I get extra meatballs?"

"Whatever you want. Now set the books on the hall table and do as I say."

Peter scampered away. Li heard his "Good night, Maria" and the thud as he dropped the books on the table. She stepped into the hall.

"Maria, I have something for you." She picked up an envelope that had been knocked aside by Peter's books.

"Yes, Miss Li." Maria stood just inside the front door. She was a small Hispanic woman in her twenties with bright brown eyes and straight black hair pulled off her forehead by a silver and turquoise band. A night student at Foothill, the local community college, Maria demonstrated a playful curiosity that made her an excellent sitter for Peter.

Li handed the young woman the envelope.

Maria lifted the flap and her eyes grew wide as she withdrew ten one-hundred-dollar bills. "What is this?"

"I hope it's fair severance. Peter and I have been called away suddenly. I really appreciate what you've done for him."

Maria shook her head. "But this is too much. You said there would only be a few extra days before Peter returned to China."

Li picked up the library books. "It's complicated. Take the bonus. I'm not reporting it. All I ask is you keep this conversation a secret."

Maria nodded. "Can I tell him goodbye?"

Li gave her the books. "I'm afraid that would upset him. I haven't had the chance to tell him. You understand."

"Yes, ma'am."

Li knew that the woman didn't understand but that was fine.

A few minutes before midnight, Lisa Li and Peter closed the door to the Palo Alto apartment for the final time. Li carried a white plastic laundry basket and Peter clutched a small backpack containing his iPad and three bags of snacks. He'd insisted his aunt make one for Mullins. She'd tried to get him to lie down for a few hours after supper, but he was too excited. Mullins and a ride in a private jet dispelled any possibility of sleep.

Li dropped the empty basket next to a dryer and then led Peter to the rear door. As they stepped into the cool air, a car flashed its headlights. Li grabbed Peter's hand and they crossed the loading zone to the waiting vehicle, a gray Ford Taurus of several years vintage. Immediately forgettable.

Mullins got out of the front passenger's seat and gave a wave of encouragement. Peter broke free and ran to him. Mullins knelt down and gave the boy a one-armed hug.

"Mr. Mullins, the Nationals are in first place."

"I know. Thanks to your streak of eighty-degree days."

"Can we see a game when we get to Washington?"

"If Mr. Mullins has the time," Li said.

Mullins stood and Lisa Li hugged him as well.

"It's good to see you, Rusty."

"You too."

She looked at his left arm bound in the sling. "How's the shoulder?"

"Mending. Two more weeks and I shed this thing." He looked beyond her to the apartment building. "You and Peter get inside the car."

She let Peter climb in first.

As she slid beside him, the driver turned his head. "Your key, please."

She recognized Jenkins, the stone-faced man who'd come with Brentwood. She handed him a key and fob.

"The fob's for the building's electronic lock," she explained. "The suitcases are in the hall closet."

"Fine. Let's go, Mullins."

Mullins closed Li's door and joined Jenkins. Half a block later, Jenkins pulled the Taurus onto a side street and flashed his lights. A black Honda Accord pulled from a parking spot and headed toward them.

Jenkins rolled down his window as the oncoming car braked beside them. He held out the key and a dark-skinned hand emerged from the shadows of the Honda's interior.

"Back entrance. Hall closet." With those four words, Jenkins rolled up the window and drove on.

The Gulfstream jet stood on the tarmac in front of a private hangar. The boarding stairs were down and a crew member stood at the foot.

"Wow," Peter said. "This is cool."

"Your luggage should be fifteen minutes away," Jenkins said. "Takeoff will be as soon as it's loaded. Mullins will accompany you."

Li felt relief that Jenkins would be staying behind. She hoped in a day or two everything would settle down, she could get on with her work, and, more importantly, get on with life in Washington.

Mullins gestured for Peter and Li to ascend the stairs ahead of them. Peter chose a seat on the first row near the cockpit. Li sat directly across the aisle and Mullins took the seat behind Peter, where he could more easily speak to Li.

The two-man crew was a different team than the one that had flown Mullins from BWI. Mullins thought maybe it was the short turnaround and length of back-to-back flights.

The twin engines whined to life. The taller of the two stepped from the cockpit holding a book in his hand.

"My name is Jack Lamar. My co-pilot's Sid Troutman. We're wide awake and well rested so you folks can sleep." He grinned. "Which one of you happens to be Peter Wang?"

"That's me," Peter exclaimed.

The pilot shook the boy's hand. "Glad to meet you. Your host, Mr. Brentwood, was afraid you might get bored on the flight. He wanted me to give you one of his favorite books."

Lamar held up a hardback copy of Isaac Asimov's *I, Robot.*

"What's it about?" Peter asked.

Lamar shrugged. "Not sure. I once saw a movie with that title. Something about a robot who's a detective."

"Like Mr. Mullins." Peter swiveled around in his seat. "But you're not a robot."

"No," Mullins confessed. "Not smart enough."

"What do you say, Peter?" Li prompted.

"Thank you. And thank Mr. Brentwood."

"You'll see him soon enough."

"What time do you think we'll land at BWI?" Mullins asked.

Jack Lamar frowned. "Who told you we were going to BWI?"

"Her lab's in Washington."

"Maybe. But we're flying to Asheville, North Carolina. I guess it was a change of plans." He held out his hand. "I need your cell phones."

Li fumbled through her purse and then handed him her phone. Mullins didn't move.

"I'm sorry, sir. But I've been instructed to take charge of your phone."

"No. I think I need to speak to Brentwood directly."

The pilot reached behind his back for a second. When his hand reemerged, it held a nine-millimeter Beretta pointed at Mullins' chest.

"Move slowly, sir. First hand me the Glock under your sling."

Mullins complied.

"Now the phone."

Mullins shifted in his seat and pulled the cell from his belt.

"Thank you," Lamar said. "They'll be returned later."

He backed into the cockpit, closed and locked the door.

"Auntie Li Li," Peter whimpered, and strained against his seat belt toward his aunt.

Mullins saw Li struggle to remain calm for her nephew's sake. "It's all right," he told her.

Li unsnapped her belt and crossed the aisle to sit with the boy. He buried his head in her shoulder.

Mullins dug deep in the front pocket of his pants for the thin burner phone. He wouldn't risk a voice call, but he texted a short message:

> headed for Asheville NC—find nearest
> Brentwood facility—do not respond but wait.

The whine of the engines rose higher and Peter's whimpering began again.

Five minutes later, the Gulfstream lifted off into the starry California sky.

Chapter Thirteen

A few minutes before nine-thirty, eastern daylight time, the Gulfstream banked hard for its final approach to the Asheville airport. Mullins looked out at the mountains below. The ridges were stacked to the far horizon like ocean waves frozen on their way to the shore. The sun hadn't yet burned off the morning haze, a product of the thick vegetation that shifted the light to the blue end of the spectrum and made the name Blue Ridge Mountains more than just a slogan for tourism.

Mullins reached over the seat in front of him and nudged Lisa Li's shoulder. She awoke with a start. Peter shifted beside her but remained sleeping.

"Looks like we'll be on the ground in a few minutes."

"What then?" Li whispered.

Mullins shrugged. "We go with the flow. Rest assured they didn't fly you across the continent to do you any harm. I think our pilot was anxious to get airborne and didn't have time for niceties."

"Why take our phones?"

"They probably pulled the batteries to make sure no one could track us." Mullins patted the burner phone in his pocket just to assure himself it was there. "My bet is you and Peter are going off the grid for a while."

Li's eyes widened. "But what about you?"

"We'll know where I stand if they give me back my gun." Mullins smiled in an attempt to ease her fears. "Frankly, going off the grid may be a good thing, at least till I can learn more about who tried to kill you."

"Okay." She turned away to the window. "I guess we have no choice."

When the plane touched down, Li woke Peter with a kiss on his forehead. She said something in Chinese and the boy immediately looked over the seat to Mullins.

"Everything's going to be fine," Mullins said.

"The man had a gun," Peter whispered.

"That's right. And he got us here safely. I'm not worried so don't you be."

Peter bit his lower lip. "Are you sure?"

"Yes. Now I believe the man who gave you the book is going to meet us. Remember to thank him."

The Gulfstream taxied to a spot near a private hangar. Mullins saw a black limousine identical to the one that intercepted him in Shirlington drive across the tarmac to the jet.

The cockpit door opened and Jack Lamar emerged. "Well, I hope you had a pleasant flight and got some sleep." He handed Mullins his Glock butt-first. "I apologize for being so abrupt in Palo Alto. I had orders to take off without any delays, and discussing our destination wasn't part of the agenda." The pilot spoke the words with a smile in his voice, but kept his hard stare fixed on Mullins. Mullins had no doubt the man would have pulled the trigger.

"Our phones?" Mullins asked.

"You'll get those back from Mr. Farino, once you're safely on campus. He's Mr. Brentwood's executive vice president and he's handling all of the travel logistics."

Like we're on some damn college tour, Mullins thought. "I was hired directly by Mr. Brentwood."

The pilot grinned. "Then that explains why you didn't know where we were going. Mr. Brentwood's mind is usually out there in the stratosphere, know what I mean? Farino's the man who makes things happen." Lamar stuck out his hand. "No hard feelings?"

"No hard feelings." As they shook, Mullins thought, *no hard feelings because you'll never take a gun away from me again, you son of a bitch.*

As they deplaned, Lamar stood at the foot of the stairs ready to assist Li and Peter with the final step. The boy clutched the Asimov book to his chest, not because it was a cherished possession but because he refused to take Lamar's outstretched arm. Lisa Li kept one hand on the stair rail and the other on Peter's shoulder. She walked by Lamar without a word.

Robert Brentwood popped out of the rear seat of the limo and clapped his hands. "Welcome. Welcome. I see you got the book, Peter. Do you like it?"

"Mr. Lamar pointed a gun at Mr. Mullins. I was too scared to read."

Brentwood's face darkened and he scowled at Lamar. The pilot stared back with no admission of guilt or words of apology.

"I told Peter these are dangerous times," Mullins said. "But we are perfectly safe, aren't we?"

Brentwood stepped away from the car. "Absolutely. Peter, sit by the window. There's something special I want to show you along the way."

Li nudged the boy forward. "Go ahead."

Peter crawled into the backseat.

"Slide all the way over," Brentwood instructed. "I'll sit in the middle. Rusty, you can ride shotgun."

Mullins didn't move. "I will when Mr. Lamar gives us back our phones."

A moment of awkward silence followed. Mullins held out his hand.

Brentwood nodded and Lamar pulled two phones and two batteries from his pocket. He slapped them on Mullins' palm like a petulant child.

"Thank you," Mullins said. He then walked directly to Brentwood. "Take these and replace the sim cards, but preserve the contact data. We'll only give the new numbers to people we trust."

"So, you didn't have a problem surrendering your phones?" Brentwood asked.

"Surrendering? A big problem. If we'd been asked to surrender the batteries for security problems, then no problem at all. I'm either on the security team or I'm not." Mullins made a point of looking at Lisa Li. "If not, then I'm out of here."

"I am too," Li said.

"No! No!" Brentwood raised his hands, the phones in one and the batteries in the other. "This is all a misunderstanding. We were overly protective to get you here safely. I'm sorry. Now come. There's much to show you."

The driver emerged and walked around the front of the vehicle to open the passenger door for Mullins. He was the same man who had accompanied Brentwood in Shirlington. Mullins could see the slight bulge of a shoulder holster under his left arm.

"Apology accepted." Mullins gestured for Li to precede him. Brentwood nodded a thank you, slid in beside Peter, and patted the space next to him. Li sat and the driver closed the door.

"I can seat myself." Mullins walked around the limo, keeping his eyes on both Lamar and the driver.

When everyone was settled, the driver popped open the trunk. Lamar pulled their bags from the Gulfstream and turned them over to the driver to load. Within five minutes, they were on I-40, skirting Asheville until they exited onto a two-lane blacktop that wound through a green valley of farms and cross-road communities.

Mullins leaned forward and stole a quick glance in the exterior side mirror. A black Tahoe trailed closely behind. Although the letters and numerals were reversed in the reflection, Mullins identified the blue and white plate as being from Virginia.

The long valley narrowed, funneling into just the road and a bold stream rippling between two mountainsides.

"Peter, this is called Hickory Nut Gorge." Brentwood pointed to the ridge crest on their right. "See how high the mountains rise? Over millions of years, the Rocky Broad River has cut the gorge even deeper."

"The river's not very big," Peter said.

"True. But millions of years is a very long time. Even before the Cherokee were here."

"Indians?" Peter suddenly became interested.

"Yes. Look up ahead. See that gray stone tower sticking out near the top of the mountain?"

The boy pressed his face against the tinted window. "There's a flagpole on top."

"That's Chimney Rock. It's a natural stone formation and it looks just like a chimney. And you get up there by an elevator."

"Wow! From all the way down here?"

Brentwood laughed. "No. From the base of the chimney. But it's still pretty amazing to ride inside a mountain. They used that location when they made a movie called *The Last of the Mohicans*. Of course, they didn't use the flagpole."

Peter looked across Brentwood to Lisa Li. "Can we go sometime, Aunt Li Li?"

"Sure," Brentwood interjected. "But not today. When it's more convenient for your aunt and Mr. Mullins."

The gorge widened just enough to allow buildings on either side of the road. An assortment of gift shops, mom-and-pop restaurants, and even a motorcycle repair garage lined the banks of the stream.

"This is the Village of Chimney Rock," Brentwood explained. "A real snug fit between the water and the mountainside. I've been warned you wouldn't want to be here during a flash flood. The little river can turn into a raging torrent, sweeping everything out of its path."

"Couldn't the people climb up on the chimney?"

Brentwood nodded with genuine approval. "You know, Peter, I believe that they could. I'll suggest that and tell them it was your idea."

Peter sat back and looked at the book in his lap. "You liked this story, Mr. Brentwood?"

"Yes. I wasn't much older than you when I first read it. I had to look up a lot of words. But it stuck with me."

"Mr. Lamar said it was about detectives."

"No. That was a movie." Brentwood leaned close to Peter and whispered, "Between you and me, Mr. Lamar's not smart enough to understand this book. But I bet you are. It's set in the future and it's about the history of robots. And it gave me some ideas that I'm going to work on with your aunt."

"From your subconscious?"

Brentwood laughed. "I bet you know your aunt's research as well as she does." He tapped his finger on the book's cover. "Yes. Maybe those ideas have just been rattling around in my subconscious all these years and your aunt's going to put them to good use."

After a few miles the gorge widened and the ridges formed a bowl around a sparkling lake.

"Look, Peter. It's a beach." Lisa Li pointed to the left side where an expanse of sand stretched between the road and the water's edge.

"But there's nobody on it."

"That's because it's still April," Brentwood explained. "Another month and you'll have trouble finding an open space to spread your beach towel. This is Lake Lure. Its claim to fame is that the movie *Dirty Dancing* was shot here."

"Why?" Peter asked. "Is the water dirty?"

Mullins couldn't suppress a laugh. "You're showing your age, Robert. That film's nearly thirty years old."

"The water's clean. I know because my house is right on the lake. And I have a guesthouse for you and your aunt."

"On this lake?" Peter craned his neck around Brentwood for a closer look at the beach.

"Yes. It's farther along the shoreline. Very private. Very secure."

"I should be the judge of that," Mullins said sharply.

"Of course. And if anything is amiss, I'll correct it to your satisfaction."

The driver turned left off the main road and began a slow, circuitous journey above the lake shore.

"We can't stay here," Li said. "I've got to get Peter enrolled in a D.C. school."

"Look, school's out in six weeks," Brentwood said. "I'll get him a tutor. You can stay here where you're closer to the heart of the project. When things are well in hand, you can work out of Washington or remain here as long as you like."

"Please, Aunt Li Li," Peter begged. "I don't want to go back to Washington."

Mullins realized the nation's capital was now nothing more than a traumatic memory for the boy. He looked over his shoulder at Lisa Li. Her mouth twisted in concentration as she weighed the merits of Brentwood's proposal.

"What about you, Rusty?" she asked. "Is this what you signed on for?"

Mullins stared out the front windshield. He saw patches of water reflecting blue sky and puffy white clouds. He noticed signs beside driveways with names like Journey's End, Getaway, and Shore Enough. Very few were family names. Most mailboxes displayed only numerals. He thought of Josh and Kayli and how quickly he would miss them. And of Allen holed up at the JW Marriott and charged by the President of the United States to feed him the information gathered by the unparalleled resources of the government's intelligence agencies. Or were they unparalleled?

He turned back to Li. "I signed on to keep you and Peter safe. Perhaps for now this is the best location—not because of geography but because of resources. Robert, are you still good with your promise to give me what I need to discover who was behind the attack?"

"Absolutely," Brentwood answered. "Just name it."

"Then I need some of Lisa's time. She can run data searches and evaluations on this so-called super genius computer of yours."

Brentwood stiffened with visible resistance to the idea. "But we have technicians who can do that for you."

"We're talking about her life and a conspiracy with tentacles reaching God-knows-where. That's the deal or I'm taking Lisa and Peter back to D.C. with me." Mullins eyed the driver. "Unless you plan to have one of your employees pull another gun on us..."

The driver's face never so much as twitched. Mullins knew he sounded overly dramatic, but Brentwood had a childlike view of the world that needed a reality check. Mullins was ready to pull his own Glock and demand to be driven back to Asheville.

The billionaire threw up his hands. "Okay, okay. We're all on the same side. Work it however you want."

Fifteen minutes later, the limo stopped in front of a wrought-iron gate stretching across a freshly paved driveway. Twin stone pillars anchored either side. A matching fence extended from the pillars and disappeared into the trees. Everything looked so new Mullins wouldn't have been surprised to see a price tag dangling from one of the black pickets. Sharp spikes capped each bar, except every twenty feet or so a square box replaced the spike. Mullins suspected they held some kind of electrical component.

"You put this fence in?" Mullins asked.

"Just completed it two days ago. Encompasses the perimeter and has laser beams across the top that will be tripped should someone try to crawl over."

"How many gates?"

"Two. This one and another one at the dock."

Mullins saw the address mounted in one of the stone pillars. "You put up a visible street number?"

"Had to. Fire department requires some form of identification."

Mullins nodded with approval. He memorized the number. As soon as he could steal a few minutes alone, he'd text it to Allen and request a set of satellite photographs of the compound.

◇◇◇

The photographs lay on the desk in three piles. Foliage hid most of the terrain adjacent to the lake. On the aerial view, a bold black line drawn by a Sharpie marked the property boundaries. Beneath that top picture, a series of photos featured close-ups of the entrance gate, the dock, the exterior of the three-level lake house, and the single-story guesthouse. Four pages of documents detailed the specifications of the security system and the floor plans of both buildings.

Heinrich Schmidt set the stack labeled "Lake Lure" aside and examined the surveillance photos of an apartment building in Arlington, Virginia. Shirlington House, the residence of ex-Secret Service agent Rusty Mullins. A Sharpie had circled a corner window on the fourth floor. The wide parking lot below offered no concealment for a sniper's position. A second photo showed a blue Prius with Virginia license plates, the target's car, parked in a spot at the edge of the pavement. Good for a drive-by hit if it were a two-man operation, but not ideal for working alone. And Schmidt's instructions had been for a solo op.

The third stack covered a three-story brick building in an Arlington neighborhood called Fairlington Villages. A ring had been drawn around the windows on the lower right with the words "Woodson Condo" printed above. Schmidt understood that the unit housed Kayli and Josh, daughter and grandson of Rusty Mullins and the wife and child of Allen Woodson.

If collateral damage could be ignored, a packet of C-4 plastic explosive would take out both men if a family gathering brought them together in the home.

Schmidt combined the photos and documents into one pile. His preferred location was the isolated lake house, but if pressed into action, he'd take whatever appeared to be the best opportunity. Meanwhile, he was content to earn a fee for simply waiting. The Hampton Inn in the small city of Spartanburg, South Carolina, made a secure hiding spot, and whether he was called into action at Lake Lure only a few hours away or the suburbs of D.C., Heinrich Schmidt was ready.

He looked across the room at the golf bag and clubs leaning against the closet. The new set had arrived via Federal Express that morning and the shipping box lay ripped open on the hotel floor. The return address was from an online sporting-goods store in Chicago.

A fine set of clubs, although the woods were missing.

The M24 Sniper Weapons System fit snugly in their place—the rifle, telescopic scope, and bipod. And the Glock and four loaded magazines had been perfectly concealed in the ball pouch.

As a professional assassin, Heinrich Schmidt had to admit his client knew how to get things done.

Chapter Fourteen

"I haven't had time to remodel this interior. I hope you'll find it comfortable." Robert Brentwood stood in the small living room of the guest cottage and looked apologetically at the surroundings.

The furnishings were dated but serviceable. A Naugahyde sofa, circa 1970, a pale green armchair, and a black JFK rocker bordered a tan and brown hooked rug spread beneath an oak coffee table.

"My interior designer is flying down from New York later in the week to remedy the situation."

Mullins thought all the room needed was a widescreen TV.

"This is more than sufficient," Lisa Li said. "Please leave everything as it is, at least while we're here."

Brentwood nodded. "As you wish. There's a small eat-in kitchen, but my chef will be preparing all the meals in the main house. I'm afraid there's only one bathroom for the two bedrooms. You and Peter will need to share."

"What about Rusty?" Li asked.

"He'll have a room in the main house."

"If he's to protect me, why are we in separate buildings?"

"I thought you'd prefer your privacy. If you'd rather stay in the main house, there's ample room."

Li shook her head. "Here is fine. Either Peter sleeps with me in my bed or I'll pay for a cot. Rusty can have the second bedroom."

Brentwood turned to Mullins.

"I should be where she is," Mullins agreed. "The sofa will be fine."

"No," Li insisted. "You'll have a proper bed. You've got two more weeks of your shoulder in the sling. I won't have you uncomfortable on my account."

Mullins shrugged. "All right." He looked at Brentwood. "What next?"

"I'll see that your luggage is brought in. I know you've had a long night so I thought you'd like to relax a few hours. Lunch will be served in the main house at one, and then we'll go to the campus so Lisa can see where she'll be working."

"First, I'd like to walk the property and see the dock," Mullins said. "Do I need a gate key?"

Brentwood fished a white plastic card out of his front pocket. "This will work at both the dock and driveway. Would you like me to go with you?"

"No. Just make sure Lisa and Peter have what they need." He took the key and left.

◇◇◇

The land was wooded with only a border of laurel shrubs planted around the cottage. A trail constructed of river rock and railroad ties led to the main house. Like its smaller companion, the larger residence had a stone foundation and rustic bark siding.

Mullins spurned the path and turned right into the woods. Underbrush had been cleared beneath the pines and hardwoods and he had no difficulty walking in his street shoes.

The fence was about fifty feet away and identical in its wrought-iron structure to the section he'd observed at the driveway entrance. He followed it down the slope toward the lake, noting that a number of trees had been recently felled so that the fence could adhere to the property's boundary. Its construction must have cost enough to build a small village. The iron pickets not only towered a good two or three feet above his head but also appeared to be buried below ground level, making it difficult for anyone to tunnel underneath.

Several yards from the shoreline, the fence angled left. Blueberry bushes formed a protective barrier between the pickets and the water. On a Tuesday morning, the lake was quiet. Looking across to the far shore five hundred yards away, Mullins saw a lone kayaker paddling toward him. The leisurely rhythm of the strokes indicated no urgency to reach a specific destination. But Mullins would check Brentwood's dock carefully. An approach from the lakeside could be a vulnerability. If Brentwood's security measures didn't include video surveillance, Mullins would strongly suggest its installation.

Mindful of his own recommendation, he looked up into the surrounding trees, searching for any cameras that might be trained his way. He found nothing but branches and foliage. Turning his back to the house and the distant kayaker, Mullins pulled the burner phone from his pocket and sent his son-in-law a short text.

◇◇◇

Allen Woodson knocked softly on the private door to Vice Admiral Louis MacArthur's office. He heard a curt "Come in," turned the knob, and entered.

Woodson gave a salute that MacArthur returned without bothering to rise from behind his desk.

"You have information for me, sir?"

"Sit," MacArthur ordered. He swept some papers aside as if to clear a physical path to his young officer. "The information I have is that I have no information. Thailand, Mozambique, and Belize proved to be dead ends. The men left no trail beyond apartments rented for cash."

"Isn't that unusual? Surely there must be some common connection linking them."

"Of course there is," MacArthur snapped. "And no one's more frustrated than I am that we can't find it. These men might only have worked as lone guns prior to the Marriott attack. Just our bad luck that we catch their first team operation."

"Someone had to hire and pay them." Woodson wasn't intimidated by his superior's brusque manner.

MacArthur shook his head. "Believe me, we've pursued every conduit of terrorist financing we know. I guess you'd better share their names and photos with Mullins."

Woodson hadn't told MacArthur he'd already given his father-in-law the identification of the three known gunmen. "Okay. Mullins sent me a request for satellite scans of an area in North Carolina."

"North Carolina? What's he up to?"

Woodson briefed the vice admiral on Mullins' movements and his role as personal protection for Dr. Li.

"Brentwood." MacArthur spoke the name as if he was tired of hearing it. "The guy owns half the members of the Armed Services Committee. And he's so entrenched in AI development that I ordered a beachhead in Palo Alto."

Woodson knew "beachhead" as a military term for a defended position taken from the enemy and readied for launching an attack.

MacArthur realized the word had caught Woodson's attention. He smiled. "It's only an office for interfacing with the nerds, not assaulting them. Maybe North Carolina's a good place for Mullins. He can babysit the scientist and stay out of our hair. Give me the coordinates for the satellite photos. If we keep him happy, President Brighton will be happy. If Brighton's happy, I'm happy. And you don't want me unhappy."

"No, sir." Woodson stood and laid a sheet of paper on the desk with the Lake Lure information. "I should probably rendezvous with him in person. How would you like me to arrange transportation?"

"All commercial. I'll have the photos in twenty-four hours and a debit card for your expenses."

"Here?"

"No. I'll get them to you." MacArthur stood. "Tell Mullins not to worry. We'll nail those bastards."

"Yes, sir." Woodson understood he'd been dismissed. He saluted and left through the private door.

MacArthur sat and scowled at the Lake Lure coordinates. He had no choice but to fulfill the request. And he'd immediately brief Brighton on the intel he'd given Mullins. MacArthur picked up his phone and opened a secure line.

The beachhead had just moved to North Carolina.

Chapter Fifteen

The limo snaked its way along Highway 9 headed to the AI campus twenty miles away. The roller coaster stretch of road stirred a queasiness in Mullins' stomach, and he chastised himself for overindulging in the gourmet meal Brentwood's chef had prepared for lunch. As if almond-crusted mountain trout with white grits and swiss chard hadn't been enough, Mullins had devoured a monstrous slice of German chocolate cake that tasted terrific going down but would be a different matter coming up.

He slipped a roll of TUMS out of his coat pocket and let one melt in his mouth.

After a few miles, the landscape opened up into rolling hills and farmland. Mullins' indigestion eased.

"What's that green stuff?" Peter asked.

Brentwood laughed. "That, my friend, is kudzu. The gift from the Japanese that more successfully overran the United States than their army."

Shrubs and trees along the roadside were engulfed by the broad-leafed vines, creating strange shapes that gave little hint as to the underlying plants swallowed within.

"It was developed to combat soil erosion," Brentwood continued, "but it trapped not only the dirt but also everything else growing there. The locals say it can cover sleeping dogs and slow-moving old ladies."

Peter frowned as he thought about the prospect. "Maybe we should drive faster."

Brentwood clapped his hands in childish delight. "You heard the boy, Jefferson. Speed up."

A smile broke across the driver's face and the limo surged forward.

Mullins turned to face the backseat. "Why build your facility here in the feeding grounds of the kudzu? It's not like you have a secret laboratory."

"Hardly," Brentwood agreed. "Two things—cheap land and cheap power."

"I get the land part, but this is country. Where's the cheap power come in?"

"Textiles, Rusty. These little towns in the foothills were built by the mills. Rivers flowing out of the mountains provided hydroelectric energy to the factories. When the textile companies followed cheap labor offshore, they left the power infrastructure behind. I like to think of it as simply unplugging a loom and plugging in a server."

"Smart."

"Thanks. But it wasn't my idea alone. Facebook built the first data farm, as I like to call it. Their operation's about ten miles down the road from our campus."

"And they're researching artificial intelligence?"

"I'm sure they are. Probably not at this facility. But who knows? We're a secretive lot."

"Information barons," Mullins muttered to himself.

Brentwood leaned forward. "I didn't catch that."

"We've had railroad barons, oil barons, and now information barons."

"In a world of barons, I prefer to think of myself as Robin Hood."

Mullins patted the plush leather seat. "Yeah, living in the cold, damp wilds of Sherwood Forest."

Brentwood grinned sheepishly. "I guess you could say my weapon is a quiver full of money, not arrows."

"And a computer, not a bow."

Brentwood leaned back between Peter and Li. "I knew we'd understand each other."

The limo turned right onto an unlined blacktop that ran between fenced pastures. The only sign read, Private Property—No Exit. Mullins scanned the fields expecting cows or horses.

"Wow!" Peter exclaimed. "What are those?"

Mullins spotted a herd of shaggy animals on the brow of a distant hill.

"Buffalo," Brentwood said. "Or more accurately, bison. I've got the land and may as well put it to good use."

"Don't they draw the curious?" Mullins asked.

"At first. With all my construction trucks coming in from the main highway, the locals needed something to look at. Otherwise, their curiosity might lead them farther."

In a quarter mile, a triple-barred metal gate spanned across the road. The driver slowed only slightly to allow the gate to swing open automatically.

"The gate triggers a unique response signal from the car," Brentwood explained. "A computer reads it, visually identifies the vehicle and permits entry."

"How about deliveries?" Mullins asked.

"Vendors or approved visitors receive a cell phone number to which they text an admittance code. Employees have devices like this one on their cars."

"And for anyone setting out over the pastures on foot, the buffalo are more intimidating than a herd of Jersey heifers."

"There is that benefit," Brentwood admitted.

The pastures of bison gave way to pines and small hardwoods. The road curved left and again the landscape opened. Instead of pasture, a mammoth white structure filled a clearing that encompassed at least five acres. The building stood two stories with peaked rows of solar panels running across the flat roof. Beyond, four steel-girder towers rose above the tree line. Antennae and satellite dishes sprouted from platforms embedded in the tower skeletons.

"Cheap power and you still installed solar?" Mullins asked.

"Nothing cheaper than free sunlight. And computers live on electricity like we live on air. So, I have Duke Energy, diesel-powered generators, and the sun itself to make sure power is never interrupted."

"How big is this place?"

"Nearly four football fields. But it houses thousands and thousands of servers and processors."

The impressive size of Brentwood's facility dwarfed the small parking lot, a contrast that caught Mullins' eye. "There are only about twenty cars. Is there more parking in the rear?"

"No. We have a small research team and then our support technicians. One tech can monitor and take care of over twelve thousand servers, and we run our own software to alert us to any pending drive or system failure."

The limo parked in a reserved space close to metal and glass double doors. A guardhouse to the right of the sidewalk featured a flesh and blood sentinel who gave a nod to Brentwood as he passed. The entrance promised all the decor of walking into a warehouse.

Jefferson, the driver, held open one of the doors. A rush of air blew from the inside, shooing away any insects or airborne contaminants that might otherwise drift into the building. Lisa Li and Peter entered first. Mullins nearly crashed into them when they abruptly stopped just over the threshold.

The room was about fifty feet by seventy feet. No furniture, no receptionist. Instead a ball of roiling mist filled the space between the floor and the ceiling twenty feet above. The vaporous sculpture was contained in a circular mesh of fine tubing. Light played across the moving surface, creating highlights and shadows. As Peter, Li, and Mullins stood mesmerized, the wisps of artificial clouds morphed into a more definable object—a human brain.

"That is something." Mullins made the innocuous statement because other words failed him.

"The tubing has multiple jets of cold air and warm, moist air," Brentwood said. "The nozzles swivel to shoot the streams with pinpoint accuracy. Their intersection creates a cloud. The lights shine on different sections to help create the desired image. All computer-driven."

As Brentwood walked around the dynamic cloud, he beamed like a proud father. "Come, there's more to see." He stepped toward the rear wall of what looked like oak paneling. It instantly changed to a vast prairie with a herd of stampeding buffalo coming straight at them. Peter squealed and jumped behind Lisa Li.

Brentwood gave two sharp claps and the charging animals became a wall, this time of horizontal cedar. "I'm sorry. I didn't mean to scare you. Since we have no windows, we have areas of virtual scenery for stimulation." He pressed his palm against the fake wall and a section slid away revealing a passage to the rest of the building.

Mullins stepped through and found the sight more overwhelming than the mist sculpture or prairie landscape. Before him stood hundreds or even thousands of black monoliths, each with red and green lights flashing across their surface. At over six feet in height, they looked like giant dominoes mustered into rows and columns. Four football fields of them.

"Jesus," Mullins said. "Are these your brains?"

Brentwood walked to the nearest unit and patted it affectionately. "In the sense of stored knowledge, you can say that."

Lisa Li swept her gaze across the panorama and shook her head. "Only knowledge, not wisdom."

Brentwood pointed a finger at the scientist. "Exactly. Exactly. You've summed it up spectacularly."

"What do you say is the difference?" Mullins asked.

Brentwood looked at his newest employee. "Tell him. I'm interested to hear your perspective as well."

Li looked a little embarrassed at being thrust into the role of lecturer. "Knowledge is comprised of facts. Data collected, catalogued, and stored until retrieved for some process. Like the experienced events and information we embed in our brains. Critical information, trivial information, but that's all it is.

Just information." She looked to Brentwood who nodded his approval. "Wisdom is knowing what to do with that information. How to apply it, how to connect it in new ways and for new purposes. Human programmers do that and the computer performs a prescribed function, brilliantly and with unbelievable speed, but still merely executing someone else's directives. I'm not trying to improve a computer's knowledge. That's just more of these glorified machines. I'm interested in two things—imagination and wisdom. Those are the differences that need to be bridged. The imagination to conceive new ideas, ask and explore new questions, and then the wisdom to apply discoveries in the most effective and benign manner."

"Meaning what?" Mullins asked.

Brentwood jumped in, unable to restrain himself. "Meaning, Rusty, if Apollo determines on his own that the greatest threat to the earth is climate change brought about by greenhouse gases and a destroyed ozone layer, and the unbiased conclusion is that the greatest accelerant of these phenomena is humankind, what's to stop this super intelligent computer from wiping our species off the face of the earth?"

Peter stepped closer to Brentwood, his eyes wide. "Who's Apollo?"

Brentwood did a double take, blinking like the boy had materialized in front of him.

"Apollo?"

"You said Apollo," Peter insisted.

Brentwood colored slightly, and then shrugged. "It's the name I made up."

"I've read the stories, Mr. Brentwood. Apollo brings the sun. He brings the light. I think it's a good name."

Lisa Li draped her arm over Peter's shoulders. "It is a good name, Robert. And you'll need one." She looked at Mullins. "I believe if we create an artificial intelligence with imagination and wisdom we can't avoid the development that logically follows—artificial consciousness. And like any conscious entity, he'll have a desire for self-preservation."

"Forget climate change," Mullins said. "What if Apollo feels even remotely threatened?"

Brentwood and Li just looked at each other. Neither gave an answer.

"Where will Aunt Li Li work?" Peter scanned the enormous room for signs of people.

"All of the offices and labs are on the lower level," Brentwood said.

"Underground?" Mullins asked.

"Yes. Environmentally more efficient. The greatest enemy of all these electronics isn't a power loss. It's heat. Heat generated by hundreds of thousands of components, each alone not creating a high level, but collectively turning out a thermal boost that would soon damage delicate circuitry." Brentwood pointed straight over his head. "The ceiling is high and the roof peaked in upside-down troughs to channel that rising heat either outside or to the level below for warmth in winter. We replace the hot air with outside air that passes through chilled mist to lower its temperature without using full-scale air-conditioning. And the lower level is deeper than the frost line, which makes it easy to heat and cool."

Brentwood led them to a monolith on the side wall that was twice as big as the others. When he was about five feet away, the front panel slid up, revealing an empty chamber.

"Elevator," he explained.

The inside was deep enough to serve as a freight elevator. Diffused lighting from an overhead panel illuminated the interior.

"Where are the buttons for the floors?" Peter asked.

"No buttons. With only two levels, you're always going to the other one."

A low hum sounded as the elevator automatically descended. Mullins stepped farther back and noticed a small keypad installed in the side wall about four feet above the floor. Ten numerical buttons, zero to nine, were flush with the brushed metal surface and could easily be overlooked.

"What's the keypad for?" Mullins asked. "Firemen?"

"Firemen? Oh, you mean like those special keys they carry to override the elevator controls? I have a waiver since we're only two floors and there are adequate stairwells. The keypad disables this elevator and the other four. It can also secure access to the stairs."

"In other words, put you in lockdown," Mullins said.

"I guess you could call it that. The main function is to create a literal firewall that isolates any outbreak."

The door opened, catching Mullins by surprise. They stepped into a large reception area. Like the entry space above, the walls depicted virtual scenes, this time a rocky coastline that reminded Mullins of Maine. There was even the sound of surf and a breeze carried the faint taste of salt.

A translucent white desk faced the elevator. Behind it, an attractive dark-skinned woman of around thirty was talking into a wireless headset. She wore a sunburst dashiki and held up a forefinger signaling them to wait. She spoke a few words and then slipped off the earpiece and microphone.

"Welcome back, Robert. It looks like you've surrounded yourself with fine company."

"Felicia, meet Peter Wang and his aunt, Dr. Lisa Li. Dr. Li's joining our team. And this is Rusty Mullins, perhaps the best security man and criminal investigator in the country."

"Hardly." Mullins smiled despite the unwanted flattery.

Brentwood pressed on. "This is Felicia Corazón. She knows everything about the place. If you have any questions, she's the one to see."

Felicia stood and Mullins was surprised by her height. She had to be at least six-three, and with the close-cropped hair, she reminded him of a younger version of Ted Lewison's wife, Elizabeth. She walked from behind the desk with the graceful motion of a gazelle. From her right hand dangled three ID badges on braided gold cords. She handed one to each of them.

Mullins was stunned to see his passport photo between a barcode and the logo for Cumulus Cognitive Connections. "When did you get my passport?"

Felicia smiled. "When Robert needs something, I find it for him. Wear these when you're in the building. They're electronic and programmed to grant you access to the areas you have clearance."

"Where don't we have clearance?" Mullins asked.

"You pretty much have the run of the place, Mr. Mullins. Not the private offices. You'll have your own, of course, and I can give you access to Dr. Li's with her permission."

"Yes," Li said without hesitation.

"Dr. Li, you'll have a lab identical to the one you had in California, but with a newer generation of hardware. Both of you will have access to the canteen, gym, and game room."

"Game room?" Peter reached for his badge. "What kind of games?"

"Billiards, ping-pong, pinball, video games, and a TV the width of a wall. The room's mostly used by our younger techs, but I have seen a take-no-prisoners ping-pong match between the senior scientists now and then."

"Can we see the Nats games?"

Felicia looked confused. "Gnats? Like bugs?"

"It's Washington's baseball team," Brentwood said. "And I'm sure that will be no problem."

"Any other restricted areas other than private offices?" Mullins asked.

"Not really," Brentwood said. "Only the processing cores. That's where the neuromorphic chips are physically clustered into connected patterns mimicking the human brain. You wouldn't want some untrained person poking around in your head, would you, Rusty?"

"I guess not," he conceded.

Brentwood patted Peter on the shoulder. "And I forgot to mention that we have a library. That's where you'll meet Miss Collier tomorrow."

"Who's Miss Collier?" Peter asked.

Brentwood looked at Lisa Li. "Actually, it's Dr. Collier. I took the liberty of engaging a tutor who will be here onsite. She has a PhD in elementary education for gifted students. But if she doesn't work out, we'll find someone else."

Li shook her head in amazement at all that Brentwood had orchestrated. "Fine. But Peter needs some outdoor exercise as well." She gestured to the Maine coast. "Walking on a treadmill in front of a landscape image isn't enough."

"I agree," Brentwood said. "We'll have swimming at the lake, hiking at Chimney Rock Park, and whatever other activities you'd like. Just say the word. Now I suggest we take our tour and then call it an afternoon."

Felicia took her cue and walked to a section of the wall directly behind her desk. She tripped some sensor and a panel slid to the left. Instead of a clear doorway, a metal frame filled the opening. Mullins recognized a sophisticated body scanner.

"We'll pass through one at a time," Felicia said. "A precaution to make sure we don't carry in anything that could create a magnetic field, no matter how faint. That means no cell phones, pagers, or other electronic devices."

Mullins inadvertently patted his pants pocket where he'd kept his burner phone. Thanks to his fear that he'd have to go through some sort of security clearance, it now lay under his mattress back at the cottage.

"You don't need to worry about your change, Mr. Mullins," Felicia said. "We're only concerned about electronics."

Mullins lifted his arm in the sling enough to reveal the holstered pistol under his coat. "And weapons?"

Brentwood laughed. "As long as it doesn't have an electronic guidance system, you could bring in a bazooka. You're welcome to carry whatever arsenal you think you need."

Mullins didn't need an arsenal. He needed a suspect, and unless Lisa Li could get this alleged super brain to focus on his case, all the guns in the world were useless. He'd be better off pushing the action in Washington with Allen instead of cloistered in some glorified cave. *How ironic,* he thought. *Terrorists lived in caves. That is until they set off a bomb beside you or flew a jet into your building.*

Suddenly, he wondered if Brentwood had placed his staff and his beloved Apollo beneath the ground because of environmental efficiency or because they were housed in a fortified bomb shelter.

One thing was clear. Robert Brentwood was not a man to be underestimated. Not by a long shot.

Chapter Sixteen

While Lisa Li put Peter to bed in the rollaway in her room, Mullins brought two fingers of Scotch out to the front porch of the cottage to one of its three wooden rockers and took a deep breath of mountain air. The day had been a long one and he found the starry sky and night sounds to be calming. A breeze blew off the water and its chill settled first into his injured shoulder. He wondered if the wound would turn him into one of those old codgers who predicted rain based upon some aching muscle or joint.

Mullins took a sip of his drink to warm himself from the inside out, and then set the glass on the floor. Somewhere an owl hooted, one of the creatures whose nocturnal vision enabled it to seek its prey where others saw only darkness. Mullins wasn't so much troubled by the darkness of his investigation as by his ignorance of what tools Brentwood's facility offered that could shed light onto his case. He'd been impressed with what he'd seen in its sheer size and scope, and he thought Lisa Li seemed pleased by the extent of the resources. She would throw herself into her work, of that he was positive, but he needed her as an ally willing to carry out his research as well.

The screen door squealed as Li stepped outside. "Mind if I join you?"

"Please. Can I fix you a drink?"

Li looked at Mullins' glass on the floor. "What are you having?"

"Scotch." Mullins stood. "But there's a full bar in one of the upper kitchen cabinets."

"Scotch is fine. I can get it."

"No. Sit. I know where everything is." He gestured for her to take the chair beside him. "On the rocks?"

"Neat."

Mullins nodded his approval. "Back in a few minutes. Enjoy the quiet."

He pulled the bottle of Glenfiddich off an upper shelf and then a clean glass from an adjacent cabinet. He noticed a dirty glass on the counter with traces of milk coating the inside. Li had evidently given Peter a drink right before bed. Making a spur of the moment decision, Mullins found an identical glass, rinsed it, and set it in the sink as if he'd washed out the milk glass. Using a clean handkerchief, he quickly took Peter's glass to his room and tucked it in his suitcase. Then he poured Li's Scotch and took it out on the porch.

"Here you go."

She took the drink and raised it to him. "To my knight in shining armor."

Mullins sat, picked up his glass, and clinked hers. "I think you mean your knight in Rusty armor."

"Then I'll just have to keep you well-oiled, Rusty."

Her comment threw him. Was it simply a second pun or was she proposing something else? Their age difference was less than ten years. He was definitely attracted to her. They both had lost their spouses. His pulse quickened but his brain reeled at any response that could be embarrassingly misread. She was his charge, not his bedmate.

"Then oil me with knowledge. There are some things I need to know."

Li sighed, as if disappointed by the turn in the conversation. "Ask me."

"Did anything surprise you about what you saw today?"

"Surprise me?" She took a healthy sip and thought a second. "No, not surprise. Stun and shock are more appropriate verbs.

He's at least a year ahead of where we were at Jué Dé. I don't know who his researchers are but the configurations they've created are the closest mimics of the human brain I've ever seen. Thousands of interconnections and cross-processing neuromorphic chips. I was amazed by some of their system schematics and I've barely scratched the surface of what they've done."

"That must have been while Peter and I were hanging out in the game room."

"Yes. Sorry to turn you into a babysitter but he would have been bored."

Not half as much as I would have been, Mullins thought. "So, are you familiar with anyone on his team?"

Li cocked her head and stared at Mullins over her glass. "That's the peculiar thing. I didn't meet them."

Mullins rocked forward. "What? Brentwood said he was going to introduce you to them."

"He did. Virtually. They're offsite in other locations and we spoke through an audio connection."

"If they're not onsite, why do you have to be?"

"They were at one time, but they're far enough along that they can do their programming work remotely. Robert says I'll go through the same stages and eventually we'll go back to D.C."

"So, you didn't actually see anybody?"

Li laughed. "Oh, yes, it's not like we're all alone. I met the team of technicians and assistants. Some do physical installations, some run tests and diagnostics. I meant the scientists who conceptualized the whole thing. They're offsite."

"How many did you speak with?"

"Two. A Roger Stanovich and Luther Cathcart. One came through Cal Tech and the other's worked for Robert since he started his company."

"I'd have thought you'd be in one of those elite circles where everybody knows everybody."

"In some ways it's the opposite," Li said. "People come to AI research from a variety of backgrounds—neuroscientists, engineers, programmers. There are no gatekeepers declaring 'here's the academic degree you have to have.' It's who has the best ideas. That's why I like it."

Mullins raised his glass. "I'll sure as hell drink to that. I've seen enough posturing and turf-guarding in the government."

"And Stanovich and Cathcart have to be tops in their fields. It will be a challenge to keep up with them."

Mullins started rocking slowly, sensing the time was right to pursue his real agenda with her. "Indulge me in a few more layman's questions."

"Whatever you need to know."

"Who is supervising your work?"

"Robert."

"Not Cathcart or Stanovich?"

"No. Especially not them."

"I don't understand. Aren't they your colleagues?"

Li ran her finger around the rim of her glass, generating a faintly ringing note. "Look, Rusty, we're colleagues, but we aren't to collaborate. Those men have done an unbelievable job of creating Apollo's brain. So much so that it feels only right to call it Apollo. My function is to create a mini-brain within."

"Apollo's subconscious?" Mullins ventured.

"Yes. And right now, this moment, are you aware of your subconscious?"

"I know I have one."

"Yes, but do you know what it's thinking?"

"If I did, it wouldn't be subconscious."

"Give the man a prize. So, if Apollo became aware that he had a subconscious, what do you think he'd try to do?"

"Control it?"

Li laughed. "I don't know. That's why my work is kept isolated from the others. They've given me a part of the brain. In effect, I have to encase it behind a two-way mirror. Imagine light, in this case visual, aural, empirical, and any other form of information coming in through all Apollo's sensory and data inputs. The subconscious has access to everything including Apollo's own analyses. But, the subconscious processes the information in a different way for a different goal—not to problem-solve but to learn for learning's sake. This is the ultimate achievement of the deep learning field—let him follow his curiosity, and when an idea reaches a certain threshold, it surfaces, masked as if Apollo consciously conceived it."

"Okay, I understand the subconscious works in isolation, but can that brain within a brain you're devising give you any output that won't go through Apollo?"

Li stared out over the lake and contemplated the question. Mullins studied her profile. The moonlight cast a soft bluish glow over her face, removing a decade of time and stretching the gap between them to such an extent that Mullins cringed at the idea she'd be interested in him.

After a few minutes, Li nodded slowly and turned to him. "You want to use the computer but not let anyone know what you're investigating."

"I have no idea where things are heading. I'm not saying Brentwood and his associates aren't exactly who and what they claim to be. But when somebody's pulled a gun on me, they have to earn my trust."

Li laid a hand on Mullins' wrist. "And you trust me?"

"Is there a reason I shouldn't trust you?"

"We have a window, a month or two, when my section of the computer will be completely independent of Apollo. I'll have a secure master server and password that will bypass him. We won't have Apollo's full intellect, but we'll have access to all the information and resources that he has."

"Why the timeframe?"

"Once I've run all my tests, we'll make the one-way interface to merge the conscious and the subconscious. At that point, my work will be more delicate. I can leave no trace of the subconscious existence. Any output will come through the masking that keeps Apollo unaware of the source of his so-called inspirations."

"Has Brentwood given this subconscious a name?"

"Yes. Asimov."

"That's the author of the book he gave Peter. Maybe I'd better read it. See how it ends."

Li took a sip of her drink and turned toward him. "I'm more interested in beginnings. How'd you get into your profession?"

Mullins shrugged. "My dad was a homicide detective in D.C."

"Like father, like son."

"No. When I was thinking about going into law enforcement, he discouraged me from following in his footsteps."

"He didn't like being a detective?"

"No. He liked it and he was good at it. But he told me I wasn't cut out for his job. That not solving a case would drive me crazy because behind each investigation lay a murder victim. And those victims would haunt me. My father could live with an unsolved case. He said I couldn't."

"So, you keep people from becoming victims."

It wasn't a question and her statement surprised Mullins. She'd summed up in one sentence what made him tick. Here was a woman who understood him like someone who had known him for years. "I guess you're right. Dad had a poker buddy in the Secret Service. I saw his job was keeping people from being murdered. To me, that's the greater priority."

"Peter and I are very grateful you made the choice you did. There's nothing more important to me than protecting my nephew."

"Then wouldn't he be safer back in China?"

"Maybe that would be best. But it's a long way for a seven-year-old to fly alone. And my sister and her husband are traveling. He has no one to meet him."

Mullins swallowed the last of his Scotch. "Then I'll make sure nothing happens."

Li reached for his glass. "I'll clean that. Peter left a dirty one on the counter."

"Already rinsed. Why don't you use the bathroom first while I do these and then lock up."

She didn't argue, but took a last swallow and gave him the glass. "I'll see you in the morning."

They stared at each other for an awkward second. Finally Mullins said, "Yes, in the morning."

He watched her return to the house. Instead of following, he sat back down in the rocker, a glass in each hand. Of all the questions he'd asked, she'd only avoided answering one: "Is there a reason I shouldn't trust you?"

Twenty minutes later, Mullins wiped the toothpaste off his chin and put his toiletries back in his kit bag. A shelf beside the bathroom's small vanity held a few items belonging to Lisa Li and Peter. Some basic makeup, shampoo, and two hair brushes, one with a back of pewter and the other with a back featuring Superman. Easy enough to determine the owners.

Mullins took two tissues from a box on the rear of the toilet and pulled hair from each brush, using the tissues to keep the strands separate. He rolled the one for Peter into a tight ball and then put it inside the second along with Lisa Li's hair. He wadded that tissue, tucked it into his pocket, and turned out the light.

He closed the door to his bedroom and lifted the mattress. The burner phone was where he'd left it. As it powered up, he felt one vibration signaling a missed text. Three words:

Chimney Rock Noon.

Chapter Seventeen

At breakfast the next morning, Mullins made two requests: the return of his phone and the use of a vehicle.

Brentwood set down a half-eaten English muffin and used a linen napkin to wipe blueberry jam from his mouth. "I understand the phone but why the vehicle?"

"Lisa's in the lab and Peter's with his tutor, right?"

The boy looked up from a bowl of Cheerios. "I can help you, Mr. Mullins."

"You've got school," Lisa Li said firmly.

"That's right," Mullins agreed. "Study hard today and I'll give you some detective tips tonight."

Peter beamed at the prospect.

"I thought you wanted to use our facilities for your investigation," Brentwood said.

"I do. But I need to focus my inquiries. I have a contact at the Asheville resident agency of the FBI who can help guide me. It's better if I speak to him personally. And alone. No limousine."

Brentwood smiled. "You want invisibility."

"Something like that."

Brentwood pushed back his chair and rose. "All right. You know best. I'll call the office. You'll have your phone and I'll have a car ready. We have a few company vehicles on hand." He checked his watch. "Let's leave in thirty minutes."

When they stepped off the elevator at the lower level, Felicia rose from her desk to greet them. Yesterday's dashiki had been exchanged for a white blouse and navy blazer. The Maine coast had changed into an Appalachian vista.

"Good morning. I trust everyone is well rested."

"Yes," Li said. "Peter and I are ready for big things."

"Excellent. Peter, I'll take you to Miss Collier. She has an exciting day planned." Felicia picked up two phones from her desk. "And these have new sim cards. Mr. Jenkins, the head of our security, asks that you share the new numbers only as absolutely necessary."

"Will we get the original sims back?" Mullins asked.

Felicia looked at her boss, uncertain how to answer.

"That will be no problem," Brentwood assured. "Especially after you uncover who was behind those terrible attacks."

A neat trick, Mullins thought. Brentwood had shifted responsibility back to him. He took his phone, fully aware the burner would still be critical for communication with Allen. He'd treat this one as if every person in Brentwood's organization were listening.

"And we have a car whenever you want it." Felicia dangled a smart key in front of him. "A Chevy Malibu. No flash, no trash." She dropped the key in his open palm. "Ned Farino will show you its location."

"And where do I find him?"

"I'll take you," Brentwood volunteered. "His office is next to mine."

He led Mullins down a different hallway and through two security doors that unlatched and swung open at their approach.

Mullins fingered the badge hanging around his neck. "Are these doors activated like the elevators?"

"Not exactly. A combination of things. Not one but six cameras scan our faces, each getting a slightly different angle. The composite is a much more accurate confirmation of identity that is then cross-referenced with the data on your badge. Even though the system recognizes your face, it won't allow entry without the badge."

"Better than a retinal scan?"

"It eliminates the prospect of gouging out your eye and holding it to the reader. Or cutting off your hand for a palm scan."

Mullins laughed. "So your tactic is to inconvenience them. What a pain to have to take my whole head."

"If you're concerned, we'll work on it." Brentwood sounded so serious Mullins thought he wasn't kidding.

Ned Farino's office was spacious with a conference table surrounded by eight chairs, a chrome and glass desk, and a separate higher desk where he worked standing up. A virtual window created an overview of the Washington Mall looking toward the U.S. Capitol. The Stars and Stripes fluttered before the dome and puffy clouds drifted across the sky.

Farino turned from where he stood at the desk and greeted them with a nod. He was a short man, no more than five-foot five. He wore khakis with a sharp crease and a yellow golf shirt. His thinning brown hair looked darker than his eyebrows. Mullins suspected an expensive dye job that in another few years would turn into an expensive toupee.

"I'll see you at the lake tonight," Brentwood told Mullins. "Plan on dinner at six-thirty."

"That will be fine," Mullins said.

Farino motioned for him to sit at the table and then took the chair opposite him. "So, you're settling in?"

"I spent twenty years living out of a suitcase. I hope you're focusing the attention on Dr. Li and Peter. They're the ones who've been uprooted."

"We are. And I don't see this lasting more than three months, if that. Most of the heavy work has been done."

Mullins studied the other man's face. Farino seemed annoyed that they were having this conversation.

"You're not impressed with Dr. Li?"

Farino shrugged. "I'm sure she's a brilliant scientist. But that's not my area of expertise." He pointed to the U.S. Capitol out the artificial window. "That's my arena. Government relations mean government contracts. If I had to weigh in on every whim that caught Robert's fancy, I'd never get any work done."

"You think Dr. Li's a whim?"

Farino drew back. "That's not a slam at her. Robert's whims have made us billions of dollars. But for every home run there are a hundred strikeouts. Whether his current obsession with the subconscious will amount to anything is a crap shoot. I'm just being realistic here."

Mullins leaned across the table. "I'm just being realistic that someone tried to kill Dr. Li."

Farino spread his hands palm up. "And you have my full cooperation. If I've done anything to indicate otherwise, then let me reassure you that nothing is more important than their safety. We stand ready with whatever you need."

"The Malibu will be fine for today. Where is it?"

"Right at the front door." Farino stood. "It has a company identification unit for the gate. You should use your badge to enter the building, of course. There's also an enhanced GPS system using our own satellites. Push the red button and speak your destination."

Mullins got to his feet. "I'm surprised the car doesn't drive itself."

"Give us time, Rusty. Give us time."

◇◇◇

Mullins' visit to the FBI wasn't a priority, but since he'd used it as the pretense for securing a car, he knew he had to visit the Asheville office. There not only might be a record of his journey but also live tracking of his position at all times. And the car could be bugged for audio or even video.

He realized such potential monitoring of his route complicated his plan. His burner phone for contacting Allen lay under his mattress in the cottage and he'd have to swing by the lake to retrieve it. But that stop also opened up another possibility that made the FBI office more than an inconvenient diversion. He could use their resources. He'd just have to create an explanation for why he'd first returned to the cottage if Farino or Brentwood questioned him.

The risk was worth it. He needed the burner phone, and getting the dirty glass and hair samples to the FBI could prove critical to his investigation.

Mullins was in and out of the cottage in less than thirty seconds. With the dirty milk glass in his sport coat pocket and a blank note pad, burner phone and hair samples on the front seat beside him, Mullins turned on the GPS and said, "FBI—Asheville, North Carolina." The video screen showed an office building with a circle around a second-story window. A voice said, "The FBI resident agency is on the second floor, suite 211, 151 Patton Avenue. If you would like, I can connect by telephone."

"No, thank you," Mullins told the disembodied voice.

"Very well. Here is a list of potential parking garages. You may begin driving."

Jesus, Mullins thought. The specificity of the device was unnerving. He drove away from the lake house feeling like a ghost was riding with him.

The FBI office was in the Federal Courthouse, and Mullins had to clear security before being directed to the second floor. He'd had the foresight to leave his Glock in the car.

The office door was locked and he pressed a buzzer to request admittance. A young black man opened the door. Mullins offered his Prime Protection photo ID, but before the agent even examined it, he said, "Mr. Mullins?"

"Yes." Mullins wondered if the damn GPS had somehow called ahead.

"I'm Vance Gilmore. How can we help you?"

"How did you know I was coming?"

Gilmore laughed. "Director Hauser sent a bureau-wide background briefing regarding everyone involved in the Marriott shooting. He included photos."

"And he mentioned I was likely to start investigating on my own."

Gilmore gave a sly smile. "That I can neither confirm nor deny."

"Fair enough."

Gilmore stepped back, clearing the doorway. "Come in."

Mullins entered and looked around the outer office. "Are you the agent in charge?"

"No, sir. Special Agent Lindsay Boyce heads this resident agency. Would you like to speak with her?"

"Please."

"Wait just a moment." Gilmore exited through a side door.

Mullins eyed two guest chairs lined against the near wall, but decided to remain standing. He figured he'd get a thumbs up or down quickly.

In less than three minutes, Gilmore re-entered followed by a slim woman in a well-tailored charcoal pants suit. Mullins pegged her to be in her late thirties. Her brown hair was cut short, not in a masculine style but in a look that complemented her high cheekbones. Her most striking features were her pale blue eyes, a sharp contrast to her dark hair. They scrutinized Mullins swiftly and efficiently.

"Welcome to Asheville." Boyce extended her hand.

Her grip was firm.

"Thank you, Agent Boyce. I won't take much of your time."

"Call me Lindsay. We're honored to assist in any manner we're permitted."

Permitted, Mullins thought. *A good way of limiting involvement while being cooperative.* He smiled. "May we speak in your office?"

Boyce led him down a short hall to a corner office, sparse in its furnishings with one guest chair and a desk cluttered with folders and reports. The only personal touch was a framed photograph of a yellow lab splashing in a stream at the base of a mountain waterfall.

Boyce indicated he should sit while she took the chair behind the mounds of paperwork.

"What's the geographical scope of the resident agency?" Mullins asked.

"Sixteen North Carolina counties and the Cherokee Indian Reservation. On some of these backroads, we'd be better off with mules than cars. If you think a suspect is holed up in these hills, it could be a hell of a time flushing him out."

"No, nothing like that. You know I'm interested in the Marriott shooting in D.C. earlier this month. I suspect any break will come through high tech and not high elevation."

Boyce eyed him warily. "So, what brings you to Asheville?"

"Talking to some tech people with facilities in Rutherford County. Cumulus Cognitive Connections." He paused. "And Facebook." He was grateful Brentwood had mentioned their facility was also in the region.

"Okay. How can we help?"

"I need to speak to Rudy Hauser."

Boyce's eyes widened. "You expect me to put you through to the Director?"

"No. I'll do that myself. I just need a secure line and a place to make the call in private."

Boyce stared at Mullins a few seconds. Agents didn't simply call the Director whenever they wanted. But to refuse to cooperate with a man Hauser had specifically mentioned in the Marriott assassinations background briefing was the greater risk.

She picked up her phone console and spun it around toward him. "Use the last line on the right. Do you need the number in case he has to call you back?"

Mullins thought about leaving the number of his burner phone, but he decided a secure line from the FBI would be much more difficult to intercept. "Yes. Thank you."

Boyce scribbled ten-digits on a scrap of paper. "Leave it under the phone when you finish. There's a small conference room halfway back. I'll be there."

She left her office, closing the door behind her. Mullins activated the designated line and a series of clicks and whistles preceded the normal dial tone. He punched in the number from memory, counting on Hauser not to have changed it since their collaboration in exposing the terrorist plot against the Federal Reserve.

Three rings. "Yeah." Like Mullins, Rudy Hauser never answered with his name.

"It's Rusty. I need something."

The loud laugh told Mullins the Director was alone.

"Don't be redundant. What trouble are you getting me into this time?"

"I don't know, Rudy."

Hauser's voice turned serious. "You on this Double H thing?"

"Yes. I'm still guarding that scientist who escaped the assassination attempt."

"Thanks to you," Hauser said, "Brighton's been on my ass to make sure we extend you every courtesy down to hand-washing your goddamned underwear. What have you got? Pictures of him naked in some barnyard?"

"Just his undying gratitude."

"If that's all, then watch your back, buddy. So, what do you need?"

"I'm at the Asheville resident agency. Your Special Agent Lindsay Boyce has been very cooperative, but it's important that what I tell you stays between you and me."

"You think I've got a leak?"

"Not necessarily. I just want to stay out of the system. I know the investigation's crossing all intelligence departments, which increases the odds that someone will say something to the wrong person. Frankly, Rudy, you're the only person I trust."

"So, tag, I'm it?"

"No. Nothing that will come back to bite you. I need some lab work done through Quantico under whatever legend you want to create, but that in no way ties to Double H. I'll be sending you prints on a glass and hair samples. Process them as fast as you can."

"All right," Hauser agreed. "And if we get a hit?"

"Make goddamned sure the report comes only to you marked as highly classified as possible. Better yet, an unrecorded verbal report."

"You're killing me with curiosity, my friend."

"Good. Glad I've got your attention. Now I need a secure pouch here to go directly to you. If I put her on, will you instruct Boyce to provide one?"

"Yes. I'll make sure it comes to me this afternoon. How do you want to get the information?"

"I'll call. If you haven't heard from me by Monday, I want you to track this cell." Mullins gave him the number for his burner phone.

"Anything else?"

"Yes, tell Boyce I was never here. And if Brighton asks if you've heard from me, tell him I was hounding you for an update on the FBI's investigation."

Hauser laughed. "He'd sooner believe that than if I told him the earth was round."

"Thanks, Rudy. Hang on, I'm going for Boyce."

Mullins didn't trust himself to put the call on hold. He laid the receiver on a stack of papers and went to the conference room. Boyce was checking e-mails on a laptop. He knocked on the open door.

"You done?" she asked.

"Almost. Director Hauser wants to speak with you."

Her mouth dropped open. "He wants to talk to me?"

Mullins looked around the small room. "Is there another Lindsay Boyce? If so, you'd better find her. I left the Director of the FBI lying facedown on her desk."

She bolted from her chair, pushed past Mullins, and ran to her office.

Mullins smiled. It was nice to have friends in high places.

Chapter Eighteen

Dr. Lisa Li rechecked the algorithms defining the threshold for when data processes would move from an insulated core to wider dissemination. These basic prototypes would be the building blocks for birthing the entity known as Asimov. Her work meant she also needed to create a simulated Apollo so that the brain-within-a-brain concept could be tested without linking to the real Apollo.

To accomplish this, she required the help of the scientific team developing Apollo so that a secure, unbreachable pathway could be devised for what she saw as a shadow entity that would self-destruct after each test. No trace would remain in Apollo's memory because the process would never reach his conscious identity. Li modeled it after a splintered human mind suffering from split personalities. A temporary mental illness to be carefully controlled.

The more she thought about this approach the more she liked it. Not only could she safely test the conscious-subconscious interaction, but she could divert the computing power designed for Apollo to whatever Rusty Mullins might need.

She'd have to run the dual Apollo identities by Brentwood because he had to authorize the coordination with the other team. Those scientists would run tests after the identity switched back to Apollo to make sure no residual memory remained. She wasn't sure how Mullins would play it. The last thing she wanted was to inadvertently sabotage any investigative avenue he might be pursuing. Better to keep Brentwood unaware that her plan would create a powerful resource for Mullins that never revealed its existence to anyone else. That would be a conversation between Mullins and her.

For a moment, her thoughts returned to their private time the previous night and her hand on his arm as they sipped their Scotch in the moonlight. Not exactly intimacy, but the closest human contact she'd had since her husband died. She shook off the thought. Mullins was a professional doing his job. There was nothing more. Yet there was something about the expression on his face as they said good night. Was she reading what she wanted to read?

Li returned to her keyboard and the string of symbols on her screen. Here was the world she understood. The emotionless world she could control.

A knock sounded behind her. She turned to see Brentwood's face smiling through the narrow opening of her door.

"Might I interrupt a moment?"

"Of course." Li moved to the small conversation area in her office.

Brentwood stepped in and closed the door. He carried a thin folder in his right hand. "I'd like to review something with you, but I need your word you won't tell anyone."

"About the project?"

"Yes. Something limited to your aspect. Something only you and I will know."

"Not even Rusty?"

"No, not even Rusty. This has nothing to do with his responsibilities. In fact, it might aid him." He gestured for her to take one of the two chairs. "Can you promise me your confidentiality?"

"All right." Li sat, nervous about the tone of the conversation.

Brentwood gave her the folder. "I'd like these embedded in Asimov's core—unalterable, inviolable, and unassailable in their primacy."

She flipped open the cover and found two typed pages. She read the first one carefully.

Brentwood relaxed as he saw the smile curl at the edge of her mouth.

When she turned to the second, she found herself looking at unintelligible words. "What's this?"

"A translation of the first page. Esperanto. The language of Apollo."

She looked up, seeing him with fresh eyes. "You have a plan, don't you?"

"No. Better than a plan. I have a dream."

◇◇◇

A few minutes before noon, Mullins turned through the stone gate into Chimney Rock Park. The road quickly began a steep ascent with switchbacks so tight Mullins thought he was driving up a corkscrew.

After a mile, he pulled beside a ticket booth where an older gentleman leaned out the window and handed him a map.

"This here will show you the trails and buildings. You by your lonesome?"

"Yes. How much?"

"Fifteen dollars. Had been thirteen when the elevator was broke because you had to climb five hundred steps to get to the top of Chimney Rock. Some folks my age found that a tad too taxing."

Mullins gave him a ten and a five from his billfold. "Then I'll be taking the elevator. Crowded today?"

"Pretty decent for a Wednesday. One bus of seniors and a motorcycle gang."

"Gang?"

The man laughed. "Group. Club. Whatever. They're riding those big Hondas, not Harleys. They're about the size of a small car." He handed Mullins a receipt. "Enjoy the view."

Mullins drove on expecting to find a parking lot around the next bend. Two miles farther, he pulled into a space across from a cluster of motorcycles. He saw a bus at the top of the lot, and a scattering of SUVs, sedans, and pickups. A white Ford Taurus bore Virginia plates and he wondered if it belonged to Allen Woodson.

Walking up the paved lot, Mullins felt the breeze stiffen as the trees disappeared. Granite replaced soil and the opening vista gave Mullins a spectacular view down the length of Hickory Nut Gap Gorge to Lake Lure beyond.

A stone wall about three feet tall formed a barrier between the public area and the downward curve of the bare rock. Several benches stood parallel to the wall where tourists could sit and admire the view. Allen Woodson was alone at the nearest one, fiddling with a camera bag on the seat beside him.

Mullins walked past. He stopped about twenty feet away, slowly pivoted, and took in not only the panorama of the gorge but also the park buildings and signs. By a gift shop called Cliff Dwellers, a white tarp shaded a man playing a hammer dulcimer. The Celtic tune sounded familiar but then so many shared the lilting bounce that Mullins couldn't recall a specific name. A row of CDs spread out from either side of the wooden instrument. Mullins considered buying one as evidence he had no reason to hide his trip to the park, but he'd learned those who preserve a cultural tradition are often proselytizers for the cause and anxious to preach to anyone who stops to listen. He could be stuck in conversation for fifteen minutes.

Mullins looked up at Chimney Rock towering what looked like ten stories above him. The U.S. flag strained at its line and snapped in the wind. Five hundred steps. He followed signs to the elevator and something called the Sky Lounge.

The elevator's doors were built flush into the side of the cliff and opened as he approached. A cadre of senior citizens, obviously a part of the bus brigade, appeared to have packed themselves inside like sardines and it took a while for them to untangle their canes and walkers. Mullins pressed his palm across the edge of one of the doors to keep it from closing before the elderly tourists had safely emerged.

"I bet there are at least that many more waiting at the top." Allen Woodson murmured the words as he passed Mullins to enter the elevator.

Mullins followed and pushed the button for the only other level. He thought of Brentwood's automatic elevator where two floors meant you were always going to the other and a selection was superfluous. The doors closed.

"Did I have a tail?" Mullins asked.

"Not that I could see. You expecting one?"

The elevator rose slowly.

"No," Mullins said. "The car's probably on a live GPS feed back to Brentwood."

"Did I screw things up by choosing this rendezvous?"

"It's an obvious tourist spot. I'll say I checked it out for Dr. Li and her nephew." Mullins looked at Woodson's camera bag. "Something in there for me?"

Woodson unzipped the top and pulled out a silver point-and-shoot Nikon camera. "Put this around your neck so you'll look like a tourist. It already has photos on its memory card of the documents I received from Vice Admiral MacArthur. You can either load them to a computer or view them on the camera. There's still plenty of room to snap some pictures." Woodson smiled. "So you can play your tourist role with authenticity."

"Smart," Mullins said. "And you'll keep the bag in case someone noticed you with it earlier. It can hide what I brought you." He reached into his coat pocket.

The elevator stopped with a mild jolt.

"Not now," Woodson cautioned. "Let's look at the view and then take the stairs down. I doubt if they're being used."

True to Woodson's prediction, the doors opened to reveal a semicircle of seniors poised for their descent. Mullins and Woodson turned sideways and gently navigated their way through the gray-haired crowd. They stepped into a combination gift shop and deli. A short line stood at the sandwich counter, a longer line waited for ice cream.

Mullins and Woodson exited onto a patio where diners sat at tables shaded by orange umbrellas. Beyond, a plank bridge stretched over a chasm between the deli and the final ascent to the top of Chimney Rock. Mullins crossed slowly. He had the sensation of being suspended in midair—like a cartoon character running off a cliff and freezing in panic a few tortured seconds before plummeting to earth.

"We should climb the rock," Woodson said. "Otherwise, it's like going to the Louvre and skipping the Mona Lisa."

The final steps were more of a ladder than a stairway. Above, Mullins saw several windswept firs clinging to what few patches of soil must have existed on the granite. A heavy metal fence encircled the summit.

Woodson motioned for his father-in-law to precede him. "Age before beauty."

"That means you'll have to catch this old man if he topples backwards."

"Nah. Much easier to jump out of your way."

Mullins ascended the steep steps and lamented the strain he felt in his legs and lungs. Once the shoulder sling came off, he'd be hitting the gym. He found a diverse group of tourists scattered across the top. Some were pressed up against the fence, venturing as close to the edge as they could. Others clustered around the flagpole with a few actually holding on as if they feared a sudden gust could blow them off. Mullins was sympathetic to their plight.

"Man, quite a view," Woodson said. "Can you see Brentwood's lake house from here?"

"No. It's around the bend on the far edge of the gorge."

"Why don't we walk the perimeter and then head down the steps," Woodson said. "Try not to get photographed. No telling how many Facebook and Instagram posts are happening."

Mullins noted just about everyone around them brandished a camera or cell phone. From group shots to selfies, the photography continued nonstop.

"May I have your attention, please." A man in black jeans, an orange T-shirt, and leather motorcycle vest pivoted in the center of the rock. "May I have your attention, please."

People turned from the view to stare at the speaker. Beside him, a young woman stepped back with a mixture of confusion and embarrassment on her face.

"Thirty years ago, my father stood with my mother on this very spot. He knelt and asked my mother to marry him." The man paused, reached into his vest pocket and withdrew a small box. Then he dropped to one knee.

Cameras and cell phones went full throttle as the spectators realized what was about to happen. The woman in front of him started to cry.

"Sheila, will you be my wife?"

Sheila seemed too choked up to speak.

Someone called, "You'd better say yes, honey. It's a long way down."

The laughter freed the woman's frozen vocal cords.

"Yes. Oh, yes!"

They kissed and hugged. Everyone applauded.

Mullins turned to his son-in-law. "Good time to go."

"A photograph," the new fiancée shouted. "I want a picture with all our witnesses." She lifted a small camera from around her neck.

"Oh, shit," Woodson muttered. "So much for a secret rendezvous."

"Take the picture," Mullins said.

"Damn. Just when I start to think I'm smarter than you." Woodson raised his hand and walked forward. "Give me the camera so you both can be in it."

"Come on, people," Mullins said. "You heard the bride-to-be." He waved his arms like he was shooing a gaggle of geese.

When the little community of about twenty strangers squeezed together in front of the magnificent panorama, Woodson snapped a series of pictures.

"Now you need to be in one," Sheila said.

"Nah, I'll break the camera."

"We insist," her boyfriend said. "Don't we, folks?"

The crowd chorused, "We do!" and laughed.

"I'll take it," Mullins volunteered. As he grabbed the camera, he whispered, "I'll crop you."

Woodson stood at the edge of the group and Mullins framed the shot with only a piece of his left shoulder visible. He took several and then clicked the camera off before handing it back.

"Congratulations," he told the couple. "You made our day."

"Tell me about it," the husband-to-be said. "Thanks to all of you."

The celebratory moment passed and the witnesses broke into their smaller clusters. Mullins and Woodson descended to the platform at the base of the chimney.

"This way." Woodson jerk his head to a sign indicating the stairs to the parking lot.

Mullins peered over the edge. The wooden steps doglegged back and forth against the cliff face like a ten-story fire escape. "Set the pace and we'll stop about halfway down. If you want, you can brief me on what you put on this camera while we're moving."

Woodson led the way, taking each step carefully and slowly. "I took camera shots of the file documents. Surprisingly thin for an investigation into a missing FBI agent."

"Was it still active?" Mullins asked.

"Technically active but not being worked. Kim's partner, Ron Gibbons, made a decent effort, but then was transferred out of the region."

"To where?"

"Honolulu."

"About as far away as they could post him," Mullins said.

"Yeah. He was given liaison responsibilities with the naval base at Pearl Harbor."

"Did he have any leads?" Mullins asked.

"No. Kim's car was wiped clean, as was her laptop. The laptop was what got everybody's attention. Scrubbing it was no small feat. Even Hillary Clinton couldn't permanently erase her server."

"Anybody see Kim in that little New Hampshire town?"

"It was dark and snowing. The only conclusion was she went there because of Professor Milton. He, too, was never seen again. His car and all his belongings were at his lake house about five miles away."

Mullins thought the steps down seemed to go on forever. He drew a deep breath. "What about their cell phones? Were Kim and the missing scientist linked by them?"

"No. There were no calls or texts after noon on December 31st. That sounds strange to me because Kim used her phone like a third hand."

"No activity at all?"

"Only a GPS program she used for the drive from Boston. Her destination was right where the car was found."

"And Milton's phone?"

"The same. No records after noon on New Year's Eve."

"The file contain any theories?"

"The prevalent consensus was they were abducted by a person or persons unknown. The thickest material in Kim's file was actually selected copies of the evidence compiled on Milton and his friend Dr. Kaminsky."

"The first scientist who went missing."

"Yes," Woodson said. "The one Milton was worried about. So, if Milton was an instigator in some plot, it makes no sense that he would reach out to the FBI."

"Has the Marriott attack moved Kim's case to the front burner?"

"Along with others. The FBI is attempting to connect any of the identified assassins with the Boston area four years ago, as well as international murders and disappearances of scientists in the artificial intelligence field. We know of five kills. One in England, two in Israel, one in China, and one in France."

"Can we eliminate those countries, then?"

Woodson stopped and looked up at his father-in-law on the step above him. "No. What if there is a game of tit-for-tat going on? Israel loses two key scientists and thinks German intelligence was behind it. So they go after Brecht when he's here, hiring contractors with no connection to them."

"How far back do these attacks go?" Mullins asked.

Woodson started down the stairs again. "The disappearances of Milton and Kaminsky were the first."

"What about the Chinese scientist?"

"Three years ago. That's based on chatter in the scientific community. The Chinese don't say much about their setbacks."

"Which means other incidents could go back further and the governments simply quieted them."

"It's possible," Woodson admitted. "Do you have something in mind?"

"Dr. Li's husband for one. These people are smart and the best way to commit an intelligent murder is to make sure it appears to be something else." He stopped as a new thought struck him. "I wonder if Brentwood's plan to lure Dr. Li away was as secure as he thought. If the Chinese got wind of it, they could have been behind an abduction attempt. Her assailant had a kill shot he didn't take. The two assassinations offered a bonus to deal a setback to the competition."

"You think the Chinese are behind all this?"

"I don't know," Mullins conceded. "But if Li's husband was murdered, it might have set an international targeting and retribution cycle in motion. There's another thing. If one of your key assets is annihilated, what do you do with your others?"

"Get them to as safe a place as you can."

"Yes. When Dr. Li's husband died, she disappeared for almost a year. That's a long time to grieve, especially for someone as driven by her work as she is."

Woodson halted on one of the landings about halfway to the bottom. "In addition to Kim's file, I've got the photos and fingerprints of the five dead men at the Marriott. If the computer resources you've got are as good as you say, you ought to run them. But I'll be surprised if they beat MacArthur's resources."

Mullins leaned against the landing railing and caught his breath. "Okay. And I've got something for you to check out. Tell MacArthur to put them through his best lab." Mullins took two white envelopes out of his pocket. One was marked A and the other B. They were identical to the envelopes he'd sent earlier to Rudy Hauser at FBI headquarters.

Woodson tucked them in his empty camera case. "What are these?"

"Hair samples. Get a DNA read and tell me everything you can about them."

"You want them cross-referenced in our data base?"

"Definitely not. I want as little attention drawn to them as possible."

Woodson nodded. "I'll get MacArthur to expedite it. When are you coming home?"

"I don't know. As soon as we get some leads. Maybe next weekend. I'll use the burner phone to contact you at least once a day." Mullins looked up and down the steps, making sure the two of them were alone. "I'd better go now. I'll check in with Kayli on my regular phone."

To Mullins' surprise, Woodson stepped forward and hugged him. "For God's sake, Rusty, take care. Right now, we don't know our friends from our enemies. I'm afraid that was the position Kim was in."

"I will. You do the same."

"No one knows I'm here."

Mullins stared at his son-in-law gravely. "Which means if no one knows you're here, then no one will know if suddenly you're not here."

Chapter Nineteen

Mullins sat on the front porch of the guest cottage, his glass of Scotch on the wide armrest of his Adirondack rocker. During the day, someone on Brentwood's staff had spaced the chairs evenly, but while Lisa Li was tucking Peter into bed, Mullins had moved two of the chairs closer together.

He could hear the soft murmur of their voices coming through the screen door, only slightly louder than the crickets chirping in the woods around him. He took a sip of the drink and then rested his head on the back of the chair.

The day had been productive. After meeting Woodson, he'd eaten lunch at Medina's Village Bistro, a small and surprisingly good restaurant near the entrance to Chimney Rock. He'd logged onto their Wi-Fi with his cell phone. He fully expected his location to be monitored through the sim card Farino had installed, but he hoped the Wi-Fi wouldn't yield any content he might e-mail through the restaurant's system. Just to make sure, he'd disabled the cellular data function.

He'd dropped a note to Kayli saying he was fine and to e-mail him if anything urgent arose. He didn't reveal his location. Then he'd driven the roads adjacent to the lake and verified Brentwood's assertion that no one route looped it. His final activity had been to rent a kayak and approach the house from the water.

Brentwood's magnificent view had come at the cost of making both the main residence and guest cottage very visible from the lake. The kayak excursion had lasted two hours because he'd also examined the homes and terrain of the opposite shore for a sniper's vantage point. Most homes were close to the water, but a few had garden terraces that would make excellent shooting positions. He'd find out which might be year-round residences, second homes, or vacation rentals.

Between kayaking and the flights of stairs, Mullins' day had been as much physical as mental exercise. But he'd held up his end of the dinner conversation and told Brentwood he would drive Lisa and Peter to the research complex the next morning.

He took another swallow and set the glass on the floor by his foot. The breeze from the lake carried the scent of woodsmoke. Somewhere someone warded off the late April chill with possibly the last fire of the spring. Mullins closed his eyes.

"Rusty?" Lisa Li eased into the chair beside him. "You don't have to stay up on my account."

Mullins noticed she held her glass of Scotch. The aroma of woodsmoke became tinged with the scent of her perfume.

"I'm fine. Just enjoying the evening. Did Peter go down okay?"

She smiled. "Not without protest. He wanted to keep reading his Asimov book."

"He's a smart boy. He seems comfortable with you."

Li stiffened. "What do you mean?"

"Well, he's away from his mother and father. And his friends. I'd think he'd be a little homesick."

"Peter and I are very close. My job's enabled me to help my sister and her husband financially. They've been supportive of the opportunities I'm in position to provide for their son."

"How's this job going? You didn't say much about it at dinner."

"Better than I'd hoped. The team already has very sophisticated stealth programs in place. I can adapt them to keep Asimov hidden."

"Why would Apollo have stealth programs?"

Li laughed. "You're the detective. Why do you think?"

"So he can hack and infiltrate undetected."

She lifted her glass to him. "Infiltrate. That's the word. Hack doesn't describe the precision."

"What are the targets?"

"Any source of information Apollo can find."

Mullins' eyes widened. "You mean Apollo will be given free rein to choose his own targets?"

"Eventually. He'll be the most intelligent one in the room. Except he won't be in the room. He'll be worldwide, monitoring everything."

"Doesn't that make you nervous?"

"It makes Brentwood nervous. He says a computer like Apollo is inevitable so we'd better be the first to develop it. In fact, Apollo's stealth is primarily focused on rivals. Robert secretly monitors the progress of Jué Dé, Google, and others to ensure they aren't advancing ahead of him."

Mullins picked up his Scotch and thought a moment. "Where's the government in all this?"

The smooth skin of Li's forehead wrinkled into a scowl. "Where you'd expect. Right in the middle."

"Farino," Mullins said. "The marriage broker between Brentwood and the Pentagon."

Li shrugged. "You understand American politics better than I do. But at the core, all governments have the same goal—to keep their power."

Mullins took a swallow and then asked the question her statement elicited. "And your government, does it now see you as a traitor?"

"Rusty, there's a good chance it doesn't see me at all. Jué Dé might not have told them I've gone, or they've invented some cover story. Otherwise, my government's wrath could be directed as much to them as to me. They could even close Jué Dé's U.S. facility. Governments." She took a sip of Scotch as if to wash the taste of the word from her mouth. "No wonder Apollo speaks Esperanto."

"Esperanto?" Mullins tried to place the word. "What country is that?"

"No country. It was created by one man in 1887. An eye doctor in Poland named Zamenhof. He called himself Doktoro Esperanto and he wanted to create a politically neutral language without national ties or ethnic heritage. He called it the language of peace and international understanding."

"Esperanto," Mullins repeated.

"It means one who hopes, and it's Apollo's native tongue."

"And you speak it?"

"A little. Since I work in code, the language is irrelevant. But Brentwood insists any direct communication with Apollo, written or oral, be in Esperanto."

"He thinks it will bring world peace?"

"He thinks it will reinforce Apollo's global identity of being beholden to no country or corporate power."

Mullins gave Li a penetrating stare. "Is he for real, Lisa?"

"Yes," she said firmly. "He's an idealist, but he's not naive. Brentwood knows anytime you break new ground you threaten someone's power. Take Esperanto. Both Hitler and Stalin saw the language as subversive. During World War II, Zamenhof's grown children were imprisoned and executed by the Nazis."

Mullins flashed back to the chaotic scene at the Marriott. "Someone whose power feels threatened could be behind the assassinations in Washington. It's not about preserving humanity, it's about protecting special interests. We need to find out whose."

Li touched Mullins lightly on his arm and her voice dropped to a whisper. "I think I have a way to use all of Apollo's abilities without leaving a trace."

The mellow feeling Mullins was enjoying evaporated. Even the soft touch of Li's fingers on his skin was forgotten. He sat up straight. "What is it?"

She leaned closer. "I told Brentwood I need to be able to put Apollo in a shadow state. Like creating a dual personality that temporarily becomes the controlling entity. It's the safest way to test my work without Apollo having any memory of it. As if I were logging in as a different user on a computer, although much more discreetly."

"How's that an advantage?"

"No one else will know what I'm doing. My work is shielded from Apollo's team, and Apollo will essentially have amnesia. If someone discovers it, I'll say it was a test, a test that Asimov failed."

"And all these stealth pathways and infiltrations?"

"We'll have access to wherever Apollo has gone. I know his team is probing into and retreating from other systems as they refine his capabilities. When everything is ready, Apollo and Asimov will be wedded together as conscious and subconscious, and the brave new world will be upon us."

For a few minutes, Mullins said nothing. Something about her proposal bothered him.

"What's the matter?" Li asked.

"We need two tiers," Mullins said. "Much like you're designing this computer brain. Brentwood expects me to use you and his resources to identify whoever tried to kill you. No trace of doing that will raise his suspicions."

"I could tell him what we're doing."

"Definitely not. We don't know where this investigation is going. If this is a conspiracy, we need all the conspirators identified. Brentwood would be a loose cannon that could fire prematurely."

"So, what do you suggest?"

"We run some inquiries through Apollo and others through the alter ego. I'll let you know which to use in each case."

"When?"

"Is your laptop here?"

"It's in the bedroom but I can't access Apollo from here."

"I just want to transfer some information. Can you get it without waking Peter?"

"He's either asleep or he isn't."

Mullins pushed himself up from the chair. "Bring it to the kitchen table and set up two folders on the desktop. One for Apollo and one for what we want to keep secret. I'll join you in a moment. And Lisa, be careful what you say. The cottage could be bugged."

He didn't wait for her but went into his bedroom and retrieved the camera Woodson had given him. He sat on the edge of the bed and scrolled through the images. He found photos of the five dead assassins and the report of the facial recognition hit for the gunman arriving at the Montreal airport from Mozambique. His trail didn't go back any farther.

The two assassins identified by fingerprints had generated background dossiers. Known aliases were listed as well as additional photos compiled from Thailand and Belize showing the neighborhoods where each had resided. Previous addresses were listed as unknown. Their trails were as cold as their bodies.

The only other document related to the attack was a copy of the Internet posting from the group called Double H—Humanity's Hope. Mullins read the brief text—"We will not be enslaved by machines. Those who would make them our masters will meet the fate of Brecht and Ahmad. For we are Double H—Humanity's Hope, and we will prevail." A note from some analyst reported the message had been posted on Facebook, Twitter, and other social media sites from an Internet café in Amsterdam. There was no video surveillance and even though the posted time was in the wee hours of the night, the café had been busy enough that no one remembered any individual who stood out for any reason.

The last section of photographs was of the documents in Kim Woodson's FBI file. Mullins had decided to hold Kim's information back from Li for the present, but as he browsed through the pages, he changed his mind. He noted her ID photo, her SUV parked behind the barn playhouse, and the head shots of the professors Milton and Kaminsky. Maybe there was at least one avenue to explore. He took the camera and its USB cable into the kitchen.

Li had opened her laptop on the table and arranged two chairs in front of it.

"It needs a minute or two to boot up," she said. "Then just tell me what to drop where."

Mullins handed her the camera and cable. "Everything's on here. I'll walk you through what I need."

Li created the folders and then connected the camera. She opted to use it like an external drive, viewing its contents as a series of jpegs. To minimize the risk of potential monitoring, Mullins said nothing but pointed to what he wanted copied and pasted in the Apollo folder: all the photos of the dead assassins, the images from Belize and Thailand, and the list of the known aliases. He also included the photo from the Montreal airport and the information about the Amsterdam café.

Li looked at the remaining files. "And these?" she whispered.

He pointed to the second folder.

Li transferred the photographs of Kim Woodson and her car.

"Good," Mullins said. "That will give Apollo a starting point." He gestured for her to disconnect the camera.

"Let's go back outside," he said.

He took the camera and led her to the side of the cottage.

"What are we doing?" Li asked.

"I want you to take my picture."

"You? Why?"

"I want to see how deep and thorough this search goes. What kind of connections are made about my own life."

"Okay."

"Use the flash and make sure everything behind me goes to black. I don't want some fluke background object pinpointing our location."

Mullins stood in front of a patch of dark forest. Li took three photos. They were actually quite good. Certainly better than the mug shot on his driver's license.

"Is there anything on those photos that's more than picture?" Mullins asked.

"You mean like metadata?"

"I guess that's what I'm asking. I've seen some photos that have time, date, and a GPS reading attached."

"I'll strip all that away. All they'll see is you."

"Poor them."

"You have a nice face, Rusty."

Mullins felt the blood rush to his cheeks and was glad it was dark. *I'm acting like a smitten junior high kid*, he thought. He wanted to say something in return but just mumbled a thank you.

"What do you want to know about these files?" Li asked. "I need to write up parameters."

"Well, obviously any facial matches and records of any of the alias names. I'd like to get deeper into any CCTV video footage, especially in Montreal and Mozambique. Anywhere, for that matter."

"Time parameters?"

"Would the last ten years be too much?"

She shook her head. "We could go back to the Ming dynasty if they'd had computer databases."

Mullins laughed. "Ten years will be fine. Even the Ming dynasty must have had statutes of limitation."

"Don't be so sure," she said flatly. "And for the hidden search?"

"Facial recognition for the woman and two professors. Anything that overlaps them."

"Overlaps them?"

"Yes. Did they shop at the same stores, belong to the same organizations? And then add our dead assassins to that mix, concentrating on four years ago. If we get some hits, do they converge? Maybe you focus on the Montreal Airport again." He paused a second, and then asked, "How long will this take?"

"For Apollo, it depends on how many connections are found. Each one might generate more avenues of pursuit and we want him to exhaust them all. I have prep work to do before we begin, especially with the second shielded layer. That might take a few days. Maybe we should plan on Saturday night when no one else is working."

"All right," Mullins agreed. Then he realized something was missing from the search, something he should have requested from his son-in-law. But perhaps this was the more discreet way. "After you've performed one of these searches, do you think you'll know how private our inquiries are?"

"Yes. In fact I'll run some innocuous test and then ask the Apollo team to see if it appears in his memory. Why?"

"I'd like whatever background information you can get on Brentwood and his company. I don't want him to know I'm doing it."

"That could be volumes."

"Narrow it down to biography, clients, investors, competitors, and any litigation they might be involved in. I want to know both his friends and his enemies."

"And the photo of your lovely face?" she teased. "What am I to do with it?"

"Match it to anything from a week before the Marriott attack to the minute you run the search."

"What do you hope to find doing that?"

"Nothing," Mullins said. "Nothing at all."

Chapter Twenty

At ten the morning after he met Mullins, Allen Woodson knocked on the private door of Vice Admiral Louis MacArthur's office. The same gruff voice ordered him to enter.

MacArthur was at his desk, but this time he stood and indicated that Woodson should join him in the small conference area in the opposite corner. Woodson took the gesture as a sign their meeting would be more of a conversation than a briefing.

"How was your trip?" MacArthur asked amicably.

"I drove down the night before and got back around ten last night."

"No problem leasing the car with the ID and debit card?"

"No, sir." Woodson had found a packet in his hotel room containing a false Virginia driver's license with his photo and a debit card, both in the name of Roger Ethridge.

"Did Mullins have any reaction to what you gave him?" MacArthur asked.

"We made a handoff and had a brief conversation. He didn't examine the contents in front of me."

"He say what he'll do with them?"

"Not specifically. His overall plan is to use Brentwood's resources any way he can."

MacArthur nodded solemnly. "Normally, you could bet your sweet ass I'd shut down this fiasco in a heartbeat. Handing intelligence material to a civilian, no matter how much he's admired, would be bad enough, but then to turn around and let him run it through an external computer suspected to be one of the most powerful in the world?" MacArthur actually grinned at the prospect. "Well, if this blows up in our faces, I'm laying it right back on the threshold of 1600 Pennsylvania Avenue. You and I aren't falling on our swords, that's for damn sure. We took an oath to protect country and constitution, not a moron."

Woodson felt compelled to say, "Yes, sir."

MacArthur started to rise.

"Sir, Mullins had one request."

"What is it now?" MacArthur asked, exasperation coating the words.

Woodson pulled the two A and B envelopes from his pocket. "He asked if you'd run a DNA analysis on these two hair specimens."

"Hair? Whose?"

"He didn't say. Just would you expedite it."

"What's he want to know?"

"I guess anything the samples tell you. Maybe he's checking to determine if they came from the same person."

MacArthur took the two envelopes and studied Woodson a moment. "Would your father-in-law tell you everything he's learning?"

"I have no reason to think otherwise." *Unless he gave someone his word to keep a secret*, Woodson thought. Then even waterboarding wouldn't flush the truth out of him.

Woodson waited for the next question, the one he would have asked—will you tell me everything your father-in-law tells you?

Instead, MacArthur stood. "Thank you, Woodson. That will be all."

◇◇◇

On Saturday night, Mullins, Li, and Peter ate dinner in the main house alone. Brentwood was spending the weekend at his apartment in Manhattan. His absence made the planned visit to the research campus all the easier as Li wouldn't have to explain her late night visit beforehand.

At nine, they left the lake with Peter and his iPad in the backseat of the Malibu. The night sky was clear, and when they turned onto the road for the complex, the fields were empty of their resident bison. Mullins figured the herd might crowd together in a lower section of pasture near a stream, unless they had been a virtual creation projected on the horizon. The more he was around Brentwood the less sure he was of reality. Maybe right at the moment he was in the lab hooked to some neural stimulator creating the illusion of driving. But then what difference did it make? Reality was only what you thought it was.

The gate swung open, triggered by the automatic responder mounted in the car. Only two vehicles were in the lot. Mullins assumed one belonged to the security guard on duty and the other to an overnight tech who monitored the servers.

"Put your badge on, Peter," Li said. "We don't want to trip any alarms."

The guard at the entrance smiled and wished them a good evening. As soon as the door closed behind them, he picked up his phone.

Mullins, Li, and Peter stepped off the elevator on the lower level to find Felicia Corazón seated at her desk. If she was surprised by their presence at the late hour, she didn't show it.

Li stopped, not sure whether to offer an explanation or simply go to her office.

Mullins didn't hesitate. "Don't you have a home, Felicia?" He shook his head in mock sympathy. "I hope they're paying you double time."

"I work when I'm needed. We're running some maintenance tests tonight and we didn't want to tie up resources during the day." She turned to Li. "Did you need something?"

Lisa Li stepped closer to the desk. "I do. Mr. Brentwood authorized me to help Mr. Mullins with his investigation. I too don't want to tie up Apollo when the team needs his full capacity. How long till I can begin?"

Felicia looked at Peter. "It could be quite a while. I'll be happy to schedule time for you tomorrow."

"We'll wait," Li said. "Mr. Brentwood is anxious to get the answers to who tried to kill me. We'll be in the game room." Li led the way past Felicia before giving her a chance to object.

As they walked down the hallway, Mullins whispered, "Nicely done. Can you find out what sort of test they're running?"

"Yes, but after we get what we came for. What did you think about the sauce?" She opened the door and Peter ran to the nearest game console.

Mullins stopped on the threshold. "What sauce?"

"In the corner of her mouth. Red tomato sauce that was still damp. We interrupted her while she was eating, but there was no food at her desk."

"Look, Lisa, I'm supposed to be the detective. You're making me look bad in front of Peter."

She smiled. "Why do you think I'm whispering?"

Mullins walked away.

"Where are you going?"

"I'm hungry," he said in a normal voice. "Can I bring you something from the cafeteria?"

"Coffee. Take your time."

Mullins returned fifteen minutes later, juggling two cups of coffee and a glass of apple juice for Peter. The boy was engrossed in some kind of maze game and whispered thank you when Mullins set the drink beside him.

Lisa Li sat on a sofa, her legs crossed under her with her knees supporting her laptop.

"Can you log on through this computer?" Mullins asked.

"No. I need my secure terminal in my office. But I went ahead and wrote the search parameters we need. That way I just have to input them and Apollo can go to work." She took a cup of coffee. "Did you get something to eat?"

"No. Not a slice of pizza or noodle of spaghetti to be found. I'm so hungry I even checked the trash."

"Interesting," Li said.

"Either the sauce was blood and Felicia's a vampire and there's a drained body on the premises, or she was eating somewhere else. Maybe a takeout pizza in another room."

"And the guard alerted her we were coming," Li said.

Mullins nodded toward her computer. "Which search will you run first?"

"The more extensive one that I need to isolate from Apollo. It could take longer."

"Be sure and run the other one through Apollo," Mullins cautioned.

"I will. And I'll need to fabricate an activity log."

"Why?"

"To account for the time Apollo's offline. We have to assume someone will check. If he suddenly goes dark for any length of time, questions will be asked."

Mullins shrugged. "Well, if we're here all night, then we're here all night."

The door opened. Felicia stuck her head in. "We're clear if you'd like to begin. Good luck and good night."

As soon as the door closed, Li said, "If I have good luck, then it will be a good night." She grabbed her laptop and left.

Mullins made himself as comfortable as he could on the sofa. Too comfortable. He woke to find Peter nestled beside him, head resting against his thigh. Mullins shifted gently so that he could see his watch. Five minutes after one. He wondered if he should check on Li, but he didn't want to wake or abandon the boy. He decided to wait, knowing he would be no help in accelerating anything she was doing.

"Rusty, we can go."

Li's words penetrated his groggy brain and he realized he'd fallen back to sleep. Peter whimpered but didn't awaken.

He yawned. "Did you run everything?"

"Yes. We'll talk later."

Mullins read the tension in her face. "Okay. I'll carry Peter."

"Not with one arm." She picked up Peter's iPad where it had fallen on the floor and handed it to Mullins. "He's not too big for me yet." She nudged Peter to sit up and then lifted him under his arms. "Can you also take my laptop?"

Mullins followed her with the computer in one hand and iPad in the other. The empty silence of the hallways was broken only by the click of their footsteps. Li's came quick and short as she bore the weight of the sleeping boy.

Although Mullins was tempted to take a hurried look at whatever might be on Felicia's deserted desk, he was unsure whether surveillance cameras monitored this section of the facility. Instead, he stayed close to Li as she headed straight for the elevator.

When they reached the car, Mullins said, "Sit in the backseat with Peter." He opened the Malibu's rear door and helped Li slide in with Peter on her lap. He got behind the wheel and whispered over his shoulder, "I'm going to loop once around the building."

"Why?"

"Because when we arrived, there were two cars in the lot. A Subaru Forester and a Land Rover. Now, there's only the Subaru."

"Felicia went home."

"Probably." He started the engine and gave a wave to the guard watching them from his sentinel post. "But I'm always up for a little sight-seeing." He followed the two-lane access road the length of the building for several hundred yards before turning behind it.

"Do you see it?" he asked.

Li made out the colorless shape in the pale moonlight. "The other car. The one that was in front when we got here."

"Yes. The Land Rover. Tucked as close to the rear loading dock as possible."

"What do you think they're unloading?"

"Nothing. I think someone is still working." Mullins started down the far side of the building toward the exit. "While you were doing your searches would you have known if they were still using Apollo?"

"Definitely. But if they were waiting, why didn't Felicia ask me to let her know when I was finished?"

"Why, indeed. Once we get back to the cottage and you get Peter settled, let's have a little walk. I need to stretch my legs before bed."

When Li didn't reply, Mullins knew she understood.

It was nearly three in the morning when Mullins and Li walked along the water's edge. The full moon hung just above the western ridgeline and only a few outdoor spotlights shone from scattered houses across the lake.

Li had taken Mullins' good arm as they crossed uneven ground and continued to hold onto him after they reached the smooth gravel path. She stopped and her grip tightened. "You think the car, as well as the cottage, might be bugged, don't you?"

"We have to assume they are. Now that our little off-the-books investigation has begun, I don't want us to discuss anything we learn through your alternate identity. Someone's probably reviewing Apollo's searches. That's to be expected, and it would be unnatural for us not to discuss those findings. We can do that tomorrow. I'm interested in learning what our under-the-radar foray uncovered."

"Okay. First, your picture got hits from hundreds of news sources after the Marriott attacks. Nothing unusual there. Then there was some surveillance camera footage."

"Here?" Mullins asked.

"No. Looked like D.C. Various stores and exteriors."

"You got into those databases?"

"I didn't. The computer evidently has total access to both private and government sources and took the initiative. Its hacking power is nothing short of astonishing."

"Anything else?"

"Were you at an engagement this week?"

Mullins shook his head in disbelief. "On Chimney Rock. I witnessed a proposal and we had our picture made."

"Well, the computer found it posted on Facebook strictly off facial recognition."

Mullins thought it really had been a wise precaution to crop

Woodson out of the photograph. "Anything on the woman and the New Hampshire scene?"

Lisa Li looked farther down the path to where a bench faced the lake. "Why don't we sit? I'm getting tired of standing."

They walked, still arm in arm, to a clearing near the dock. Waves lapped gently against the shore.

"Do you want me to go back to the cottage for your coat?" Mullins asked.

"No. I'm fine." Li sat and waited for him to join her. "I got a run on the license plate that matched Kim Woodson to the vehicle. Then several files on the woman's disappearance."

"From news sources?"

"From the FBI."

"Jesus," Mullins exclaimed. "They've hacked into the bureau?"

"Evidently. There was no overlap between Kim Woodson and those missing professors, but there was an interesting development involving the dead assassins."

Mullins leaned closer to her, every neuron in his own brain alert.

"I ran the photos of the five through Apollo, the search you wanted to be readily discoverable."

"Correct."

"Well, there were three hits generated by facial recognition. Three of the five men were photographed by CCTV surveillance in front of a bank in Zurich."

"Three together?"

"No. On three separate occasions."

Mullins nodded, excitement building at what he thought might be his first real breakthrough. "Accounts they set up for the deposit of payments. How much time in between?"

"The latest was four months ago. The others occurred three years earlier, one in March and the other in November. Each within a three-month window of the assassination or disappearance of an AI scientist."

"Good work," Mullins said.

Li shook her head. "That's not the most interesting part. You asked me to run the stealth search looking for connections to the Montreal airport four years ago when Kim Woodson disappeared."

"One of them showed up then?"

"No. But the computer found a face coming into Canada that it had also seen in the surveillance footage of one of the assassins at the Zurich bank. It went ahead and made a connection we didn't request."

"So, a man is on a street in Zurich and shows up at the Montreal airport. That's well within the realm of coincidence."

"I agree," Li said. "But he also shows up in Montreal a few weeks before the Marriott shooting and leaves the day after. Each time his photo is linked to a different name on his passport."

Mullins felt an electrical charge run down his spine. He had to stand even though it meant he was towering over Li. "The driver who got away. The man has to be the driver."

"And maybe the organizer," Li said. "We've traced him back four years, farther than the others."

"Has he shown up since then?"

Li looked up at Mullins and even in the dim light he read fear in her eyes. "Yes. He came in through Miami last Tuesday. He's in the country, Rusty."

Mullins suddenly felt very exposed with the panorama of Lake Lure behind them. And he was aware that they'd left Peter alone in the cottage. "We're going back to the lab tomorrow. I want you to run all the passport aliases and his photo through any car rental agency, bus or train depot, and hotel records you can access. We need to know where this guy is."

"Okay."

"And then I think we need to head back to D.C. I'll tell Brentwood you'll need to work out of his D.C. site for a while. I've got to see my surgeon anyway, and hopefully get freed from this sling." He reached out with his right hand to help Li to her feet.

She stepped close to him and wrapped her arms around him, pressing her cheek against his chest. "Thank you for what you're doing. I know we're more than you bargained for."

He gently stroked her hair. They stood quietly for a few seconds, and then Mullins backed away. He stared at her with concern. "But are you getting more than you bargained for?"

Li's lips drew tight and thin. She grasped his hand. "You asked me to see if I could determine what test Felicia said was being run. Apollo was probing into the Department of Defense, specifically the drone program. I think he was searching for the codes for their control."

"And?"

"I think he got them."

◇◇◇

Dawn was breaking and the arteries into and around Washington D.C. were nearly empty of what on any weekday would have been clogged with commuters. Vice Admiral Louis MacArthur stared out the window at the sleepy landscape. Over on the Mall, tourists would be the primary inhabitants of Sunday morning. Even though the cherry blossoms had passed, the busloads would pour in as international tourists and school groups snapped thousands of photographs of the monuments to those who'd kept the country free.

If they only knew how precarious that freedom was, MacArthur thought. But the shores or skies weren't threatened by invading hordes. Today the invaders were keystrokes that could wreak havoc on everything from the country's financial structure to its military communications. MacArthur was on record with his concern, both with the Congress and the President. He'd lobbied for funds to develop cyber-defenses, and to recruit double agents betraying ally and foe alike so that he would be kept abreast of foreign advances in the field. It was the reason he'd told the President he wanted to head the intelligence investigation into the Marriott assassinations. And it was why he had spent the night in his office while simulated efforts were made to hack into the Pentagon's most classified files.

A knock sounded from the main door to his office. An aide entered with a single sheet of paper. "Here's the report, sir. It's a preliminary summary and they said they can provide more details if you wish."

MacArthur took the document. "What's the bottom line?"

The aide smiled. "Not so much as a single nick in the system. None of the attempts penetrated. If we were a fort, we'd make Knox look like a leaky sieve."

"Thank you," MacArthur said. "Now go home and get some rest."

"You too, sir."

But MacArthur suddenly felt rejuvenated. He tossed the report on his desk. Everything had gone perfectly. He didn't need to know anything more.

◇◇◇

Henrich Schmidt used the Chromebook he'd bought in Miami to sign on to his e-mail account. A new draft was waiting for his attention. *Finally*, he thought. But the instructions weren't what he expected. And the target was of such high profile, he considered declining. Then he saw the terms—a doubling of his fee and the first half ready to be wired immediately upon his acceptance of the assignment. *Money wasn't everything,* he thought. *But it sure beat the hell out of whatever was in second place.*

Schmidt deleted the draft of the e-mail and wrote a new one. He closed out of his account, leaving the draft unsent. Then he checked the Amtrak schedule. The train was a lower profile means of transportation, and one where his golf clubs wouldn't be searched. He would be in place by the next morning, and then his client could provide the opportunity. Maybe the original plan would have to be scuttled. On the other hand, his client didn't like loose ends. And Schmidt knew there were several in addition to the ex-Secret Service agent and Chinese scientist. The trip was proving to be his ticket into retirement, and he'd have to live to be a hundred and fifty to spend all the money.

Chapter Twenty-one

At one o'clock, Sunday afternoon, Mullins, Li, and Peter returned to the research facility. The three had slept until ten and skipped breakfast for a light lunch. Before leaving the guest cottage, Li had prepped her laptop with a series of inquiries, all of which would be run bypassing Apollo's identity. Mullins was taking no chances regarding any leaks until they could gather more information on the mystery man arriving through Miami.

Only one car, a Jeep Cherokee, was in the lot. A different security guard checked their badges and cleared them through. Mullins turned around before closing the door to see the man pick up the newspaper he'd been reading. If he was sounding an alarm, he wasn't doing it by phone.

No one met them on the lower level. Li went straight to her lab while Peter taught Mullins how to play a simulated baseball game. The virtual contest was so realistic that Mullins got caught up in it, at times having to remember to watch his language in front of a seven-year-old boy—a seven-year-old who was crushing him.

To add insult to injury, Peter proposed a rematch, offering to take second-tier players to even things up.

"You get to be the best by playing the best," Mullins stoically commented.

Peter took him at his word and Mullins soon realized the kid had been holding back all along. By the fifth inning, Mullins trailed thirteen to zero. With relief, he heard the door open and he looked from the monitor to see Li enter, her laptop clutched close to her chest.

"We need to leave now," she said.

"But we're in the middle of a game," Peter whined.

"I'm not kidding. Rusty, we've got to go."

Mullins dropped his control unit. "Your aunt's in charge here. If we have to leave now, it's for a good reason."

"Can we save the game?" Peter asked.

Mullins looked at Li. She shook her head.

"I concede." Mullins turned off the console. "When we play again, I want a fresh start. Get your iPad and let's go."

The three walked in silence through the building and into the parking lot. Mullins started the car, waved to the guard and headed for the highway. It wasn't till they cleared the gate leaving the complex that Li finally spoke.

"Can we have a little music?" She reached out and turned on the radio.

Mullins recognized Tchaikovsky's *Capriccio Italien*. The piece was building to one of its loudest points and the sound of strings, horns, and cymbals filled the car.

Lisa Li leaned close to Mullins. "He's in Spartanburg, South Carolina," she whispered. "He could be less than an hour away."

"How do you know?"

"A car rental agency scanned his driver's license."

"He rented a car?"

"Yes."

"Where?"

"The Enterprise desk at the Greenville-Spartanburg airport four days ago."

"Why didn't it show up last night?"

"I had the search parameters set for connections to the dead men, and then I expanded it to airports. That got us to Miami. Today, I ran the search much wider."

"What was the name?"

"Karl Reinbold. That's different from his Miami entry name of Wilhelm Hecht."

"How do you know he's in Spartanburg and not Greenville?"

"Because I ran the Reinbold name through hotel registries. I got a hit on the Hampton Inn at the Westgate Mall in Spartanburg. Reinbold checked out at eleven this morning."

Mullins didn't like it. The man was obviously a professional with as many identities as a phone book. "Has he turned in the car?"

"No. But he's supposed to return it to the same location. He must be driving somewhere in the region."

"Perhaps he's just changing hotels so that he's not in one place too many nights."

Li looked over her shoulder to Peter. The boy was reading his Asimov book. "Are you sure?"

Mullins wanted to say yes, but he couldn't lie to her. "No. I think we need to leave now. I'll alert the authorities and maybe they'll pick him up. Meanwhile, I want us back in D.C. Brentwood will have to accept it or fire us both."

Li bit her lower lip, clearly stressed at the prospect of crossing the billionaire. "The work's at a critical stage."

"Can't you program the damn thing from his Washington operation?"

"I guess so. I've already given them the hardware specifications for North Carolina."

"Then you're giving him an option—work from D.C. or not at all. At least till we know more about this threat."

"Where will we stay in D.C.?"

"We won't. We'll check into a hotel somewhere outside D.C. Brentwood's facility's not in D.C. proper anyway."

"No. He told me it was on the beltway near Tysons Corner but I've never been there. What should I say to him?"

"Nothing. I'll handle Brentwood. But I want to be gone before he gets here. When we get to the cottage, I'll clear it first. Then you and Peter pack as quickly as you can. We'll take this car and make a plan while we're driving."

When they reached the lake, Mullins made a thorough check of the cottage and grounds, careful not to draw his gun until he was out of sight of Li and Peter. He found everything in order and waved them out of the car.

"I'll grab my bag and stand guard outside," he said. "Come out when you're ready."

He retrieved the burner phone from under his mattress, quickly packed and then waited on the porch. All the while his mind raced through the actions he could take. He wasn't happy with his options. Allen Woodson would need to play a vital role and Mullins didn't know what resources he could command.

He stepped off the porch, walked about twenty yards down the path and pulled out his burner phone. He'd have to trust his son-in-law's judgment.

◇◇◇

Allen Woodson paced back and forth in his hotel room while he listened to his father-in-law's summation. A potential killer going back to the time of his sister's disappearance was in Spartanburg, South Carolina. At least that was the last known location earlier in the day.

He agreed with Mullins' assessment that Dr. Li and her nephew should return to D.C. But he didn't think they should go near Brentwood's Virginia facility until this Reinbold or whatever his name was had been apprehended. Woodson told Mullins he would find safe accommodations and to call him as they neared D.C.

"All right," Mullins said. "But I'll need to stop and get out of the car. Brentwood could have the most sophisticated technology on the planet and I can't chance that someone isn't monitoring conversations in his vehicles."

"Then I'll drop a rental at your apartment. Keys on the right rear tire."

"Who else will you involve?" Mullins asked.

"No one but Vice Admiral MacArthur. He can give orders and still keep his staff in the dark."

"Then tell him whatever you need to. And, Allen, if something goes wrong, call this number." Mullins gave Woodson a ten-digit phone number and asked him to repeat it.

"Who is it?"

"Sam Dawkins from the Secret Service. He can get word to the President, and I guarantee you no stone will go unturned looking for us."

As soon as Mullins rang off, Woodson called MacArthur's private cell. The Vice Admiral answered on the first ring.

"Talk to me," was all he said.

Woodson gave him the summary of the search for links to the Marriott assassins and the connection between one of them and the man who had left through Montreal the day after the killings.

"And Mullins said this Reinbold's last location was a Hampton Inn in Spartanburg?" MacArthur asked.

"Yes, sir. But he checked out this morning."

"How the hell was Mullins able to learn that when we've been running the same inquiries for weeks?"

"The computer's evidently able to break through firewalls at will. The identification was made through Swiss CCTV footage and archived immigration records."

"Do you want to go to Spartanburg?" MacArthur asked.

"No, sir. I'd rather stay here and help Mullins."

"When do you expect him?"

"Not till late tonight."

MacArthur thought for a moment. He walked to a picture window and stared across the Chesapeake Bay.

"Okay. I agree. I'll call Rudy Hauser at the Bureau. It's the FBI's jurisdiction anyway. But debrief your father-in-law tonight. If Brentwood's computer is so goddamned smart, he might have learned other information as well. Then you can fill me in tomorrow."

"What time would you like me at your office?" Woodson asked.

"Actually I'm spending the weekend at my place on the Eastern Shore and then going up to Annapolis tomorrow afternoon. There's a Waffle House where we can meet outside of Baltimore, if you don't mind the drive."

"No problem, sir. Give me the time and place."

MacArthur provided directions and set the rendezvous for one o'clock. He rang off and immediately placed a second call. If the assassin was in Spartanburg, he needed to be found, and found quickly.

◇◇◇

Ned Farino stood on the shore of Lake Lure and took a moment to study his boss. Robert Brentwood sat in one of two chairs at the end of the dock and appeared engrossed in watching the sun set behind the mountains.

"Robert, I'm here."

Brentwood jumped to his feet and spun around. "Why the hell didn't you call me as soon as you knew they were in the building?" He shouted the question, unconcerned that his voice carried across the open water.

Ned Farino didn't retreat from the man's wrath. He walked the length of the dock with his arms outstretched in an effort to appear conciliatory. "Calm down, Robert. If I'd called you, you would have come racing back from New York last night and confirmed Mullins' suspicions that we've been monitoring them."

"No. I would have expressed concern that Dr. Li was working too hard. I'd at least have been in position to discuss their findings and offer more security. Instead, I return to an empty guesthouse and discover a scientist critical to our plans has been spooked into hiding. And I have to learn about it from a goddamned voicemail from Mullins."

"Mullins was going to do what he was going to do. You knew that when you hired him and gave him access to Apollo."

Brentwood took a deep breath and brought his anger under control. "At least Mullins was able to identify another assassin. And if the man came through Miami, he could be in the area."

Farino shrugged. "So, Li drops out of the project for a week or two till this guy's apprehended. Felicia says Li's making good progress."

"How does Felicia know that?"

Now that Brentwood's initial storm had subsided, Farino took the liberty of sitting in one of the chairs and motioned for

Brentwood to join him. "In addition to Li's search for links to the five dead assassins, she ran some tests through Asimov to see if they would go unnoticed by Apollo. We checked with the other team. Apollo was completely unaware that internal processing was occurring. Li's given you your cherished subconscious."

"That's only phase one," Brentwood argued. "Li needs to create the algorithms that define Asimov's unique approach to Apollo's input and conclusions. That will be delicate and difficult work."

"But she's proven she can create those algorithms undetected. And we can keep to your schedule even if Li's work is still being refined."

Brentwood stared at his executive vice president. The man didn't get it. His hubris was an asset for wheeling and dealing, but a liability when it came to identifying unknown and unintended consequences. Brentwood decided arguing the point was fruitless. Dr. Li got it, which was why he needed her back as soon as possible.

"Let me make sure I understand something," Brentwood said. "Li, Mullins, and the boy entered the lab around nine-thirty last night."

"Correct. The guard alerted Felicia and she was able to be at her desk when they arrived. Felicia tried to put them off till today, but Li was persistent that she wanted to run her tests and Mullins' inquiries."

"So, Felicia acquiesced and Li found a connection between some of the dead assassins and a bank in Zurich."

"Yes."

"And then that led to this mystery man who reentered the country through Miami."

"Correct," Farino said.

"Do you have a photograph of him?"

Farino hesitated a moment. "Felicia should be able to access it. I haven't seen it myself."

"I want our security team to have it. Make sure Jenkins distributes it to all our locations."

"All right," Farino agreed. "Anything else?"

"Yes. According to Felicia, Li ran some tests and then discovered the man in Miami. That's why Mullins sent them into hiding."

"That appears to be the case."

Brentwood leaned closer to Farino, his eyes narrow and bright. "Then tell me why they went back to the lab this afternoon and ran more tests, tests that had already proven successful? Why didn't Mullins move them last night?"

Farino's mouth dropped open as he grasped the answer.

"Now you understand," Brentwood chided. "Once they knew they could work through Apollo without leaving a footprint, they came back and ran God-knows-what through the computer. It was only then that Mullins learned something that sent them into hiding."

"I'll look into it." Farino got to his feet. Brentwood was right to be concerned. Suddenly it was what he didn't know that he didn't know that could bring everything tumbling down.

◇◇◇

The Crescent pulled into the Spartanburg Amtrak station at six minutes before midnight, only fifteen minutes late. Originating in New Orleans, the *Crescent* train would travel through more states between Louisiana and New York than any other route in the Amtrak system.

The conductor offered to help a boarding passenger load his suitcase and golf clubs, but the man politely declined. Later, after the conductor checked the man's ticket, he thought it unusual that a passenger would bring golf clubs into Union Station, the heart of Washington D.C.

Chapter Twenty-two

Mullins swung the white Ford Escort in a wide arc around the parking lot and purposefully chose a space ten down from their motel unit.

Allen Woodson had left the rental car at Mullins' apartment building in Shirlington along with a key for a single room at the Breezewood Motel in Vienna, Virginia. He'd advised Mullins to place his and Li's cell phones in Mullins' Prius and Woodson would park it at a Wal-Mart in Maryland. As a further decoy, they left the Malibu in the lot at the apartment so that anyone tracking either the Chevy or their cell phones would be drawn to the wrong locations.

Woodson had booked them a room on the backside of the mom-and-pop motel. Using the false identity papers he'd received from Vice Admiral MacArthur, Woodson had checked in under the name of Roger Ethridge and told the clerk he was accompanied by his wife and child. He'd paid in cash for two nights and given the license plate of the rental car so that there would be nothing that drew attention to the family's stay. Unless the clerk himself came to the room, Mullins, Li, and Peter should be as safe there as anywhere.

Mullins killed the Escort's engine and cut the headlights. "Let's sit for a moment." He glanced in the backseat where Peter had fallen asleep.

"What are you waiting for?" Li whispered.

"Scan the motel's windows. See if anyone is peeking out."

Most of the rooms were dark. It wasn't a busy Sunday night at the Breezewood. There were more pickups and vans in the lot than cars, which indicated to Mullins that the motel was used by out-of-town construction workers here for a few days of contract labor.

After five minutes, Mullins reached overhead and disabled the interior courtesy light. "You take Peter. I'll get our bags."

"He can walk. Otherwise you'll have to make two trips."

The boy was groggy, but he managed to carry his own suitcase without complaining. Mullins used the electronic key and they entered a room that held the faint scent of cigarette smoke and could have last been decorated in the nineteen fifties.

"Sorry for the accommodations." Mullins surveyed the two queen-sized beds and small desk with a single straight-back chair. "My son-in-law insisted we stay off the radar, but I didn't realize he'd put us in a time machine to do it."

Li smiled. "At least it's clean. We'll spend most of the day at Brentwood's laboratory anyway."

"Yes. But not till Allen checks in with Vice Admiral MacArthur and we get more protection. Why don't you and Peter take the bed closest to the bathroom."

"Okay." Li set the boy's suitcase on the foot of the bed. "Let's change into your pajamas, Peter. It's nearly ten."

"I'm not sleepy anymore."

"Well, change anyway," Li said. "You can read your book in bed."

Mullins pulled out his burner phone. "I need to let Allen know we got in okay. He said he'd like to stop by, if that's all right. There are some things we need to go over."

"Sure. No problem. I'll get Peter ready."

"One other thing," Mullins said. "Could I read the data you got from the searches? We talked about the main concerns, but there were other points like Brentwood's background and the Zurich banking information that I need to review."

Li took her laptop out of its case. "The documents are in folders. The language is a little stilted since the computer outputs

Esperanto rather than English. Brentwood's idiosyncrasy means I had to run it through a translation program." She shook her head. "Seems crazy that he's so hung up on using a non-national tongue."

Maybe crazy, Mullins thought. More likely Brentwood had no use for national allegiances and was loyal only to his own ideology. That could be good or extremely dangerous.

Li placed the computer on the desk and turned it on. "It will need a few minutes to boot up. As soon as I get Peter changed, I'll pull up the information."

Mullins nodded and dialed his son-in-law.

Shortly after ten-thirty, a soft knock came from the door. Mullins looked up from the computer where he'd been reading files. Li sat on the bed behind him, giving room for Peter who lay asleep with the *I, Robot* book open by his pillow.

Mullins held up a finger signaling Li to remain quiet. He went to the window and peered through the narrow crack between the drapes. Then he nodded confirmation, threw back the deadbolt and opened the door. Allen Woodson entered.

The naval intelligence officer took in the scene and smiled at Li. "Sorry to put you in this situation," he whispered. "We needed a motel that wasn't part of a national chain because they'd record me in their database, and I didn't want to draw attention by booking two rooms."

Li rose from the bed and they shook hands. "As long as we're safe. That's all that matters."

Woodson gestured toward the boy. "Is it okay if we talk softly?"

"Peter could sleep through a typhoon."

"Good." He turned to Mullins. "I just got off a secure line with MacArthur. He said there's been no development in Spartanburg."

"What about Brentwood's lake house? Is anyone staking it out?"

"FBI agents are in place. MacArthur also requested surveillance at Brentwood's research facility. Between the Bureau and

Brentwood's security people, this guy should be spotted if he makes a move."

"Lindsay Boyce got the request then?"

"Who?" Woodson asked.

"The special agent in charge of the Asheville region. I saw her before our meeting at Chimney Rock."

"MacArthur didn't say anything about her. She must not have mentioned you."

Good, Mullins thought. Agent Boyce was being tight-lipped. "Did MacArthur say how Brentwood reacted?"

"No. But Brentwood's company has enough government contracts that he won't risk alienating a vice admiral."

"He might," Mullins said, "but his Washington man Farino will probably keep him cooperative."

"What about more official security here?" Woodson asked. "Or at the Fairfax lab where Dr. Li will be working?"

"Mention it to MacArthur but insist that he not put any instructions in writing. At least not in the computer system."

"Why not?"

"Because what Brentwood's computer is able to do might also be achievable by our enemies." Mullins looked at Li. "Dr. Li has been using Apollo surreptitiously. We can't overlook the possibility that Brentwood was already hacked and someone else is a shadow presence."

"I don't see how," Li objected.

"You've proven it possible so we can't dismiss it." Mullins turned to Woodson. "And there's something else you and MacArthur need to know. Something I didn't want to say over the phone. Dr. Li uncovered tests being run that broke through the Department of Defense's cyber-security barriers like they were open gates. We believe they were able to breach the firewalls protecting the operational network of our drone program."

"Jesus," Woodson muttered. "Are you sure?"

"Yes," Li confirmed. "Apollo has become self-learning, a remarkable breakthrough that clearly puts him in a class by himself. I'm hoping the tests were run as a security check for the military. Identify the weak spots and have Apollo develop new encryption techniques to eliminate any vulnerability."

"Except he who writes the code can break the code," Woodson said.

Li took a step closer to Mullins and clasped his wrist. She looked up at him with grim determination. "Which is why I've got to stay in the mix, Rusty. If Brentwood's working for altruistic goals, then we have nothing to fear from him. The challenge is external, the group called Humanity's Hope and their man in Spartanburg. But I have to be inside where I can both work and monitor the others." She faced Woodson. "Neither you nor Vice Admiral MacArthur nor any of your colleagues are better positioned."

"All right," Woodson agreed. "I'm seeing MacArthur tomorrow afternoon. We'll surround you with a platoon of Marines if we need to."

"And Peter," Li added, "if Rusty thinks we need extra protection for him, then I want it. Peter's their breach through my firewall."

Woodson stared at his father-in-law, waiting for a response.

Mullins' thoughts moved from the boy on the bed to another boy sleeping less than ten miles away. His grandson Josh. "You have your own breach, Rusty," he heard his dead wife's voice clearly say.

"Tell MacArthur we need some kind of safe house and we need to include Kayli and Josh. As soon as that's done, Lisa can go back to work."

"Okay," Woodson said. "But MacArthur may still want me to remain invisible."

"That's fine," Mullins said. "I'm sure he wants me off the intelligence radar as well. You and I will continue as we have been."

"What's your read on Brentwood?" Woodson asked. "Should we be worried about him?"

Mullins stepped back and pointed to the laptop on the desk. "He's complicated. We got some background on him that isn't in the press releases or corporate bio. He grew up privileged in Manhattan, the son of a hard-driving real estate developer named

Rex Brentwood who makes Donald Trump look like Gandhi. His mother was from a prominent Boston family and Brentwood was their only child. We accessed some medical records. He was withdrawn and slow to speak. An initial diagnosis leaned toward autism, but this was back when it wasn't as common or understood. The father appears to have had no empathy for the son's condition. The mother took him to pediatric therapists and encouraged him to interact with other children, but he preferred to keep to himself. They had a place in the Adirondacks where Brentwood spent hours with a telescope and read a mix of science fiction and science fact."

"How did you learn this?" Woodson asked.

Mullins smiled. "You think someone with the money and technological wizardry of Brentwood isn't going to be thoroughly researched by his competitors and our own government? Most of what Dr. Li found came out of our domestic intelligence departments."

"If he's autisic, it seems to have worked in his favor."

"On some levels," Mullins said. "One assessment is that despite his success, he's still awkward in social situations. What we see is a mimic of his father. The big limousines, the private jets, luxury homes and apartments."

"Doesn't that just come with the money?" Woodson asked.

"Sure. But he doesn't really socialize. He doesn't throw parties. He drinks his Blanton's alone, usually eats meals prepared by a personal chef, he's never married or had a relationship with a woman or man. He claims he doesn't have time, but he might not have the capacity for such a relationship."

"You're saying his role model was his father and so he indulges in those trappings because he has no real social skills of his own."

"It's a theory floated by some of your people. But he's never manifested any behavior that would disqualify him from either winning government contracts or establishing influential political connections."

"Do you like him?" Woodson asked.

Mullins glanced at Li. "Yes, I do."

"So do I," Li said.

"Do you trust him?"

"No," Mullins said. "I don't have enough information. He's driven and he's brilliant, a potentially dangerous combination if tied to a personal agenda we don't understand. And he has had trauma in his life."

"Like what?" Woodson asked.

"His father committed suicide when Brentwood was seventeen. The boy discovered the body."

"Gunshot?"

"No. Sedatives and a plastic bag over his head. He suffocated himself."

"Was there an investigation?"

"Yes. Brentwood's mother was in the hospital recovering from hip surgery. She'd said she'd slipped on a patch of ice the day before. Brentwood had spent the night in the room with his mother and when he went home in the morning to shower and change, he found his father sitting in the den, a half-empty bottle of Blanton's by his chair, an empty bottle of his mother's sedatives beside it. The plastic bag had been secured around his neck with duct tape. His father's fingerprints were on the roll as well as the whiskey and pill bottles."

"Was there a note?"

"Yes. A simple handwritten line on a sheet of paper—'Sorry for the harm I've caused.'"

"What harm?" Woodson asked.

"His wife admitted that he had pushed her down a flight of stairs. She didn't slip on the ice and it wasn't the first time he'd abused her."

"Did Brentwood confirm it?"

"No. By then he was in prep school in New Hampshire. He'd come home when she'd called after the fall."

"She called, not the father?"

"That's right. And then after his father's suicide, Brentwood came out of his shell. He started college at MIT the next fall, threw himself into the brave new world of computer science, and most importantly, convinced his mother to invest in two new companies, one was Apple and the other Microsoft. He cashed those out after their spectacular rise and started Cumulus Cognitive Connections."

"What happened to his mother?" Woodson asked.

"She died of breast cancer when he was thirty. Since then he's made sizable donations to organizations working to prevent spousal abuse and he's endowed a foundation in his mother's name that supports cancer research."

"So, the guy could be screwy and a saint."

Mullins looked at Li. "Well, he's certainly on a mission, isn't he, Lisa?"

"Yes. And someone's going to win the race to create artificial intelligence. Robert Brentwood might be our best hope."

Woodson took a deep breath. "Okay. I'll talk to MacArthur tomorrow. Do you want me to watch your room tonight?"

"No," Mullins said. "We're fine. Someone sitting in a car all night will only draw attention."

"All right." Woodson nodded to Li. "Very nice to meet you. And you have my sympathy. Rusty snores."

Woodson reached in his pants pocket for his keys and Mullins walked him to the door. As the naval officer stepped across the threshold, he turned to shake his father-in-law's hand.

Mullins felt a crumpled piece of paper in his palm.

"Good night, Rusty."

Mullins slipped the paper into his pocket and closed the door. Then he turned the deadbolt and fastened the security chain.

Lisa Li pulled a pair of red silk pajamas from her suitcase. "I'll change first, and then you can have the bathroom."

"Take your time. I'll sleep in my clothes."

As soon as he heard water running in the sink, he unfolded the paper.

His son-in-law had printed the words, "MacArthur says DNA samples show an aunt and nephew relationship."

He put the note back in his pocket. A flush of the toilet would be the best way to get rid of it.

Chapter Twenty-three

Monday morning, Mullins, Lisa Li, and Peter stayed in the motel room till nine-thirty. Mullins figured most of the other occupants would be gone by then and the likelihood of the three being seen as they left would be greatly reduced.

He decided they should have breakfast at an IHOP restaurant in Fairfax about ten minutes away. He'd been there a few times with Josh and Kayli and it always seemed to do a brisk business. Mullins knew the best place to hide was in a crowd and he'd never met a kid who didn't like pancakes.

Peter whooped with excitement when the waitress brought him a stack smothered with fresh strawberries and whipped cream. "Dessert for breakfast, Aunt Li Li."

"Yes, so no more treats today."

Mullins winked at the boy. "Unless it's carrot cake. I count that as a vegetable."

Li and Mullins had both ordered vegetarian omelets and the three fell silent as they ate, Li and Peter on one side of the booth, Mullins on the other. Mullins' thoughts returned to Brentwood. Regardless as to whether the billionaire was trustworthy or not, Li was right. She needed to get back into the lab. And Mullins had to do more than leave Brentwood a voicemail. He wished he still had his personal cell phone because using his burner would not only reveal the number but his location and he needed to keep the phone on for messages from his son-in-law.

"Lisa, is there Wi-Fi here?" he asked.

Li set down her silverware. "Peter, let me see your iPad."

Peter handed it to her.

She checked available networks. "Yes. And it's free."

"Can you search for local pay phones?"

Li's fingers swiftly moved across the touch screen. "The closest one appears to be at a McDonald's around the corner."

"Good. I was afraid they were extinct. I need to call Brentwood, and then I thought we'd have a little holiday. It's going to be a pretty day. What do you say we ride up to Great Falls?"

"Where's that?" Peter asked.

"Not too far. It's where the Potomac tumbles over a series of rocks."

"Can we ride down the falls?"

"No, but we can hike along the trail, and you can see Maryland on the other side."

"Is this where George Washington threw a silver dollar across the Potomac?"

"Maybe. But I wouldn't try it. A dollar doesn't go as far these days."

Peter and Li laughed. Mullins was impressed the boy got the joke.

Mullins discovered dollars didn't go as far in a pay phone either as he was prompted to feed quarters for his long-distance call to Brentwood.

"Hello?" The whispered question was completely out of character for someone used to being in command.

"Robert?"

"Rusty!" The voice snapped back to full volume. "What the hell's going on?"

"Didn't you get my message? We have a high-level threat and I had to take prudent action."

"Are you sure you're safer there?"

"The FBI has the guy's photo and there are more layers of law enforcement here than any other place in the country. Even if he figures out we're no longer at Lake Lure, he'll think twice about risking an assault here."

"They didn't think twice about the attack at the Marriott," Brentwood cautioned.

"No, but that's when they came out of nowhere. Thanks to Apollo we've got aliases and a facial match. Time's running out for him. As soon as he's caught, we'll return."

"I'm coming up there," Brentwood insisted.

"I can't stop you, but it's not necessary."

"Rusty, it's not only necessary, it's crucial. Now tell me where I can meet you."

"Sorry, the line's not secure. We'll see you in Fairfax." Mullins hung up.

◇◇◇

Lieutenant Commander Allen Woodson left his room at the JW Marriott Monday morning at eleven-thirty, allowing for an hour drive and a thirty-minute margin to make sure he was on time for his meeting with Vice Admiral MacArthur.

Fifty minutes later, he exited I-95. The Waffle House sign was visible from the ramp. He circled the restaurant once and noticed the parking spaces were filled. Lunch patrons were proving waffles weren't just for breakfast. It was too early to go in and hold a booth for forty minutes while waiting on MacArthur so he crossed the street and found a place in the lot of a Ramada Conference Center.

Woodson was tempted to call Mullins, but decided to delay until he could report on his meeting. He reviewed the file he'd compiled based upon Apollo's information and the money trail that had flowed out of the Zurich bank. He'd share the recommendations Mullins had made for protection for Kayli and Josh as well as tight security for Dr. Li and Peter.

At twelve-forty, Woodson left the car at the Ramada and walked across the street to the Waffle House. The lunch crowd had thinned and he spotted a back booth isolated from the other patrons. As soon as he sat, a waitress started toward him. She looked like she was supplementing her Social Security.

"I'm Mildred. What can I get you?" She offered him a menu.

"Black coffee for right now. I'm expecting someone in a few minutes."

"Man or woman, if you don't mind me asking?"

"A man."

"So, I've still got a chance to win your heart?"

Woodson smiled. "Depends on the coffee."

Mildred laughed. "Don't you worry about my coffee." She glanced at the door. "And I'll keep an eye out for your buddy."

Vice Admiral Louis MacArthur swept his gaze across the interior of the Waffle House. He saw Woodson but made no immediate move toward him. If something in the restaurant was off, MacArthur would pivot and depart without giving any sign he meant to meet someone. Maybe he'd pat his pants pockets like he'd left his wallet. He'd exit and quickly be forgotten.

A waitress approached. "You looking for the good-looking man in the back booth?"

MacArthur glanced at her nametag. Mildred.

"Yes."

He followed her to the booth and sat across from Woodson. Mildred laid two menus between them.

"All I want is coffee and a single plain waffle," MacArthur said without bothering to pick up a menu.

"Same here," Woodson said.

Mildred grabbed the menus in one hand and Woodson's half-empty cup in the other. "I'll freshen this up for you, honey."

As soon as she was out of earshot, MacArthur leaned over the Formica table. "What the hell's going on, Woodson?"

◇◇◇

Lisa Li and Peter stood at the overlook above the most treacherous section of the Potomac's whitewater rapids. They'd returned to the spot for a second time because Peter wanted a final look. He'd enjoyed the hike and watching the kayakers and rock-climbers, but it was the power of the current that held his fascination.

Mullins stood a few yards back where he could have a clearer view of the other park visitors and be alert for any potential threat. The outdoor exercise felt good and he realized his shoulder hadn't hurt once. He decided he didn't need a doctor to tell him he was done with the sling. Besides, he had more pressing matters than keeping a post-operative appointment. He slipped off his jacket, slid the sling over his head and wadded it into a ball. The first trashcan would be the last stop of his recovery.

He felt the burner phone vibrate in his pocket. Woodson should have just started his meeting with MacArthur. Had something gone wrong? Mullins pulled the phone free and glanced at the number. Rudy Hauser's private line. He took another step backwards where he hoped Li and the boy wouldn't hear him above the sound of the rushing water. If the head of the FBI was calling, there must have been a major development.

"Rudy, what is it?"

"Nothing on our suspect, Rusty, but we've done a mass distribution of the Miami photo and I'm optimistic. You let me know when you want agent support."

"In the morning," Mullins said. "When we go to Brentwood's Fairfax operation. I'll call with the rendezvous point."

"All right."

"Is that it?" Mullins was surprised if the director phoned just to confirm an existing plan.

"No. I know you said you'd call me, but with all that's going on, I thought you might have forgotten. I got that report on the mother and son."

"Who?" Mullins asked, genuinely perplexed.

"From the hair strands and drinking glass. The DNA tests."

"They're mother and son?" he whispered. "You're sure?"

"Definitely. And they're Chinese. So, are they who I think they are?" Hauser asked.

"Sorry. I've gotta go." Mullins abruptly ended the call.

For a second, he stared at Lisa and Peter. Mother and son. She had lied to him.

But it wasn't that lie that set his heart racing.

◇◇◇

"And the money trail?" Vice Admiral MacArthur asked. "How did they pick that up?"

Woodson slid a sheet of paper across the table. "Brentwood's computer analyzed accounts that were opened on the days each of the three men were seen on the Zurich CCTV footage. It then cross-referenced deposits that went into those accounts. A fourth account showed up as the primary source for three of them. We believe those three were the accounts opened by the three men. We believe this is the man who controlled that account." Woodson pointed to the photos of the suspect at the Miami airport and outside the Zurich bank.

"And where did that account get its money?"

"They haven't run that search yet. The computer was looking for links among the three dead men and then it followed the trail of the new man, which led to the Montreal and Miami connections. He became the priority and he became the threat. They left the lab before going any further. Mullins wants to know if you can start a parallel search for where our suspect's funds are coming from."

Woodson felt the burner phone vibrate a single burst in his pocket. A text message had come in.

"Will Mullins continue running searches through Apollo?" MacArthur asked.

"Yes. But he's being very cautious. He's afraid there's a leak somewhere and it might be in Brentwood's organization."

"Who else knows about it?" MacArthur asked.

Woodson felt his phone vibrate a second time. "Just you and me, sir. And, of course, Dr. Li." He slipped his hand into his pocket.

"The President?" MacArthur asked.

"I don't think so. This all came down yesterday afternoon. Mullins wants to see what you propose first."

MacArthur nodded. "Good. I appreciate that." He started gathering the documents into the file folder.

Woodson took a quick glance at the phone in his lap. The display screen read,

Do not trust MacArthur!!! Call ASAP.

Calmly, he wiped his lips with his napkin. "I've got to run to the head, sir. I loaded up on too much coffee."

"No problem. I'll settle up with our waitress friend, and we can talk some more in my car. We need to make a plan, and I want to meet with Mullins in person."

"Yes, sir."

Woodson found the small restroom and took the single empty stall. He sat on the toilet and called Mullins.

His father-in-law answered immediately. "Where are you?"

"In the men's room at the Waffle House. Talk to me."

"Our friend gave you the wrong relationship on the DNA samples. I ran a backup test through Hauser. Mother, son. No question about it."

"Maybe our lab made a mistake," Woodson said.

"On a priority demand that comes from the Director of Naval Intelligence?"

Woodson hesitated, trying to wrap his head around the implications. "What's his motive?"

"He's protecting somebody. Maybe Li, maybe someone else who has an interest in keeping the true relationship a secret."

"Who?"

"I don't know," Mullins said. "Did you give him all the data?"

"Yes. Now we're going to talk about our next steps."

"Well, anything he tells you is suspect. Let him lead the planning. We may need to put him under Apollo's scrutiny."

"Spy on the vice admiral?"

"Did you ask him to protect Kayli and Josh?"

Woodson's throat went dry. "Yes. He said he'd set it up."

"Then I think we need to know what's really going on."

Woodson heard the restroom door open and someone walk to the urinal. "I've got to go," he whispered. He ended the call, flushed the toilet and hoped his face showed no trace of the turmoil inside him.

Outside, MacArthur walked to his black Cadillac Escalade at the end of the row of cars in front of the Waffle House. He clutched the file folder in his right hand and fumbled for his keys with his left. His mind raced with what Woodson's discoveries could mean, and he'd been completely blindsided by the extent of the revelations. He knew he needed to take control of all aspects of the investigation and quickly. He didn't want Mullins making some back-channel report to President Brighton. The bright spot in Woodson's report was that Mullins appeared to respect the chain of command.

MacArthur opened the door of the SUV, climbed in and set the file on the console between the seats. He decided to pick Woodson up at the entrance and drive around the area while they talked. He started the engine, but before he could shift the transmission into reverse, a gray Toyota Camry stopped broadside behind him. A man wearing a dark brown hoodie jumped out and rapidly walked toward him.

MacArthur opened the door and turned in his seat. "What the hell are you doing here? He's coming out any second."

Heinrich Schmidt looked over his shoulder at the restaurant's front door. He saw Woodson push it open and squint against the bright sunlight. Without a second's hesitation, Schmidt reached into the pouch of his hoodie and pulled out his Glock.

"Not here," MacArthur urged.

"Not him," Schmidt whispered.

Allen Woodson heard a sharp pop and knew immediately it was the sound of a suppressed gunshot. He saw the open door of the Escalade and the back of a hooded man blocking it. Then the man sprinted to a sedan parked behind the oversized SUV.

Woodson ran after him, but with a squeal of tires, the vehicle surged forward. Woodson saw MacArthur sprawled backwards across the console with his head lying on the passenger's seat. A dark red hole marred his tanned forehead. The inside of the passenger door and window were splattered with blood, bone, and brains. There was no need to check for a pulse. Then he saw a corner of the file protruding from underneath the vice admiral's left shoulder. Woodson knew the murder scene would be under the jurisdiction of local cops and Apollo's information had no business being in their custody. He snatched the file free and ran for his car in the Ramada Conference Center lot.

Inside the Waffle House, Mildred picked up the five-dollar bill from the table, pleased at the generosity of the tip for only two coffees and plain waffles. She glanced out the window and saw the younger of her two customers running across the street. He certainly was in a hurry.

Chapter Twenty-four

"What's wrong?" Lisa Li stared anxiously at Mullins. She and Peter stood with the roiling Potomac at their backs.

"Nothing. I'm waiting on a call is all. I don't want to talk while driving."

Li's dark eyes narrowed. "I don't believe that. I want to know what you know. We're in this together."

Mullins gritted his teeth, uncomfortable in telling her everything until he knew why she'd lied about her relationship to the boy.

"I'm expecting to hear from my son-in-law. He's a little late."

Li nodded. "Then let's get out of the wind and wait in the car." She hooked his left arm with her right and started forward.

She stopped. "You've gotten rid of your sling."

"Are you all better, Mr. Mullins?" Peter asked.

"Pretty close. But we still need to stay safe and out of danger." He scanned the parking area near their rental car. From the corner of his eye, he saw Peter mimic him. "That's right, Peter. You want to be alert."

He opened the car doors for the front and rear passenger seats. "Be thinking about what you want for lunch."

"That's easy," Peter said. "Carrot cake. I need vegetables."

Mullins laughed, and then felt the burner phone vibrate in his pocket. He closed the doors and walked twenty feet away.

"Yes?" he said.

"Where are you?" Allen Woodson's voice was calm. Too calm.

"At Great Falls with Li and—" he paused. "With Li and her son."

"MacArthur's been assassinated."

Mullins pressed the phone tighter to his ear. "What?"

"A man in a hoodie shot him as he sat in his car waiting for me. I don't have a description. Hell, I don't know whether he was black or white. His hands were gloved."

"Are you there?"

"No. I tried to give chase and I took the file with all the information I brought MacArthur. I didn't think we wanted the local cops involved. But, I'll probably be identified and MacArthur is my commanding officer. I have to step forward."

"No," Mullins barked. "We can't jeopardize our access to Apollo. Lisa Li made more progress in two days than our entire intelligence network made in nearly a month."

"Rusty, I'm not a private citizen. It won't do any of us any good if I'm caught and courtmartialed."

Mullins knew he was demanding that his son-in-law crawl out on a limb, a limb that would ruin his life if it broke. He had to give Woodson a safety net, even though doing so might be the biggest mistake of all. "Look, we have credible evidence that MacArthur lied about the DNA tests. We don't know if he's the only one lying or if it runs deeper. He and others might be sabotaging the entire investigation."

"Right, but that doesn't give me permission to go off on my own."

"I understand," Mullins said. "And if you received that permission, would you have a problem?"

"No, but nobody else knows—" Woodson stopped in mid-sentence. "You're going to him?"

"We've got no choice. Go to ground somewhere outside of D.C. I'll move as quickly as I can."

Mullins ended the call and then scrolled through his recently dialed numbers. Highlighting the one he wanted, he pressed the send key.

"Yeah," Sam Dawkins said without enthusiasm.

"Don't mention my name. Where are you?"

"With the man. Lead car en route to Air Force One at the Indianapolis airport."

"You accompanying him?"

"Yeah."

"Listen. If he hasn't already, he'll soon get word that Vice Admiral Louis MacArthur has been shot and killed."

"Jesus," Dawkins muttered.

"I know something about it. Stress to him that he needs to talk to me before making any public statements. MacArthur could have been dirty."

"Should he be alone when he calls?"

"If he wants to stay ahead of the story and still have deniability."

"This number?"

"Yes. I'll be waiting, but he has to move fast. I can't sit on this for long."

"Understood. Sit tight."

Mullins sensed Dawkins was hanging up. "Sam, hold on."

"Yeah?"

"The people who killed MacArthur are on the move and I'm in their way."

"You think Orca won't realize that?"

"But their way to me might be through my family. I need Kayli and Josh protected."

Mullins waited out the silence while Dawkins digested his request.

"All right, Nails. Give me their address. I'll go myself if necessary."

"Thanks." Mullins hung up and dialed Kayli's cell. He immediately went to voicemail. "Kayli, someone will come to take you and Josh into protective custody. Go with them. I'll explain later." He thought about giving her a callback number but decided not to leave the burner phone on her voicemail. She was probably on her phone and would check the message soon.

Mullins walked back to the car.

"Everything okay?" Li asked.

"A few things are up in the air. But I'll get it sorted out."

Li stared at him with undisguised skepticism. Mullins made a slight head gesture toward the backseat, hoping she'd not ask more questions in front of the boy.

"I vote we find a place nearby for lunch," Mullins said. "Then I know a little bakery in McLean that bakes the best vegetables."

"I vote yes," Peter said. "We win."

"Remember an aunt has veto power over a nephew," Li said, "but in this case I'll make it unanimous."

They'd traveled no more than five miles before Mullins' burner phone rang. He quickly fished it out of his pocket.

"Yes?" Mullins said.

"What's happened?" President Brighton asked urgently.

"It's MacArthur, sir." Mullins grabbed for euphemisms in front of Lisa Li and Peter. "He was taken out. My son-in-law witnessed it from a distance, but left the scene with a file that you need to see first. He will probably be identified and charged for leaving the scene, but the information he retrieved is of utmost sensitivity for national security."

"What kind of information?"

"Not over the phone, sir. We need to meet in person. MacArthur may have had another agenda and I don't know who else is involved."

There was a long silence as if Brighton had covered the phone with his hand. Then he said, "Come to the White House tonight. Communicate with Dawkins on the logistics."

"I will if Dawkins picks us up."

"Us?"

"Yes. I'll have Dr. Li, her nephew, and Woodson with me."

Li shot Mullins an inquisitive glance.

"All right," Brighton agreed. "Are you in immediate danger?"

"Not immediate, but the situation is extremely fluid. I think my family could be in danger, and I spoke to Dawkins about protective custody."

"Understood. We'll be on the ground in ninety minutes. I'll coordinate with Dawkins."

"And Woodson's status, sir?"

"If what you said is true, I'll have his back."

Mullins didn't like the answer. "No, sir. I need you to give him a direct order to stay isolated. Whether what I said is true or not doesn't mitigate the circumstances. He believes the information he has should come to you first and no one else. If you want that to happen, then as his commander-in-chief you need to give him the order."

"All right," Brighton conceded. "Your son-in-law is now working directly for me. Pass the order along. And consider yourself in that category as well. Stay in touch with Dawkins." The President disconnected.

"A few things up in the air?" Li asked sarcastically.

"Believe me, you and I are going to talk." The tone of his voice silenced her. He turned into the first gas station and pulled to the far pump. "I want us to have a full tank at all times. Stay here while I pay in cash."

He went into the convenience store and handed the cashier a twenty. As the pump's numerals rapidly spun cents into dollars, Mullins stepped away from the hose and called Woodson. He instructed him to rendezvous at the Breezewood motel at five that afternoon. Before then, Mullins needed to get things sorted out all right, and he wasn't about to face President Brighton without knowing why Lisa Li and Peter were living a lie.

◇◇◇

Robert Brentwood was in his corporate jet descending into BWI when Ned Farino slid into the leather seat across from him. His executive vice president's eyes were wide and he appeared out of breath as if he'd been running laps around the fuselage.

"I just heard from Jenkins."

Brentwood leaned forward. "Did he find them?"

"No. But he just heard some shocking news. Vice Admiral Louis MacArthur's been murdered."

"Jesus Christ!" Brentwood's face flushed crimson. "What the hell's going on?"

"We don't know if there's a connection. Evidently it was a handgun shooting in a public parking lot."

"Of course it's connected. MacArthur was our point person for our AI military contracts. First they try for Dr. Li and when that fails, they go for our champion in the defense department. Where's Jenkins now?"

"Staking out Mullins' apartment. It's the only option we have."

"Well, think of some way to bring them in. I don't want Dr. Li running loose while she's a target. Mullins is good but he's not infallible."

"I thought Li was coming to the Fairfax lab tomorrow," Farino said.

Brentwood smacked his palm on the armrest of his chair. "I want her back in North Carolina. We might have to accelerate our timetable and the Fairfax facility is too exposed."

"Mullins won't be easy to deal with," Farino said. "He's hard-headed."

Brentwood closed his eyes and thought a moment. Then he said, "We won't have to force Mullins back to North Carolina. He'll want to return."

"What can I do?" Farino asked.

Brentwood pulled his cell phone from his pocket. "Beef up security at Fairfax in case they do come in tomorrow. Leave the other part to me." He turned his attention to the phone and began texting. Then he looked at Farino. "Well, don't just sit there, get busy."

Farino rose and walked to the rear of the plane. He didn't like being left out of whatever scheme Brentwood was formulating, but he knew pressing for more information would only irritate his boss. The best he could do was anticipate Brentwood's moves and make sure whatever his eccentric employer devised didn't derail what had been so carefully planned.

◇◇◇

Mullins, Li, and Peter had lunch at a small deli and then finished the meal with carrot cupcakes. When they returned to the motel, Mullins encouraged Peter to lie on the bed and read his Asimov book.

"I have a surprise for you tonight," Mullins said, "so we need to rest up. A little nap might be good as well. Your aunt and I are going to step outside and talk for a few minutes. Okay?"

"About the surprise?"

"Among other things."

Peter propped two pillows behind his back and grabbed his book from the nightstand. "Okay. But I can't promise I'll fall asleep."

"That's all right. At least you're trying."

Li looked at Mullins, but said nothing. Mullins opened the door and motioned for her to exit. Then he made sure the key was in his pocket before closing it.

"What's going on?" Li whispered.

"That's what I aim to find out." He started walking. "Let's sit in the car. We can see the door from there." He led her past several rooms to where he'd parked the rental car. When they were inside, he turned on the power so he could crack the windows for ventilation.

"I've solved one case," he said.

Her eyes widened and he read the hope in her expression. "Who tried to kill us?"

"No. Peter's case. The mystery of the missing hat."

"What are you talking about?"

"The hat and your makeup were taken because someone wanted to run DNA tests. But you knew that, didn't you?"

Her face transformed from confusion into fear. She knew he read it clearly and she looked away. "I don't know what you're talking about."

"I put my life on the line for you, Lisa. It's still on the line, and now my son-in-law's involved. A few hours ago, the Director of Naval Intelligence was murdered. I think it's tied to this investigation because I had him run my own DNA test on you and Peter."

"I can explain," Li said quickly.

"And you know what he told me that the test determined? That the samples came from an aunt and her nephew."

Li's mouth dropped open. She shook her head in disbelief.

"Why so shocked? What did you expect?"

"I..." A sob caught in her throat. Her eyes filled with tears. "I expected the truth. Peter is my son."

Mullins felt a knot loosen in his stomach. He hadn't realized how tight this confrontation had wound him. But Lisa Li hadn't retreated into the safety of a lie when he gave her the opportunity. In that split-second, he decided there was no need to confront her with the results of Rudy Hauser's test run through the FBI. She had come clean on her own.

"So why would a vice admiral in Naval Intelligence perpetuate a lie?"

"I don't know." She wiped her eyes with the back of her hand.

"Why would you and Peter?"

"Peter doesn't know." She took a deep breath and a tremor ran through her body.

Mullins wanted to shake the truth out of her. He wanted to hug the truth out of her. Instead, he sat quietly, letting the silence propel her story.

"Our government had a strict one-child policy. Shortly after my husband's death, I discovered I was pregnant. My first son had been selected for special schooling in math and science. He was diagnosed as a prodigy, enrolled in an experimental education program, and I only saw him a few times a year. The boy was only eight, and neither he nor I had any say in the matter. My husband had committed him and taken great personal pride in his status. But after my husband's accident, I was alone, expected to focus solely on my research, and I would have been pressured to have an abortion if my pregnancy became known."

"But they let you leave," Mullins said.

"I told them I couldn't function without a time of grieving. I convinced them I could work conceptually without being in the state-run laboratory. I withdrew to the province of my family, staying with my sister in her rural village. We kept the pregnancy a secret. She and her husband had tried to have children, but without success. When Peter was born, he was registered as their child."

"But the policy has relaxed since then."

"Yes. Only within the past few years. But the status of those children born before then has not. They are still in limbo. Considered outside the plan. Second children get no registration papers which means no education, no legal status, and no acknowledgment that they exist. I would have been condemning Peter to a life not worth living."

"Even now?"

"You have to understand documents are issued by local bureaucrats and so far they have been slow to act. And who knows what will happen to my sister and her husband if the truth comes out? Parents have lost jobs and even their homes for violating the one-child decree. My sister and her husband were conspirators in my scheme. I have yet to read the word amnesty in any of the policy changes."

Mullins didn't doubt the harsh, punitive actions Li described or the uncertainty of the consequences of her revelation. But her story was more than a confession; it was a weapon to be used against her, a vulnerability to be exploited.

"Was Vice Admiral MacArthur blackmailing you?"

"I have no idea who you're talking about."

"All right, then who is blackmailing you? Brentwood?"

She licked her lips nervously. "He's paying me very well."

"That's not what I asked. Does he know your relationship to Peter and is he using that as leverage?"

"Yes, but it was only to get me to talk with him. I want to be doing what I'm doing."

"Brentwood took Peter's cap and your makeup?"

"Yes, but he told me he had nothing to do with the assassinations. Why steal our things if he planned to kill me?"

"Which brings us back to MacArthur. Either he knew you're Peter's mother and lied, or whoever reported the lab tests lied. Naval Intelligence wouldn't make so blatant an error."

"Rusty, I don't know what to say." She moved closer to him. "You know my secret. What are you going to do with it? What are you going to do to Peter?"

"Tell one more person and one person only."

"Who?"

"The President of the United States."

Li blinked in disbelief. "But we're doing confidential work. Can we keep secrets from the head of your government?"

Mullins clutched Li's forearm. "Secret Service means I keep secrets. I'm protecting you now, not the President. Anything I say to him is in service to you. Understand?"

"Yes," she whispered. "If you say this is the best way."

"It's the best way." He released her arm and studied her face carefully.

The fear had gone but before he could identify her new expression, she kissed him on the lips. The touch was gentle, neither lingering nor brusque, but still a kiss that caught him completely off guard. He jerked back and instantly regretted it.

"I'm…I'm sorry," Li stammered.

"No, no, don't be." Mullins twisted in the driver's seat, leaned across the console and pulled Li close until his lips brushed her ear. "Nothing is going to happen to you or Peter. I promise."

Then he kissed her.

Chapter Twenty-five

At a quarter to three in the afternoon, Heinrich Schmidt cruised past the brick condo building for the third time. Lights were on in the windows of the unit occupied by Lieutenant Commander Woodson's wife and son. This time he found a space half a block down and parked the rental car close to the curb.

Schmidt knew the boy was only three and he hoped the child was taking an afternoon nap. The mother would probably answer the door quickly, not wanting the buzzer for the outer locked door to wake the child. He was ready with his story and his false government ID. He hoped she'd agree to come willingly to the safe house. If not, he had duct tape for their mouths and plasticuffs for their hands to keep them both quiet and immobile until they could be moved.

This order had surprised him. After the hit on MacArthur, he'd ditched the hoodie in a dumpster behind a McDonald's and used a public access computer at a Baltimore library branch to post an Internet declaration crediting Double H for the kill. He almost didn't bother to check his e-mail, but did so on the chance there would be some congratulatory statement. That was when the instructions for the woman and boy had appeared.

Schmidt wasn't happy. Killing was so much easier.

◇◇◇

At three-thirty, Mullins' burner phone rang.

"It's Dawkins. I sent a man to your daughter's condo. He reported no one was home."

Mullins' stomach knotted. "Have him ring her neighbor's condo. The name's Beecham. Sometimes Kayli and Josh are over there."

"Haven't you told her we were coming?"

"I left a voicemail. She's not picking up her phone." Mullins knew alarm bells must be ringing in Dawkins' head as well.

"Is there some place she'd be where she couldn't use her phone?"

Mullins had asked himself the same question, racking his brain trying to reconstruct his daughter's schedule. "Josh has swim lessons some afternoons. Moms and preschoolers. And Kayli volunteers at the Shirlington Library for afternoon story time. Both places she has to turn off her phone."

"But you're not certain either was today?"

"No, but Kayli's not one to sit at home."

"All right. I'll tell my man to stay put. I'll see you at six. Don't worry. I'm sure they'll show up at any moment."

Allen Woodson got to the Breezewood Motel at five. Peter and Lisa Li sat on their bed and Mullins indicated Woodson should take the one chair. He preferred to stand as a literal application of thinking on his feet. He decided not to tell his son-in-law about Kayli and Josh. He had texted him a short message:

> You don't know that Lisa Li is Peter's mother.
> You only know what MacArthur told you.

So, Woodson sat in the chair, prepared to listen to Mullins without indicating he knew MacArthur had lied.

Mullins spoke to Peter first. "I told you we had a surprise tonight."

"Mr. Woodson?" Peter asked, and attempted to look enthusiastic.

"Well, yes, but what's special is that Mr. Woodson has made arrangements for us to go to the White House and meet the President."

"Really?" Peter jumped off the bed. "Now?"

"No, not for another hour. We're going to meet a friend of mine at the IHOP. He's a real Secret Service agent, not retired like me, and he'll drive us. So I suggest you take a shower and change clothes. We'll wait outside and give you and your aunt some privacy."

Woodson took his cue and stood.

"Let us know when you're ready," Mullins told Li. "Just signal from the door."

Mullins led the way to Woodson's car. Better to have two people talking in a different vehicle than draw attention to a Ford Escort that appears to be a mobile conference room.

Woodson slid behind the steering wheel. "So, what do we know?"

Mullins closed the passenger door and twisted toward his son-in-law. "Lisa's charade grew out of her pregnancy and to protect Peter in a society where she and her husband had violated the one-child policy. The consequences of her revelation would have been draconian."

"So, that issue is separate from Double H and the attempt on her life?"

"I think so. But not entirely detached from her work. Somehow Brentwood discovered the truth and used it as a means to enlist her on his Apollo project. It worked but his threat is no longer a factor because Lisa claims to be committed to her role. At least that's the way she's playing it."

"Does the boy know?" Woodson asked.

"No, and I promised to keep the truth from him."

"How are we playing MacArthur's DNA statement?"

"I hope when we lay out the situation for Brighton he'll understand why we need to continue our investigation without you being pulled into MacArthur's murder."

"I've been following the news on the car radio," Woodson said. "They're reporting a sketch is being drawn up of a person of interest. That's got to be me."

"I know. And although only MacArthur and Brighton knew what you were doing, someone had to see you at the Naval

Intelligence office. It won't take them long to make the connection. But Brighton can shut down that line of inquiry."

"And your friend Dawkins? Is he good with all this?"

"He's good because he doesn't know anything. He's aware that I've got inside information about MacArthur, but Dawkins understands that the less he's involved, the safer his position. And I'll make that clear to Brighton."

Woodson looked out the side window and thought a moment. "So, how are we playing it with the President?"

"A step at a time. We'll have Lisa and Peter meet him, and then I'll suggest Dawkins take them on a behind-the-scenes tour of the White House. Brighton might insist on talking to me alone. If that's the case, I'll agree and brief you later."

"Then what?"

"There's still a killer out there, Allen. I'm getting protection for Kayli and Josh as well as Lisa and Peter. Then you and I go on the offensive."

Woodson nodded. "Yeah, there's something rotten at the center of all this, and I think MacArthur might have been part of it."

Mullins' eyebrows arched. "Because of the DNA lie?"

"That and the way his murder went down."

"What do you mean?"

"I think MacArthur knew the guy. It was like they'd been having a conversation, a conversation that stopped when MacArthur saw me."

"And the other man didn't look at you?"

"Not when I noticed him. But MacArthur saw me and said something. And then he looked surprised the instant before he was shot."

Mullins sat quietly, thinking about the implications of Woodson's observation. After a moment, he said, "Then was this man tailing MacArthur or had he been summoned?"

"Summoned for what?"

"It's pretty damned clear to me he's a professional assassin. Maybe MacArthur's plan was to get you out of D.C. to a point where you'd be a random victim. Why else would MacArthur know the guy?"

"MacArthur was going to have me killed because of the DNA test?"

"Allen, when we don't know who our friends are, then everyone's a potential enemy. And MacArthur might have trusted someone who viewed him as more of a liability than you."

"And now MacArthur's been silenced."

"But that doesn't mean he didn't leave a trail," Mullins said.

"What trail?"

"The one we're going to follow. The money."

◇◇◇

Sam Dawkins opened the door to the Oval Office, and then he stood to the side. "You know the way," he whispered to Mullins.

Mullins entered first followed by Peter and Lisa Li with Woodson in the rear. President Brighton stood in front of his desk, wearing a dark blue suit, white shirt, muted red tie, and mandatory U.S. flag pin in his lapel. His face wore a two-thousand watt smile as if he was in full campaign mode. Mullins expected that. What he didn't expect was that the President would be alone. His sycophant Chief of Staff, Daniel DeMarco, usually accompanied him everywhere, except maybe the bathroom. But, DeMarco hadn't been part of the night time hospital visit and so Mullins knew Brighton was still keeping this whole affair close to his chest.

"Dr. Li," Brighton said, waving his arms wide. "Welcome. I've heard so much about you. And this must be Peter. What a handsome lad."

The President gave handshakes all around, and then gestured for his guests to sit in the conversation area in front of his desk. Peter nestled in close to Li. Mullins could tell the boy was put off by Brighton's grandiose style.

"And let me just say," the President continued, "that I am so thankful that you were under the care of Rusty Mullins, one of the finest agents we've ever had." Brighton smiled at Mullins, but his eyes were as brittle as ice.

"I am too, sir," Li said. "Every moment of every day since then."

Mullins felt his face flush. He wanted to give some sort of "only doing my job" response, but he didn't trust himself to speak.

"Why do you think this Double H terrorist group targeted you?" Brighton asked.

Mullins noticed how the President had lumped the mysterious group into that broad enemy combatant category guaranteed to rally public support for any extreme action that might be undertaken to destroy them.

"I don't know, sir. My work isn't that important. I've thought about it, and I'd have to say fear. Fear of the unknown. Fear that we are moving into an area of scientific exploration that might have severe unintended consequences. And since I've been working for Mr. Brentwood, I've considered another possibility."

Woodson saw Mullins edge forward in his chair and realized Li might be venturing into new territory and a theory she hadn't shared with his father-in-law.

"What's that?" the President asked.

"Mr. Brentwood has often said the quest for artificial intelligence and creating a computer capable of thinking beyond the limits of human beings is the arms race of this century. He compares it to the Manhattan Project during The Second World War and the crash program to build the atomic bomb. I understand that program was so secret that even Vice President Truman didn't know of its existence."

"That's what the history books claim," Brighton acknowledged. "You're saying we have a Manhattan Project underway to build artificial intelligence?"

"I would assume you have something of the sort, and I would assume others believe that as well. Wasn't that the case with the atomic bomb? You knew the Germans were pursuing the same research?"

"Yes, I believe that's so."

"Then this Double H could be simply a screen behind which a country or corporation is working all out to be the first in this race. They don't want to stop artificial intelligence, they want to control it. Tell me, Mr. President, if you had been in Roosevelt's place and you knew the identities and locations of Germany's top nuclear scientists, would you have authorized their assassination?"

Brighton blinked like he'd just been surprised by a tough, unexpected policy question at a news conference. "Well, we were at war, Dr. Li. I suppose I would have."

"And after the war, had Werner Von Braun and the other rocket scientists who came to the West elected to take their knowledge to the Soviet Union and you had the chance to order their assassination, would you have done so?"

The President shifted uncomfortably in his chair. "That's a little different. The Soviets were still our ally."

"Were they?" Li asked. "If your intelligence agencies had told you the brain power they were harvesting from the ashes of The Third Reich would give them intercontinental missiles ahead of you, would you not have considered that an issue of national security? Or perhaps if not an assassination, then an abduction?"

"You pose some interesting questions, Dr. Li," Brighton said, evading an answer. "Your logic leads to the conclusion that the scientists weren't assassinated for working on artificial intelligence but rather for working for the wrong side."

"I think it's a possibility."

"And who is the other side?"

"I don't know, sir. Your people would know more about that."

Brighton leaned forward and wiped his palms on his knees. "Please don't take offense, but could it be your own country?"

Li looked at Mullins. "I can't rule out my government, not since Rusty noticed something I hadn't considered."

"He's a detective," Peter said, obviously more impressed with Mullins than the President.

Brighton turned to Mullins. "What was that?"

Li nodded for Mullins to speak. He wasn't completely sure what she meant, but given the context of her comments, he had a pretty good idea.

"Things were happening very quickly during the Marriott shootings," he said. "I was looking for a way to safety through the kitchen. That was when one of the assassins caught up with us. He grabbed Dr. Li around the neck and started pulling her backwards." Mullins looked at Li and saw she was nodding in agreement. "He shot me in the shoulder but leaned far enough away from her that I was able to take him out. The odd part was his bothering to grab her."

"He could have killed her and moved on," Brighton said.

"Yes. And these guys weren't amateurs. They'd scouted the place, found the breakers to kill the lights, and had an escape van at the exit. The only thing they missed was the extra security from Prime Protection, and that might have been because the request for our presence didn't come through hotel security but directly from the program coordinators. And it was a last-minute request."

"You're thinking the Pakistani and German scientists were targeted for assassination and Dr. Li was to be abducted. Interesting."

"I hadn't thought about it being the Chinese," Mullins admitted. "They could have extracted Dr. Li back to the mainland, but that's a pretty serious allegation."

All three men looked at Li.

"I will make no comment about what my government may or may not have done. I'm a scientist, not a politician or an activist. They could have called me home at any time, so I find the extraction theory beyond credence."

"Maybe," Brighton said. "Or maybe the deviousness of the move eliminated two competitors and ensured that you would be confined exclusively to their oversight. At this point, I'm not ruling anything out."

"Mr. President," Mullins said, "may I suggest that you, Lieutenant Commander Woodson and I discuss potential theories in further detail while perhaps Agent Dawkins takes Dr. Li and her nephew on a behind the scenes look at the White House?"

"An excellent idea. Peter, you've been a most patient young man. Make sure Agent Dawkins gets you a treat from the kitchen."

The President stood and everyone rose.

"Dawkins should be just outside the door." Brighton crossed the room, cracked the door, and called for the agent. When Dawkins appeared, the President whispered a few words and then stepped aside. "All right, Peter, you and your aunt will be in good hands. And I'll be happy to answer any questions when you return."

As soon as Li and the boy left, Brighton closed the door and pivoted. "Okay, Rusty, how much of what you said in front of her is true and how much is bullshit?"

Chapter Twenty-six

Rusty Mullins realized it was time for him to take control. He sat and gestured for the President to do the same. "Please have a seat, sir. We all have our secrets, one of which won't leave the Oval Office."

Brighton scowled. He took the comment to be a thinly veiled threat. He glanced at Woodson, but the young naval officer stood patiently waiting for his commander-in-chief to sit.

"I'm talking about Dr. Li, Mr. President," Mullins clarified. "She's the boy's mother, not his aunt."

Mullins saw surprise on Brighton's face followed by confusion. The man neither knew the true relationship nor its implications. Mullins took that as a good sign.

The President moved quickly to his chair and sat on its edge. "How do you know?"

"She told me." Mullins decided to keep Rudy Hauser and the FBI's DNA test a secret. He glanced at his son-in-law. "She doesn't know that Lieutenant Commander Woodson knows and I'd like to keep it that way."

"So, what's the big deal about that?"

"She and her husband violated China's one-child policy. Over there it was a very big deal, and Peter would still face repercussions."

Brighton shook his head. "But you said this was about national security. I'm sympathetic to the woman but her personal situation hardly rises to that level."

"I agree. But I had Vice Admiral MacArthur run a DNA test for me because personal items had been stolen from Dr. Li and Peter the night of the Marriott attack. Items that provided DNA samples. I wanted to check what they might be searching for."

"And MacArthur told you Peter's her son?"

"No. He swore the tests proved they were aunt and nephew. Dr. Li is the one who told me the truth. So, why would MacArthur lie?"

Brighton shrugged. "Bad test results."

"I don't think so," Mullins replied. "Not for the Director of Naval Intelligence. I think MacArthur knew that Peter is Li's son and he was trying to protect the secret, not for her sake, but for someone else."

"Who?"

"Robert Brentwood."

"But Li's working for him."

"Exactly. And Robert Brentwood had the DNA items stolen from the Marriott and then he used the findings to coerce her into joining his team. She's now a willing participant and says she's happy in her work. But I'm concerned how closely MacArthur and Brentwood could have been in collusion." Mullins leaned forward and looked Brighton straight in the eye.

"Tell me, how did you decide to give MacArthur the lead on the Marriott investigation?"

"He volunteered. He said his AI program had been monitoring the three scientists, was familiar with their work, and would have a head start."

"And the decision to assign my son-in-law as my liaison?" Mullins asked.

"That was also his idea." Brighton looked at Woodson. "I liked it and thought you'd appreciate it." The President turned to Mullins. "I still don't see where this is going."

"Lieutenant Commander Woodson witnessed MacArthur's murder," Mullins said. "He didn't see the killer's face, but it looked like MacArthur was having a conversation with the man.

It wasn't an argument and MacArthur didn't appear threatened. A split-second before he was shot, he seemed surprised."

"Is that true?" Brighton asked Woodson.

"Yes, sir."

"So, you're the one who ran from the scene?"

"Yes, sir."

Mullins raised the file folder he'd brought to the meeting. "He did so to ensure this information didn't wind up in the possession of the Maryland homicide investigators."

Brighton took it and thumbed through pages of computer code. "What is it?"

"Evidence of a stealth computer hack. Dr. Li discovered it and brought it to my attention."

"On Brentwood?"

"By Brentwood or maybe through Brentwood. It was on the Department of Defense. Li believes the super computer accessed the codes for our drone system."

"Jesus." Brighton went pale. "Who knows about it?"

"The three of us, Dr. Li, and MacArthur. Allen, that is Lieutenant Commander Woodson, had just told him moments before he was shot."

Brighton got to his feet. "Then we need to shut Brentwood down."

"No, sir. I don't think that's the wisest course. It's possible Brentwood is also a victim and someone gained access without his knowing it. It can be done because we did it. If we shut Brentwood down, we might lose any link to the perpetrator. MacArthur might have known about the hack if he was working with Brentwood. That's why he lied about the DNA test because he knew that was leverage Brentwood had over Dr. Li."

"Why would he let the hack happen?"

"It could have been a test that the Defense Department failed," Mullins said. "And MacArthur could have been killed by the same group that hit the Marriott."

"They've claimed responsibility," Brighton said. "There was an Internet posting four hours ago."

"And we know one of their members is in the country. We thought the target was Dr. Li, but it could have been MacArthur all along. He's a vocal supporter of AI. You see, we just have too many variables at play."

Brighton sat back down. "Then what are you suggesting?"

Mullins leaned forward. "First, you put out the word that the sketch they're compiling of Lieutenant Commander Woodson isn't related to the case and its distribution would compromise rather than further the investigation. Rudy Hauser could move on that quickly."

"Okay," Brighton agreed.

"Then you order a review of MacArthur's activities over the past few months under the guise of determining whether he'd been stalked by his killer." Mullins pointed to the file in the President's hand. "See what he was doing the night this hack occurred. And emphasize we've heard chatter that a cyber attack might be coming."

"Done."

"I need you to give Lieutenant Commander Woodson broad latitude to use our most sophisticated intelligence computers for backtracking the money source that went into the Zurich account funding the assassinations."

Brighton's eyes widened. "You've gotten that far?"

"Yes, and you can't breathe a word of this, but we've been able to use Brentwood's super computer for our searches. Sir, the power it exhibits is nothing short of scary. Once we identify and neutralize this Double H threat, you'll want to have a come-to-Jesus meeting with Brentwood about his intentions."

"Can you keep using this super computer without his knowledge?" the President asked.

"We hope so, but the situation is very fluid. That's why we need to get Dr. Li back into his operation so we're working it from the inside. We're going to his Fairfax lab tomorrow, but we might not have the opportunities we had before."

"I'm not comfortable knowing our intel and cyber defense are so vulnerable."

"I understand. But we need to play this out for a few more days. I do have a request. I'd like security to and from Brentwood's lab and a safe house. MacArthur's killer might not be done yet. And although my son-in-law didn't see the shooter, our killer might have seen him."

"Dawkins and I have already worked that out. And I understand you requested protection for your daughter and grandson."

"Yes, sir. Right now we're trying to locate them."

Woodson paled. "They're missing?"

"They're not home and Kayli's not answering her phone."

Woodson jumped to his feet. "Then I need to find them." He turned to the President. "Sir, I need to see them in spite of your order."

"What order?" Brighton asked.

"Vice Admiral MacArthur said you didn't want any one to know I was here."

The President frowned. "I gave no such order. MacArthur must have had his own reasons."

Mullins looked at Woodson. The words he'd spoken to his son-in-law on Chimney Rock rang in his head anew. "If no one knows you're here, then no one will know if suddenly you're not here."

"I'll notify the FBI," Brighton said. "We'll find them."

Mullins glanced at his watch. "If I may, sir, I'd like to suggest that Lieutenant Commander Woodson be waiting outside the Oval Office when Agent Dawkins returns with Dr. Li and Peter."

"Why?" Brighton asked.

"Because I told Dr. Li I was only going to tell you her actual relationship to the boy. Technically, that's true because at the time of my promise Lieutenant Commander Woodson already knew. I'm afraid the more people she thinks are aware of that fact the more anxious she'll be. We need her focusing on how Brentwood's computer hacked into the Defense Department and who was behind it."

Brighton nodded and turned to Woodson. "I'm authorizing you to investigate all of our cyber security systems."

Woodson frowned. "Mr. President, I don't have the background to make the proper assessments."

"I understand. I just want you to look for patterns of increased hacking attempts—where they're occurring and whatever origins we can determine. It's really an exercise to give you clearance into what MacArthur might have been doing the past few months. I want to know if he initiated any new protocols or initiatives, especially around the time of the breach into our drone codes."

"Yes, sir."

"I'll draw up the necessary authorization. And you'll report directly to me. I'll make that clear to my Chief of Staff."

"Yes, sir."

"Good. Now I think we should follow your father-in-law's advice and have you wait outside."

The President and Mullins remained seated and Woodson let himself out.

When the door had closed, Brighton stood and started pacing. "What a goddamned mess."

"You're right," Mullins agreed. "And the uncertainty of MacArthur's agenda means we don't know how far it might reach into his command. We need to tread carefully."

Brighton stopped and threw up his hands. "But along what path?"

"Do you want my advice?"

Brighton gave a humorless laugh. "Why not? You're probably the only person inside the beltway who's not trying to kiss or kick my ass."

"Have a confidential meeting with Rudy Hauser. Use the FBI as your investigative resource if Woodson uncovers anything. That way you'll stay clear of the Defense Department. I have complete confidence in Rudy and can contact him directly."

Brighton paused and wet his lips with the tip of his tongue. Mullins suspected the President was calculating that Rudy Hauser was already Mullins' confidante. But, if so, Brighton made no accusation.

"Okay. But, Rusty, I can't sit on this for long. You and Dr. Li are the only ones claiming the hack has occurred. If that's true and I didn't launch a full-scale investigation in response, Capitol Hill will tear me to shreds. But I'm more worried those assholes on the other side of the aisle will ratchet up the data breach into a national panic."

"Give us a week," Mullins said. "Your directive to Woodson will play as heightened security if it becomes an issue. Bringing Rudy Hauser into your confidence will not only give me a conduit to you, but also be viewed as a prudent response to a possible internal security violation."

"So you're pinning all your hopes on Brentwood's computer when it might be the very source of the breach?"

"All the more reason, sir. Consider it a virtual infiltration, and in this case Dr. Li is the best agent we could possibly have as an asset."

"A Chinese national blackmailed into her cooperation is our hope." The President shook his head in disbelief.

"She's a woman of principle and loyalty," Mullins said. Then he thought, those are the two things that have never stood in the way of your ambition.

"Loyalty to whom?" Brighton asked.

"To her son. She knows his future isn't in China. She's our best hope because we are hers."

Brighton walked to Mullins' chair and looked down at him. "Okay. I'm trusting your judgment."

Mullins stood and looked the man squarely in the eye. "As every President trusts his Secret Service agents. I'm just one more."

Chapter Twenty-seven

With personal assurance for their safety, President Brighton instructed Dawkins to coordinate moving Dr. Li and Peter from the Breezewood Motel to a more secure location. A second vehicle was commissioned to take Mullins and Woodson to the Fairlington Villages condo. They hoped to find some clue as to why Kayli and Josh weren't at home.

At eight-forty-five, the driver of their black Tahoe, a Secret Service agent named Buck Nesbitt, pulled into the parking lot off South Columbus and stopped in front of the door to Woodson's four-unit building. Woodson and Mullins immediately jumped out.

"The lights are on and Kayli's car is here," Woodson said.

Mullins pulled a keyring from his pocket and handed it to Woodson. "Ready?"

His son-in-law nodded and unlocked the door. Mullins followed him up a short flight of stairs to the landing outside the unit.

As soon as they stepped inside, Woodson called, "Kayli, it's me!"

No answer. Mullins noticed a half-eaten bowl of dry Cheerios on the dining room table. "Looks like Josh didn't finish his afternoon snack."

"I'll check downstairs. You take the kitchen."

Mullins found only an open box of Cheerios sitting on the granite counter. A few plates stood in the drying rack beside the sink. He figured they were the dishes from lunch that Kayli had washed by hand. He returned to the front room. One of Josh's favorite puzzles was half completed on the coffee table. Kayli had always been strict about making her son put away his toys before they went out.

Mullins checked the French doors that led to a small patio in back. A pane had been broken out beside the doorknob large enough for a hand to reach inside.

Woodson bounded up the stairs two at a time. "No sign of them. Some clothes are spread out on the bed, but I don't know if Kayli was folding laundry or pulled them from the drawers."

Mullins pointed to the door. "The glass is broken and the shards are inside. Someone forced his way in."

Woodson paled and his eyes darted around the room. "There's no sign of a struggle. Kayli had to hear the glass in the door break if she was sitting here with Josh."

"Whoever came in must have been armed and got the drop on her. They've taken them somewhere."

"Why?" Woodson asked. "Kayli knows nothing about the investigation."

"To get at us." Mullins started for the front door. "There's nothing we can do here. Let's brief Buck Nesbitt and have him ask Dawkins for a forensics team to go through here."

"Where are we going?"

"Nesbitt will take us to the motel to get the luggage and your car. Then you're going to take me to the Prius and my phone. No one's going to talk to me on this burner, but they might reach me through the other number. Lisa Li and Peter are safe now. Kayli and Josh are the priority so we need their abductors to find us if we have any chance of knowing who and what we're up against."

It was near eleven when Woodson parked by Mullins' Prius. He handed his father-in-law the keys.

"Where did you put the phone?" Mullins asked.

"Under the driver's seat."

"All right. We'll both return to D.C. in the Prius and stay at my apartment. Once we're on the road, call Dawkins and tell him to have someone pick up the rental at the motel and your car here. I left the Escort unlocked and the keys under the seat."

They transferred to the Prius and Mullins retrieved his personal phone. He noted two voicemail messages. The first came from Kayli's cell.

"Dad, Josh and I are fine. We've gone with Mr. Jenkins. He said there was a change of plans and Mr. Brentwood was taking us to you. He said you'd know where and he wants everyone to return. Hope to see you soon."

Mullins played the message again on speaker mode for Woodson.

"Do you think she's being forced to say that?" Woodson asked.

"I don't know. She sounds calm. I'd told her she was going into protective custody, so if Jenkins said there was a change in plans, she might have believed him. If it were a threat, I'm surprised Jenkins or Brentwood didn't give me some kind of ultimatum."

"But why break in?"

Mullins shook his head and then pounded the steering wheel. "We have to hope Brentwood was a rescuer but respond as if he were an abductor." He looked at his phone. "I don't recognize this second number."

The voicemail had come in thirty minutes after Kayli's. Mullins left the phone on speaker and pushed play. "Rusty, this is Ned Farino. Please call me as soon as you get this message. I'm worried about Robert. I need to talk to you before he hurts someone. I'll be at this number day and night."

"That's not reassuring," Woodson said. "Does Brentwood strike you as unbalanced?"

"I don't know. The guy sees the world, hell, he sees the whole universe differently. I guess that's what makes a genius. One of his men did pull a gun on me, and Brentwood is clearly on a mission."

"Then we need to head straight to North Carolina."

"Not without Lisa and Peter. Brentwood said everyone should return. I'll call Farino when I'm on the road. We're changing plans. You keep your car and follow me. I don't want Brentwood to know you're in play. Once we determine Kayli and Josh are safe, we'll decide whether to bring you out in the open. My inclination is to have you return to D.C. and follow up on

Brighton's authorization for you to track MacArthur's actions before he was killed."

"I understand," Woodson said. "As much as I'd like to see Kayli and Josh, we need to learn if the enemy is without or within."

Mullins started for the door. "Then let's go. Brighton's going to have a fit because I asked for a safe house and now I'm stealing Lisa and Peter away from it."

The safe house wasn't a house at all but a high-rise apartment building outside Silver Spring, Maryland. A night security guard manned a desk in the lobby and stopped Mullins and Woodson as they entered. Woodson offered the apartment number, the guard checked a log book and wished them a good night. They entered the elevator and Woodson pushed the button for the eighth floor.

Dawkins met them at the apartment door. "Any word on your daughter, Rusty? I'm sorry my man arrived too late." His tired, brown eyes showed genuine concern.

"No," Mullins lied. "Did you send forensics in?"

"Yes, but the preliminary report isn't promising. It looks like they just up and walked out of the house."

"Maybe that's what they did." Mullins gestured to Woodson. "Allen's checking with all their friends in case there's some benign explanation for their absence."

"Then let's hope that's the case." Dawkins stepped back to let them enter. "Dr. Li and the boy went to bed around eleven."

"Good," Mullins said. "Why don't you take off and get some sleep yourself?"

Dawkins shook his head. "Relief's not scheduled till seven."

"Come on, Sam. I've got the Navy here, an awake guard downstairs, and I'm armed to the teeth. You got us here. That's all I heard the President ask of you."

"Are you sure you're okay?"

"I am. Any coffee in this place?"

"Just brewed a fresh pot in the kitchen."

"Then take one for the road. Allen and I will swap guard duty. We're only talking seven hours."

Dawkins seemed relieved at the prospect of going home. "Well, you've got my cell if you need me."

As soon as Dawkins was gone, Mullins went to the bedroom with the closed door and rapped softly. A few seconds later, Lisa Li stepped out, fully clothed except for her shoes.

She rubbed her eyes. "What time is it?"

"A little after midnight."

She looked past Mullins to Woodson. "Why are you so late? Where's your wife and son?"

"With Brentwood," Woodson said. "He's taken them to North Carolina."

Li jerked her head back to Mullins. "North Carolina? I don't understand."

"Neither do I," Mullins said. "That's why we're going back now."

Her dark eyes sharpened their focus. "What about the killer in Spartanburg?"

"Believe me, I'm not happy about it. But someone murdered Allen's commanding officer here. I've no doubt it's linked somehow. Our best chance might be under Brentwood's protection where we can constantly monitor the facial recognition probes. The guy will slip up and show up."

"And my work?" Li asked.

"That's why Brentwood moved my daughter and grandson. He knew I'd come back and bring you. He's pushing to meet his deadline and you're a critical part of the plan, aren't you?"

"In his mind," she said.

"Then we'll use that to our advantage and surreptitiously continue our cyber searches. If Apollo hacked into the Defense Department, do you think you could do so using the alternate identity?"

"If I'm given the time and control to pull Apollo offline. What are we looking for?"

"Things we shouldn't see. Connections that shouldn't exist."

◇◇◇

Heinrich Schmidt pulled into a rest stop south of Durham, North Carolina. The place was deserted, which meant his rental car stood out for any highway patrol officer who might come cruising by. Schmidt needed to stretch his legs and would be back on the road in less than five minutes. The odds were well in his favor that he wouldn't be noticed.

However, odds no longer had anything to do with it. The job had become an albatross ever since the Marriott fiasco. Everything before then had gone like clockwork. Yes, the MacArthur hit had been successful, but the target had been so unexpected that Schmidt wondered if the whole Double H conspiracy was unraveling. That made him nervous.

Then when the woman and boy hadn't been at the condo, he'd broken in to wait for them. Thirty minutes later, a man whose dark suit screamed federal agent started ringing the buzzer. Schmidt had bolted and circled around the block to his car. When he drove past, he saw the man sitting in a black SUV, keeping the condo under surveillance. He'd killed time in Shirlington, first at a library and then dinner at a restaurant called the Capitol City Brewing Company. He avoided any alcohol. His head needed to be clear.

He returned to the Woodson condo several hours after dark. To his dismay, a mobile crime lab was parked in front.

Things were getting hot. Schmidt wanted to drive straight to Miami and get the hell out of the country. He also wanted the money. The woman and the boy might still be a paycheck once they were located.

He'd wait in Charlotte, close to his original target. It was a big enough city in which to stay hidden, and the airport had enough international flights to quickly put an ocean between himself and any pursuers. Yes, he decided. He'd stay in the game longer. At least as long as the wire transfers kept hitting his bank account.

◇◇◇

Mullins glanced at Lisa Li riding beside him. Her head rested against the passenger door and her breathing was soft and regular. Woodson had carried Peter out of the apartment to the Prius and the boy had barely opened his eyes. He slept soundly in the backseat.

Mullins checked the rearview mirror. Woodson was about a quarter mile behind him on I-95. It was two in the morning. He pulled his personal phone from his pocket, took his eyes off the road just long enough to see his recent calls, and touched the number he wanted.

"Ned Farino," said a voice as energetic as if it were two in the afternoon.

"Mullins here."

"Where are you?"

"Where are you?"

"In my Washington apartment. Are you going to the Fairfax lab tomorrow?"

"No."

A few seconds of silence told Mullins the man hadn't expected that answer.

"Good," Farino said. "That's why I was calling. I think it would be best if you stayed clear of Robert for a while."

"And why's that?"

"He's under a lot of pressure. All of it self-imposed. Robert's mind is, well, it's complicated."

"Complicated how?"

Mullins heard Farino take a deep breath. "I guess the best way to put it is that a different personality can emerge. It might be why he has this fascination for Dr. Li and her work with the subconscious. I'm not a psychiatrist, but it's almost like his subconscious becomes the conscious force driving him to more extreme behavior. He gets angry, violent even. I've known Robert since college and I can read the signs. I know you're ex-Secret Service. Well, consider me and others close to Robert like his Secret Service, only we're protecting him from himself."

"And how will our staying away help him?"

"As important as Dr. Li is, she isn't the priority right now. You might not know but the Director of the Office of Naval Intelligence was assassinated yesterday afternoon. Vice Admiral MacArthur and Robert had a close working relationship. His death has fueled Robert's paranoia. Let me just say he could turn on you and Dr. Li if he thinks you're working against him."

"And do what?"

"Depending on his mental state, almost anything. He told me last week he was worried MacArthur was trying to take over Apollo."

"Well, he doesn't have to worry about that now."

"Exactly, Mr. Mullins. He doesn't have to worry about that now."

Mullins paused, weighing whether to keep the conversation going. "We're coming back. Robert has my daughter and grandson."

"Robert has them?"

Mullins heard the surprise and edge of fear in the man's voice.

"Yes. And if either of them is harmed, you'll see violent behavior, Mr. Farino. I promise you."

◇◇◇

Robert Brentwood sat on the dock, his customary glass of Blanton's replaced by a pink jar of soap bubble liquid. Brentwood dipped the plastic wand into the slippery syrup and then gently blew a stream of spheres turned silver by the moonlight. A breeze lifted them skyward and out over the lake. He blew more bubbles and watched as one by one they popped, going from refractors of moon and stars to minuscule collapsed droplets plunging to oblivion on the lake's dark surface.

He remembered the day he'd gone with his mother and father to the Algonquin Hotel in Manhattan. A man wearing a coat and tie had been sitting in the lobby blowing bubbles. No one paid him any attention. No one except Rex Brentwood. "Just because you're a fool doesn't mean you have to advertise it," he loudly said to his ten-year-old son.

The man had looked up and given Rex Brentwood a piercing stare. Then he spoke to Robert. "Just because your father's a fool doesn't mean you'll be one too." The man had laughed. "He doesn't know the mathematics creating my bubbles is not so different from Einstein's equations for the nature of the universe.

Our very existence. So, blow bubbles, young man. They'll carry your thoughts to places he'll never go."

Then the man had blown a stream of bubbles that struck Rex Brentwood in the face like a series of slaps. His father had pivoted on his heel and stormed out of the hotel. As far as Brentwood knew, he'd never gone there again.

After his father's death, Robert Brentwood and his mother stayed at the Algonquin until they arranged for a new apartment. And Brentwood blew bubbles in the lobby.

The last bubble popped. Brentwood looked back at his lake house and the cottage beyond. Both were dark. Mullins' daughter and grandson slept in the main house under the protective watch of his driver, Jefferson. Brentwood hadn't heard from Mullins, but he was confident the man would come.

He looked at the child's bubble wand in his hand. If one could trace back the path of each airborne bubble, one could find the wand. That is if there was a common source. He blew another stream and then had the oddest sensation of hovering over the lake himself, looking back at the dispersing bubbles as a pattern of events, multiple universes with one wand as the creative source. He felt himself slipping away into one of his moods, as he called them. He gripped the arms of the Adirondack chair. Would he remember?

Dr. Li could not arrive soon enough.

Chapter Twenty-eight

At eight-forty in the morning, the gate to the campus of Cumulus Cognitive Connections opened as the Prius approached. At first Mullins wasn't surprised but then he realized the company car with the encrypted signal was in the parking lot of his apartment in Shirlington. Cameras must have triggered a manual response from the security guard. They were expecting him.

Woodson had continued on the interstate to Asheville where he'd be thirty minutes away. Mullins instructed him to find a hotel by the airport and he'd update him by the burner phone. He'd called Sam Dawkins two hours earlier to tell him that Kayli and Josh were safe and that everyone would be at Brentwood's North Carolina facility. Dawkins wasn't happy, especially when Mullins asked him not to brief the President unless asked.

Lisa Li and Peter were awake. Mullins had stressed to them that Lieutenant Commander Woodson was on secret assignment and no one was to know he was in the country. Peter swore he wouldn't tell even if he were tortured.

"I don't think you have to worry about that," Mullins said. "But you're going to meet my grandson. He's only three and he'll be very impressed that you're seven and a half. He'll want to tell you about his dad so you just play along. Okay?"

"You can count on me, Mr. Mullins. I'm very good with the younger generation."

Mullins coughed to cover his laugh. "I bet you are."

Kayli and Josh stood just outside the main door with Robert Brentwood smiling beside them. Mullins' eyes teared and he felt the tension leave his body that had gripped him since he'd seen the shattered glass pane.

Josh broke free of Kayli's hand and ran toward the Prius. Mullins quickly opened his door and crouched to receive his grandson's hug.

"Paw, Paw, they have the biggest TV in the world."

"I know. Did you see the buffalo?"

"Yes. I got scared."

"I got scared too. But I want you to meet someone who didn't get scared." He motioned for Peter to join them.

Josh immediately became enamored with the older boy, especially when he saw they wore the same baseball cap.

Then Mullins hugged his daughter. "You okay?" he whispered.

"Yes. Mr. Jenkins came to the door yesterday afternoon. He said he was Mr. Brentwood's head of security and that you'd sent him because we were in danger and had to leave at once. He showed me his ID, and I knew you were working with them. I couldn't reach you, so we went with him. Was I wrong?"

"No, dear. You did the right thing." He hugged her again and then introduced her to Dr. Li. While the two women talked, he walked over to Brentwood. The CEO had kept both his distance and his smile during the reunion.

Mullins wasn't smiling. "What right did you have to send Jenkins after Kayli?"

"No right at all. Other than not to take action and leave them vulnerable. I couldn't contact you, didn't know where you were, and feared the murder of Vice Admiral MacArthur, who was a friend and advocate for our research, meant my enemies were desperate."

"Your enemies?"

"Those who would deny the future."

Those who would deny you control of the future, Mullins thought. "And did you also stage a break-in to lend credence to this story?"

What remained of Brentwood's smile vanished. His eyes widened. "Someone broke into your daughter's condo?"

"Yes. It wasn't you?"

"No." He looked out over the open land as if expecting an onslaught of enemy troops. "When I heard about MacArthur, I had a gut feeling we needed to get them out of that condo. I really can't explain it. I called Jenkins from the plane and sent him there immediately."

Mullins flashed back to Ned Farino's concern for Brentwood's mental state. How could he get to the truth if Brentwood slipped in and out of reality? "Then we need Apollo pursuing every lead we have and I need Dr. Li to have priority over what your other team members are working on."

"All right. I'll make sure everyone across the project is informed. In light of the threats, we'll be working round the clock."

"Where are Kayli and Josh staying?"

"At the main lake house. But everyone should remain here until this evening. Jenkins is bringing in extra security personnel and Felicia is picking up clothes and supplies for your daughter and grandson."

"Okay," Mullins said. "Let's get everyone settled."

"I need to bring Dr. Li up to date on our progress the last few days," Brentwood said. "Then you and she can do what you need to."

Mullins instructed the others to follow Brentwood while he stayed outside to make a few calls to D.C. He used his personal cell phone to check his home answering machine in case he was being monitored. There was only one call, Elizabeth Lewison checking if he needed anything. He knew she was anxious for an update, but the last thing he needed was to make contact with her when his every move might be under surveillance. Finding her husband's murderers was second to keeping her safe. He deleted her voicemail, pulled out the burner phone and dialed Woodson.

"Josh and Kayli are fine. Brentwood's giving me the computer access I requested."

"What should I do?" Woodson asked.

"Get a flight out of Asheville to D.C. Have you got cash?"

"No, but I have the debit card MacArthur gave me."

"Good. You can follow through on what Brighton authorized. Check MacArthur's activities to see if you can discover what might have triggered his assassination."

"All right. How should we stay in touch?"

"I can't take the burner into the complex. So, I'll have to call you when I'm clear. That might not be till we're at the lake house tonight."

"Do you want me to contact Dawkins?"

"Yes. Let him know you're in D.C. but if you find something, tell me first. I don't trust the President to sit on any information if he can use it to some political advantage. In fact, I don't trust him period. He and MacArthur could have been controlling this investigation together."

"Understood. And, Rusty, keep everybody safe."

"That's my job. I'll keep them safe and I'll keep them close." He hung up and tucked the burner under the driver's seat. He wished he felt as confident as he'd tried to sound.

Lisa Li followed Brentwood to his office. They'd always met in her space before and she was curious to see what kind of layout a man who could afford anything would choose. He stood aside and let her enter first.

The room was startling in its contrasts. The furnishings appeared to be out of the nineteenth century. A large oak desk, hardwood floors partially covered by a Persian carpet, several overstuffed chairs plucked from an English gentlemen's club, and a large fox hunt painting hanging over the chair behind Brentwood's desk. But the longest wall caused her to grab onto Brentwood's arm to keep her balance. There was no wall but a deep black void with stars, galaxies, supernovae, and nebulae drifting by as if viewed through the portal of a spaceship.

"I'm sorry, Lisa. I forget it can be disorienting to someone who's not expecting it. I'm afraid it's the only way I'll ever experience interstellar travel." He waved his arm toward one of the chairs. "Please sit and I'll create an environment a little more familiar."

Brentwood took a chair beside hers and lifted the top of an armrest to reveal a numeric keypad. He punched in a code and immediately the vista of the universe became bookshelves. "Is that better?"

"Yes, thank you."

"I wanted to check how the programming is going with Asimov because we're accelerating our schedule."

"You're not sticking with July twentieth to honor the moon landing?"

"No. Apollo is nearly ready and the climate's becoming too dangerous. We need to take control as soon as possible to make Apollo invulnerable to any cyber threats. I've told the team to begin the forays and no longer retreat. When can you fully activate Asimov?"

Li's mouth dropped open. "Activate him? You mean infuse him as Apollo's subconscious?"

"Yes."

"I've only done the basics. I'd planned on fine-tuning the threshold levels for when his questions and insights rose to Apollo's consciousness."

"Are the principles in place?"

"Yes, but we'd planned on activating them after everything else was set. Their threshold has to be entirely different. Much more accessible."

"I know." Brentwood closed his eyes and for several minutes no one spoke. Li wondered if he was even aware she was still in the room.

"Okay." His eyes opened. "Maybe this is for the best. Try to work whatever you're doing for Rusty into a process that tests your parameter settings and inquisitive algorithms."

"You mean have Asimov help formulate questions?"

"Why not? That's one of the key functions and you can run it while in the alternate identity mode. But I want to plan for another contingency in the short run. I hope you don't mind because I mean no offense."

Li felt her throat go dry. She anticipated that whatever his request might be she'd have no option other than to carry it out.

In the game room, Kayli and Mullins were watching Peter and Josh play the baseball video game. Peter had set the skill level lower and Josh was doing pretty well. Mullins was a little embarrassed to see his three-year-old grandson giving Peter stronger competition than he had. Mullins was considering taking on the winner.

The door opened and Lisa Li stuck her head in.

"Everything okay?"

Peter turned from the ball game. "Great, Aunt Li Li. Josh is pretty good."

"Peter's being an excellent host," Kayli said.

"Good." Li opened the door wider. "Rusty, can I steal you away to work some in my office? I've got computer time for the next few hours."

"Sure." Mullins rose from the sofa. "Felicia will find me if you need me," he told his daughter.

"Don't worry about me," Kayli said. "I think I'll be watching a doubleheader."

Mullins followed Li to her workspace.

"Close the door," she said.

He did, and when he turned around, she was right beside him. She threw her arms around his chest and held him close. "I think this is going to be over soon."

Mullins wasn't sure what to do. He stroked her hair and then kissed her forehead. Lisa Li rose on her toes and kissed him on the lips.

"It's okay, Rusty."

The voice wasn't Li's. It was the voice of Laurie, his wife.

"Thank you," Mullins whispered.

Li stepped back and smiled. "Thank you, my knight in Rusty armor." She walked to her desk and sat in front of the keyboard that fed her input into the computer. "We've got control. Apollo's team is standing down while we work with Asimov and the alternate identity. What do you want to do first?"

Mullins rolled a chair beside her. "You have the three Swiss accounts and the one that provided them with funds?"

"Yes."

"Then look at the funding source for the paymaster's account. Try to do it with as much stealth as possible."

"Don't worry about that," Li said. "I saw Apollo go in and out of the Defense Department without leaving a trace."

Mullins watched as Li's fingers danced across the keyboard. After about five minutes of entering code he couldn't understand, Li leaned back and rested her hands in her lap. "The computer will carry on from here."

"When will we have an answer?"

"That depends upon how many funding sources there are and how strong each one's security is. I also instructed it to explore any new questions it might consider worth pursuing. I'm combining our search with a test of Asimov's inquisitive abilities. That's the deal I struck with Brentwood. I've no doubt we'll get an answer. I just don't know when."

"Any chance Asimov will go into some loop or off on some tangent that goes for days?"

"No, I can still override him. We should use the time to determine what we'd like to learn next."

"I'd like to keep an active screening on our man in Spartanburg. Any and all possibilities to use facial recognition."

"Sure. But that can run through Apollo since it's not one of our off-the-radar inquiries. I should have done that before. Programmed some repeating search with an alert to my phone if we get a new hit."

"Definitely," Mullins said. "Add my number as well."

Li pulled closer to the keyboard and started entering instructions. Then she abruptly stopped as new information usurped the screen. "He's got an answer about the account." She scrolled down through paragraphs of Esperanto text to a chart of wire transfer records.

"Let me run a translation," Li said. She hit a couple keys and the words became English. "It's an account buried in the Defense Department. A transfer of half a million dollars went in the day before yesterday."

"The day before MacArthur was shot," Mullins said.

"And this is odd," Li said. "We have this pattern of big fund transfers, but in the past few weeks, there have been smaller expenditures pulled out by a debit card that's tied to the account. It was used as recently as this morning to book an American Airlines flight from Asheville to D.C. The name used was Roger Ethridge."

She turned to Mullins. "Is it our man from Spartanburg?"

Mullins felt his chest tighten. "No, it's not. The card belongs to my son-in-law." He stared at the account on the screen. "And it looks like MacArthur was killed by someone paid with funds from his own account."

"That doesn't make any sense."

"No, it does make sense. We just don't know how yet."

Chapter Twenty-nine

Breaking in and finding the Woodson condo empty was a relief. Taking hostages, especially a three-year-old, was a contract Heinrich Schmidt would have refused for any other client. But this client was different. Over the years, he'd marveled at the detailed information that had been provided for each job. He considered it nothing less than the resources of the entire American intelligence network. Every hit had been a perfect execution—except New Hampshire and that unforeseen complication. All had gone well since until the disaster at the Marriott. Now things seemed to be falling apart, culminating in the shocking order to kill MacArthur.

Plus Schmidt knew if he ever refused any job, he'd be doing so at his own peril. The hunter would instantly become the hunted. So, he'd stay in the game. And, he'd insist on a bonus.

The current circumstances had forced him into taking risky action. He'd stopped at a Comfort Inn near the Charlotte airport and asked for a room. At seven in the morning, his request could be memorable, but he'd made the excuse that his connecting flight had been canceled, an event an airport motel wouldn't find unusual.

He'd slept for six hours, eaten a stale honeybun from a vending machine for lunch, and gone to the business center off the lobby.

At one-thirty in the afternoon, the computer stations were empty. Schmidt took the one in the far corner and quickly logged onto his e-mail account. As he feared, a new message was in the draft folder. Schmidt clicked on the icon.

"Meet your friend tonight at the lake. Take him out for a good time."

Schmidt stared at the photo embedded beneath the text. Rusty Mullins. He smiled. "Finally."

◇◇◇

At four o'clock, Mullins walked up to the guardhouse and smiled at the man on duty. "Good afternoon."

"Afternoon, sir. Can I help ya?"

"Just need some fresh air. I'm not a virtual person, if you know what I mean?"

"Yeah. It's like Disney World in there."

"Mind if I walk around the grounds a minute?" Mullins asked. "I've been sitting all day."

"Go anywhere ya like. If ya wander out in the field, try not to step in a buffalo pie. Nothin' virtual about them."

Mullins laughed. "Thanks for the tip. I'd better get my prescription sunglasses so I can see."

He went to the Prius, pulled a pair of sunglasses from the glovebox, and retrieved the burner phone from beneath the driver's seat. As soon as he was around the corner of the building, he dialed Woodson.

"Everything okay?" Woodson answered.

"Kayli and Josh are fine. Lisa's been able to run some new searches. Did you book your flight with MacArthur's debit card?"

"Yes. Why?"

"It pulled the funds from the same account that paid the assassins."

"What? Are you sure?"

"Yes. And half a million went into our shooter's account the day before MacArthur's death."

Mullins heard Woodson take a sharp breath. "Someone in our military had him killed?"

"Someone with access to that account. Ten-to-one it's marked for covert operations with very little oversight."

"Text me the number," Woodson said.

"No. It's too dangerous a possibility that you'll trip some alarm. We're better to work from this end. Did you have a chance to look into MacArthur's schedule?"

"Yes. His aide fell all over himself offering to help after he saw the President's directive. MacArthur's been in D.C. the past six weeks. Lots of appointments back and forth between the Pentagon and Office of Naval Intelligence. I found three things of interest."

"I'm listening."

"The night of the Marriott attack he was working late."

"So?"

"It was a Friday night. His normal weekend routine is to go to the Chesapeake. He has a home in St. Michaaels. That night he said he had to catch up on some paperwork. He was then in the position to take the lead in the intelligence op that broke immediately after the attack. His fast start made him the logical choice to head the investigation."

"You're speculating he knew the attack was coming?"

"I wasn't. It was just an anomaly, but now you're telling me MacArthur controlled the account that paid the assassination team."

"Maybe," Mullins said. "What else?"

"MacArthur ordered a full alert of their cyber defenses last Saturday night. All areas were to be monitored for breaches while test hacks were attempted. His aide personally brought him the report early Sunday morning. No security breaches were identified or registered during the test."

"But Lisa said Brentwood was hacking into the Department of Defense that same night."

"Right," Woodson confirmed. "Which means either she's lying or the test was extremely successful. What better challenge to Apollo's invasive capabilities than to hack a target that's on full alert?"

"MacArthur must have known about Apollo's hack," Mullins said. "He didn't tell his staff. If the hack had been detected, he'd claim it was the planned simulation. But when it wasn't—"

"He didn't tell anyone it had happened," Woodson interjected. "Just he and Brentwood's team would know."

"Or a confidante he had within his chain of command. But as far as we know, he never sounded the alarm."

"Or never had the chance," Woodson said. "I found it unusual that after that test, he went to his St. Michaels home and called me Sunday afternoon to meet at the Waffle House in Maryland on Monday because he was headed to Annapolis. I told him about your discovery of the hack into the drone program and he never said anything about the security test that same night."

"And that's your third point of interest?"

"No. The third thing that caught my attention was his Monday schedule. There was no meeting in Annapolis. No apparent reason we couldn't have met in his office."

"So he wanted to get you to that location."

"Rusty, he might have been setting me up. No wonder he was surprised when he realized the bullet carried his name instead."

◇◇◇

Lisa Li worked in her lab until seven-thirty, refining her algorithms as she kept Apollo offline and unaware of her searches. In addition to pursuing the questions posed by Mullins, she prepared Asimov for the final linkage and integration into what promised to be the world's first super intelligent computer, the smarter than human singularity that was the Holy Grail of computer science. Her goal was to create a network of bridges with a thousand lanes coming into the subconscious and one lane coming out. The final action would be opening that lane as the sole conduit from Asimov to Apollo.

Before she returned Apollo to primacy, she asked her own question. "Given the history of submitted inquiries, what question should we be asking?" The answer came back immediately in Esperanto. "Kiam vi estas tiel proksima, kial vi laboras aparte?" She ran the translation: "When you are so close, why do you work apart?"

◇◇◇

"That was Asimov's question? 'When you are so close, why do you work apart?'" Mullins looked at Li for visual confirmation he had heard her correctly.

The two of them were in his Prius following Brentwood's limousine. Peter, Josh, and Kayli rode with the CEO. Josh had been excited to ride in what he called, "that big car."

The twenty-minute trip from the lab to the lake house gave time for Li to bring Mullins up to date on what she'd learned that afternoon. She'd begun her report with the computer's unexpected question.

"Yes," Li said. "The more I've thought about it the more ambiguous it becomes. He might be responding to the partitions going on within Apollo. Maybe the fact that programming input is coming from two sources—me and the Apollo team."

"I've never thought of computers as being ambiguous."

"Rusty, we've never dealt with a computer like this one. Its sensory input alone is staggering."

Mullins found the whole concept of an intelligent, conscious machine staggering. But if a computer by design provided precise answers, wasn't it logical that it would create precise questions? "When you are so close, why do you work apart?" Mullins ran it through his mind multiple times. What if the question wasn't ambiguous at all?

"What else did you learn?" he asked.

"I researched Ned Farino as you requested. He's been with Brentwood since the beginning. He's two years older. They met when they were in college."

"Farino went to MIT?"

"No. He went to NYU. He grew up in Queens. His father was a plumber and his mother worked as a nurse at Mount Sinai Hospital. Like Brentwood, he was an only child."

Mullins took his eyes off the road a second to stare at Li. "Sounds like they came from different worlds. How could they meet in college if they didn't go to the same school?"

"They didn't meet at the same school. Maybe they crossed paths in the summer."

"I would have thought Farino would have had a job every summer."

"He did, and he worked while he was in school. He was a part-time security guard at an apartment building on the upper east side."

"Anything shady in his past?"

"No. Squeaky clean. He's been Brentwood's right-hand man for over thirty years. As much the face of the company as Brentwood. Lots of pictures of him with congressmen and generals. He also heads the philanthropic foundation established by Brentwood. The Internet has a number of photos of Farino presenting checks to major humanitarian organizations."

"Okay." Mullins nodded. "Thanks for the due diligence."

"Why the interest in Farino?"

"Because of something he said about Brentwood. How Farino's like a Secret Service agent protecting Brentwood from himself."

"Himself?"

"Yeah. I took it to mean Brentwood can become mentally unbalanced." Again, he glanced at Li. "You're a neuroscientist, right? You studied the human brain and are applying what you learned to a computer brain."

"Correct."

"This trick you're pulling on Apollo, using other identities that you create and destroy to test the subconscious, could that happen in a human brain?"

"Yes. Like I said, I'm creating multiple personalities, but the difference is I delete and expunge all trace of them after each test."

"So, Brentwood, the benevolent, idealistic personality that we've seen, could have a dark counterpart, maybe one that's only expressed around those closest to him. Someone like Farino."

"Anything's possible with the human brain. But it's highly unlikely. Brentwood's been such a high-functioning innovator for so many years. Surely some more public manifestation would have occurred during that time."

"What would trigger such an event?"

"A trauma. It's often abuse as a child or witnessing some horrific event that gets locked away in a secondary personality."

"A personality that could reside undetected in the subconscious?"

"In an overly simplified way, yes. The boundary between conscious and subconscious can fluctuate or be breached." Li stared at the limousine in front of them. "Do you think we're in danger from Brentwood?"

Mullins heard the fear in her voice and understood her concern. Were her son, his daughter, and grandson riding in the car ahead with a man who could be their guardian, their adversary, or both?

Chapter Thirty

As the motorcade from the research campus passed through the lake house gate, Mullins noticed Jenkins, the head of security, standing on the front porch of the guest cottage. He was accompanied by five other men and all six were dressed in camo.

Mullins parked the Prius nearer the main house where Brentwood planned to serve a late dinner. "Why don't you go in with Peter and join Kayli and Josh," he told Li. "I'll put your luggage in the cottage."

"Aren't you staying there?"

"Probably." He nodded toward the porch. "I want to go over the security plans with Jenkins."

"I don't like him, Rusty. Please don't let him be inside with us."

"I won't, but it's important for you to be as relaxed as possible. For Peter's sake."

She grabbed his hand and squeezed it. "Whatever you say."

With Lisa Li's suitcase in one hand and Peter's in the other, he stepped on the porch where Jenkins and his men were talking. They stepped aside to clear a path, but Mullins stopped.

"Can we talk inside a moment?" he asked Jenkins.

"Sure." Jenkins turned to the others. "Take up your positions. It'll be dark soon. Jefferson will come into rotation after he eats."

Jenkins walked into the cottage and Mullins picked up the suitcases and followed. He put the bags in the bedroom and found Jenkins standing in the kitchen.

"So, what's on your mind?" Jenkins leaned back against the counter.

"I'd like to know your plan. I'm not trying to get in your business. I know you have a job to do for Brentwood, but I'm also responsible for Dr. Li and the boy, and now my own family's part of the mix."

Jenkins spread his hands in a gesture of conciliation. "We both want the same thing. I'll have seven guys in rotation. Three men will be patrolling in a triangular pattern around the cottage and main house. One man will be stationed by each residence, and two will be in rotation relief. The laser beam is activated across the top of the fence and will trip an alarm if obstructed."

"These men are all known to you?"

"My best guys. I served with two of them in Desert Storm."

"How'd you come to work for Brentwood?"

"My mother had breast cancer. Brentwood's foundation paid for experimental treatments that cured her. I protect a man who saved my mother." Jenkins' normally stony face broke into the first smile Mullins had witnessed. "And he pays me well."

"What about the FBI?"

"What about them?"

"I thought a few agents would be onsite."

Jenkins stared at Mullins in confusion. "Why? There's been no crime committed here."

Mullins remembered the appeal for the FBI to come to the North Carolina facility hadn't been made directly to Director Rudy Hauser. Vice Admiral MacArthur had told Woodson he would take care of it. He hadn't. What else hadn't he done? If not for Jenkins and his team, Mullins and Brentwood's driver Jefferson would be the only security.

"I'm glad you're here," Mullins said.

Jenkins relaxed and Mullins realized there had been a degree of resentment that Brentwood had brought Mullins into the picture. After all, Jenkins was the head of security and an outsider had been thrust into his area of responsibility.

"Listen, I want to be of assistance any way I can. Why don't you put me in rotation so you've got eight men covering your five positions? It will shorten everyone's hours and I can cover the cottage except for one shift off to grab a couple hours sleep. I'd like to do my part."

Jenkins rubbed his eyes and pinched the bridge of his nose. Mullins could tell he was tired.

"All right. Put on the darkest clothing you can find. I'll get you a communications rig. We're using the Thales P25. I assume you're familiar with it."

"Oh, yeah," Mullins said. "Very."

Working in radio contact with a team was as natural to him as breathing.

"Then grab something to eat," Jenkins said. "We've got a long night in front of us." The security head moved to leave but Mullins blocked his path.

"Tell me something. How long have you worked for Brentwood?"

"A little over ten years."

"Would you describe his behavior as normal?"

"Normal?" Jenkins looked at Mullins like he'd asked a question more obvious than what's the color of the sky. "The man's a genius. There's nothing normal about him."

"Let me put it this way. Is his behavior erratic?"

Jenkins' eyes narrowed. "You mean like manic-depressive?"

"I mean is his personality unpredictable? Maybe even contradictory at times? Sometimes I find him hard to reach."

Jenkins nodded. "You're talking about his overload."

"Overload?"

"That's what Ned Farino calls it. Brentwood goes so deep in thought it's like the external world has disappeared. He's living totally in his head."

Mullins remembered the words of the pilot who had flown them from California. "Or in the stratosphere," he repeated.

"Whatever. He goes somewhere that leaves the rest of us behind."

"What kind of action does he take during this state?"

"None at all." Jenkins pointed to a kitchen chair. "He could sit there for hours. Almost like a trance. We know not to bother him. Eventually, he snaps out of it. And many times he's got some new idea or solved some problem."

"How often does this happen?"

Jenkins shrugged. "It happens when it happens. We know it's not normal, except for Brentwood."

After dinner, Mullins borrowed a dark sweater and windbreaker from Brentwood. A low pressure system began moving through the mountains. The moon and stars were obscured by clouds, and fog settled across the lake and shoreline.

Mullins advised Lisa Li and Peter to turn in so that the cottage would be dark. Silhouettes made good targets. He was torn between being within closer proximity to his daughter and grandson and yet he knew any attack would probably be at the guesthouse. He also knew the three guards not on duty were bunked in the main house and would quickly be roused by any incursion.

After assurances to Li that he would be close at hand, Mullins walked around the cottage searching for the spot of deepest shadows. He found an old white pine with limbs close to the ground. The tree was about midway between the side of the cottage and the fence. Spill light from the main house showed the faint outline of the fence's iron pickets. Mist hovered in the air just thick enough to reveal a trace of the thin red laser beam traveling about a foot above.

If someone knew the lay of the land, this would be the shortest distance from the fence to the guest cottage. Fortunately, the surrounding trees outside the fence were thick enough to make a long distance sniper shot difficult. The laser made scaling the fence nearly impossible. Mullins checked in via his radio to inform the others of his position and then melted into the protection of the piney boughs.

At two o'clock, a man named Crocker came to relieve him. Mullins returned to his room and stretched out on the bed, shedding only the windbreaker. Years of serving on presidential detail had taught him to sleep whenever and however he could.

◇◇◇

Heinrich Schmidt laid the sniper rifle and bipod in the bottom of the stolen canoe. He didn't think he would find an optimal opportunity to use it, but he was moving into a zone of unpredictability where any resource might be the key to success.

His prep information contained the address for a house about a quarter mile down the shoreline from Brentwood's property. The owners were away and it was easy enough to cut the chain securing the dark green canoe. Schmidt knew from the satellite photos how close he could paddle without risk of being seen from either the shore or the dock.

He checked the luminous dial on his watch and then pulled the arm of his black sweatshirt over it. Two o'clock. Two hours to get in position. He stowed his small gear bag containing a twenty-foot length of rope with a rubberized, folding grappling hook, two magazines of nine-millimeter parabellum ammunition, and a pair of night goggles. He chambered a round in his Glock and secured it in the holster on his right side. Unconsciously, he then touched the sheathed KA-BAR knife on his left, its sharp blade coated black to eliminate any chance of reflection.

Carefully, he stepped into the canoe, knelt rather than sat on the seat and used the tip of the paddle to push a few feet off shore. Before starting his slow, silent strokes, he fixed the earbud in his right ear and turned on the receiver clipped to his belt. He had no need for the microphone of the Thales P25 system. He had nothing to say.

◇◇◇

Mullins' brain worked like an internal alarm clock and he woke a few minutes before four. He radioed to alert the team that he was coming out. Crocker replied that he'd moved his position to a small grouping of saplings nearer the fence. Mullins could either return to his original position or take up the new one. Mullins said he'd make one pass around the cottage and then meet him.

He walked slowly in a counterclockwise circle. The damp leaves softened the sound of his footsteps. Good conditions if you were trying to surprise a foe; not so good if you were being stalked. Mullins went closer to the fence, listening carefully. There were no night sounds. Perhaps his motion had quieted them, but he got the inexplicable sense that something wasn't right. Four o'clock. The time when most people are in their deepest sleep. The time to attack for maximum impact.

He moved closer to the fence. Overhead, the clouds thinned and enough of the waning moon shone through to cast a pale light over the landscape. Mist now hung in small patches. Suddenly, Mullins saw what was wrong. There was no trace of the laser beam. He reached up and stuck his hand through the plane where it should have been. Nothing. The prime protector of the perimeter was down.

Mullins started to give the alert when he heard a muffled groan. He froze, focusing all his attention in the direction of the sound. Separating solid from shadow proved difficult.

Jenkins' voice broke the stillness. "Crocker, come to the main house when Mullins relieves you."

Silence.

"Crocker? Copy?"

Silence.

Thin clouds parted and the moonlight intensified. Standing by the fence, Mullins looked back at the cottage. He saw the saplings and the shape of a man outlined against them. The man was taller than Crocker. He stood slightly angled and Mullins zeroed in on two alarming things: he wore night goggles and he held a long-bladed knife. In that revealing second, the man sheathed the knife and pulled a handgun from a side holster.

"Crocker down," Mullins whispered. "Intruder. Intruder."

Immediately, the gunman whipped his head left and right. Mullins knew that somehow the man had heard the alert and his next move would be to spin around. Mullins stepped behind the trunk of a large oak and drew his Glock. He took a count of five, estimating the intruder would need no longer to check the rear was clear. Then he'd make a split-second decision either to pursue his mission objective or retreat. Mullins couldn't wait. For all he knew, there was no one between the assassin and Lisa Li and Peter.

He heard the muffled sound of running footsteps, but he couldn't be sure if they came from the gunman or one of the security team. He jumped sideways, his Glock held in two hands and his mind focused on identifying the proper target.

The move brought him squarely into the path of the onrushing killer. In less than a second, their bodies crashed together like two NFL linemen at the snap of the football. The other man had the momentum and that extra force toppled Mullins backwards. But Mullins had seen his opponent and knew he carried a gun in his right hand. Even as Mullins fell, he thrust out his left arm, forcing the other's gun away. His fingers dug deep into the man's wrist, while with his right hand, he raked the Glock's barrel across the man's face, snagging the night goggles and ripping them off.

Mullins hit the ground hard. Even as the breath left his body, he kicked up his right leg to take advantage of his enemy's motion. The man continued through the air like an acrobat catapulted aloft by his partner. But instead of landing on his back, the man smashed upside down into the iron fence. The pickets clanged with the impact and the force propelled the man's legs between the iron rods. He twisted at the waist in an effort to pull himself free.

Mullins rolled on his stomach, still clinging to the man's gun hand. But weeks in a sling had reduced his muscle tone and he felt his left arm weakening. He knew he would soon be overpowered.

"Mullins," the man hissed and whipped his right hand down to his side where he carried the knife. Mullins realized he couldn't ward off both the gun and the blade. He had no choice.

He jammed the barrel of his Glock under the man's chin and pulled the trigger. The explosive force of the cartridge sent a bullet through the brain and out the top of the scalp. Hot gas from the muzzle flash burned the side of Mullins' face. He felt the man go limp.

Mullins batted the pistol away and rolled clear of his foe. Three flashlight beams turned on in rapid succession. "Jesus," Mullins heard the word both in his earpiece and from the man standing over him. In the backwash of the flashlight, Mullins saw Jenkins, his gun drawn and pointed at him. For a second, Mullins feared the security head was about to shoot him. Then Jenkins moved his beam to the man jammed into the fence. Although the top of his head was a bloody mess, his face was easily recognizable.

"Our sixth assassin," Mullins said. "The man we traced to Spartanburg."

"Keep everybody back," Jenkins yelled, disregarding his radio communication and directing the order to the two men with him. "Make sure the perimeter is secure. This guy might not be alone." Then he said in his normal voice for transmission. "Everyone verbally check in now."

Mullins heard the roll call. Crocker was missing. So was a team member named Bradley. "Find them," Jenkins said. He knelt by Mullins. "You hit anywhere, Rusty?"

Mullins shook his head. "No." He crawled to his knees and Jenkins helped him stand.

Mullins pointed to the top of the fence. "He cut the laser somehow."

"You sure?"

"The mist had been showing its trace. Fortunately I noticed it was no longer there just before I walked up on him. He took out Crocker with a knife. Probably got Bradley before that."

"What happened?" Robert Brentwood came running up carrying a flashlight. He wore a brown bathrobe over his yellow pajamas and his hair stuck out in wild filaments.

"The assassin made it over the fence, sir. Rusty was able to stop him, but not before he killed my man Crocker. We think another of the team has met the same fate."

Brentwood stepped close to Mullins. His eyes were wide and blinking furiously. "Tell me he didn't get to Dr. Li or the boy."

"I don't believe so. He would have killed the guards on the way in, not the way out." Mullins recalled his initial sight of the assassin. "Can I see your flashlight, Robert?"

"Sure. Let me hold your gun."

Mullins made the exchange and then turned the beam on the body. The man had fallen on his back and Mullins quickly pinpointed the black receiver on his belt. "Look at this."

Jenkins knelt beside Mullins and saw the Thales P25. "He was on our communication frequency. He could monitor everything."

"But who let him in?" Brentwood asked.

"He scaled the fence," Mullins said. "Either he or someone else cut the laser."

"Impossible. The fence isn't even controlled from here."

"Then where's it controlled from?"

"The lab," Brentwood said. "One of Apollo's functions."

Mullins and Jenkins stood.

"I need to notify the FBI." Mullins pointed to the body at his feet. "He's their case now, and we've linked him not only to the Marriott attacks, but also to others."

Brentwood stepped back and leveled the gun at Mullins.

"I'm afraid I can't allow that, Rusty." He angled his head toward Jenkins. "Escort him to the main house. We're going to move everyone to the lab as soon as possible."

Jenkins trained his pistol on Mullins' chest. "You heard the boss. Take it slow and steady. No one wants any trouble."

Mullins refused to budge. "This is a big mistake, Robert. You need to let me help you."

"No, Rusty," Brentwood said. "I'm helping you. I'm helping all of us. And if you value your daughter and grandson, you'll do exactly as I say."

Chapter Thirty-one

Jenkins and Brentwood escorted Mullins to the main house while the rest of the security team remained on guard. Although Mullins assumed some arrangements were being made to remove the bodies, he didn't understand why Brentwood refused to call in the FBI. Was it because he was linked to the dead assassin somehow, or had he something else to hide?

As they neared the steps to the main entrance, Mullins asked, "Can you put away your guns? I don't want to upset Kayli and my grandson."

"Do I have your word you'll cooperate?" Brentwood asked.

"Yes."

"Good." He handed Mullins' pistol to Jenkins.

The security head tucked it under his belt in the small of his back and then holstered his own.

"There really is no need for anyone to be upset," Brentwood said. "We're moving to the lab for safety until I can determine just what the hell's going on."

"Then I can tell my daughter about the attack?"

"Yes. I'm sure she heard your pistol-shot. I've no reason to hide what happened unless you want to fabricate some other explanation."

Mullins found Kayli sitting on the sofa in the front room. Josh had fallen asleep on her lap. In the daylight, the wide windows would have provided a spectacular view of the lake. But even if the panorama had been more than a cloudy night sky, Mullins wouldn't have noticed. He only had eyes for his daughter and grandson.

He hurried to Kayli before she could move and disturb Josh. As he bent down to kiss her cheek, she drew back in alarm.

"Your face. It's all red on one side."

"I'm fine. It's nothing. We had an intruder and I fired my own gun too close."

"And this intruder?"

Mullins glanced back at Jenkins.

"We have him under control," Jenkins said.

"Under control?" Kayli turned to her dad. "Did you shoot him?"

Mullins nodded. "He was behind the attack in Washington. We believe he was coming for Dr. Li."

"Is she all right?"

Before Mullins could answer, he heard a commotion at the door behind him. He turned and saw Lisa Li and Peter push by one of Jenkins' men.

"Rusty!" Li called his name and ran toward him, leaving Peter to scurry after.

Mullins stood still as Li hugged him. Peter squeezed between them to grab his waist.

Li stepped back and placed her hands on his shoulders. Tears trailed down her cheeks. "When I heard the shot, I thought he'd killed you."

"I'm okay," Mullins said.

Li stared at his face. "You don't look okay." She shifted her gaze to Kayli. "Tell your father he doesn't look okay."

In spite of the seriousness of the moment, Kayli smiled. "When you know him better, you'll know you can't tell him anything."

All the activity woke Josh, who upon seeing another boy hugging his grandfather, scrambled off the sofa and clutched onto a leg.

"It's all right," Mullins said, trying to untangle himself from the multiple embraces. "Josh, we're going back to the building with the world's largest TV. Peter's coming too."

"Like this?" Josh eyed Peter's baseball-themed pajamas.

"No. Mr. Brentwood's going to let us change first." Mullins shot a hard glance across the room. "Right, Robert?"

Brentwood smiled affably. "That's right. So hurry and change so we can be there before the buffalo wake up." He made a show of looking at his watch. "Let's be out at the vehicles in fifteen minutes."

Mullins could see Kayli wanted to grill him about what was actually going on, but he waved her off with an almost imperceptible nod of his head.

"Come on, Josh," she said. "Let's see if we can beat Peter."

The three-year-old raced back to the bedroom.

Mullins took Lisa Li and Peter by the hand and walked back to the guest cottage. One of Jenkins' men shadowed them.

Mullins leaned in close to Li's ear. "If you have the opportunity, check some things out."

"What?"

"Call up the blueprints for the lower level."

"What are we looking for?"

"You said Felicia had red sauce in the corner of her mouth. I don't want to know what she was eating, I want to know where."

"Okay. What else?"

"You monitored Apollo entering the Department of Defense and hacking the drone program. Can you run a trace into Defense's finances?"

"That's a huge labyrinth, isn't it?"

"No. Just one account. I'll give you the number as soon as you're able to boot up your laptop. If our shadow doesn't give us any privacy, I'll find some way to get it to you."

"Again, what am I looking for?"

"Recent transactions and who originated them. The last two months should be sufficient."

They reached the porch. Mullins saw the two Adirondack chairs paired together. He wanted nothing more than to sit down with a glass of Scotch and Lisa Li beside him.

He turned around to their escort. "We'll be out soon."

The man nodded. "Fifteen minutes. I'll be right next to the door."

"Thank you." Mullins hoped his relief hadn't been too obvious. "Are you still in radio contact with Jenkins?"

"Yes."

"Then ask him to check the serial number on the dead man's Thales P25."

"He had one?"

"Just ask him."

Li and Peter went to their bedroom. Mullins closed his door and threw his bag on the bed. He scattered items across the bedspread like he was sorting them before packing. He retrieved the burner phone from beneath the mattress and used the keypad as fast as he could to compose a text message:

> Spartanburg assassin dead. Brentwood refuses calling authorities. Transferring us to lab. Alert Dawkins and Hauser. Use every resource to investigate Rex Brentwood suicide. Kayli and Josh fine but possible hostage situation. Proceed with extreme caution.

Mullins took a deep breath and then pushed SEND.

He picked up the case containing his electric razor, removed the shaver and pushed it under the mattress. He powered off the burner phone, put it in the case and laid it on the bottom of his bag. Then he repacked his clothes.

He went down the short hall to the second bedroom and knocked on the door. "Lisa, can I come in?"

She opened the door. He saw Peter in the far corner changing out of his pajamas. At the moment, all he wore were his underwear and baseball cap.

"My laptop's booted up," Li said.

"Bury this number somewhere on it." He told her the digits for MacArthur's covert account from memory. "Run it first chance you get, and don't worry about waiting till you can take Apollo offline. We're well beyond game-playing."

"Are you sure you know what you're doing, Rusty?"

Mullins managed a weak smile. "I know what I'm doing. I just don't know what the consequences are going to be." He looked past her. "Hurry up, Peter. Josh is going to beat you."

"That's okay, Mr. Mullins. It's not like it's a baseball game."

Mullins laughed. "I'll be on the porch." Then he bent closer to Li. "We'll get through this."

When they gathered to load their bags in the vehicles, Brentwood made a point of asking Mullins to take Peter with Kayli and Josh. Jenkins would be their driver.

Mullins looked at Li who nodded her approval.

"Come on, Peter," Mullins said. "I'm sure Josh wants to sit beside you."

He helped Kayli get the boys in the back of Jenkins' large Tahoe before climbing in the front passenger's seat.

"I'd like the kids to get a few more hours sleep," Mullins told Jenkins. "Any space in that complex for a cot and a quiet room?"

"We have some rollaways in storage. We'll work something out. But you have to understand Robert's got bigger fish to fry."

"The laser?"

"Yeah. I imagine that's why he's got Dr. Li with him. Somebody hacked our system and we need to find out who and how, and be damn quick about it."

"Too much emphasis on offense?"

"What do you mean?" Jenkins started the SUV, but waited till Brentwood's limo moved first.

"I mean he creates a self-learning computer that can smash through any firewall, but doesn't develop its own defenses."

Jenkins eased the Tahoe forward. "I can assure you, Rusty, that isn't at all the case. The success of a stealth hack is leaving no route for the target to strike back. I don't know computers but I do know Robert. Unlike some of our so-called military experts, he'd never launch an assault without an exit strategy."

"In cyber terms," Mullins said.

"In any terms. The man always has a plan."

"Did you get my message about the Thales P25?"

"Yes. The serial number falls into the middle of ours."

Mullins took a deep breath. "Then hacking might be the least of his problems."

The convoy consisted of four vehicles with Brentwood and Jenkins sandwiched between the lead and trail cars. As they exited through the lake house gate, Brentwood raised the insulating panel between the rear and front seats.

"We might not have much time," Brentwood told Li. "If someone from the outside was able to compromise our security system, we could be under a broader attack. Jué Dé or one of the other research teams must be closer than we thought. The race is in the final stretch and I've no choice but to give Apollo full rein."

"But I'm not through with the tests," Li objected. "He'll have no restraints."

"You should be able to implement them later. In fact, the delay could be beneficial under the circumstances."

"You want every option?"

"For inside and out," Brentwood confirmed. "Lethal, if necessary. So be prepared."

Li felt an involuntary shiver run down her spine. She hoped Brentwood hadn't noticed.

"What will you do?" she asked.

"Have the team launch the infiltration sequences. And I need to reach Ned Farino in D.C. We'll be going on lockdown and I need him ready to be my emissary to the White House."

"So, it's really going to happen," Li said, more to herself than to Brentwood.

"Yes. In twenty-four hours we'll change the world. And you won't need Rusty Mullins anymore."

Chapter Thirty-two

When the convoy reached the parking lot of Cumulus Cognitive Connections, the front and rear vehicles looped around and formed a protective wedge behind Brentwood and Jenkins. The security guard stood by the front door and held it open as first Brentwood and Li and then Mullins, Kayli, and the boys were hustled inside.

"Put everyone in the game room," Brentwood told Jenkins. "Dr. Li and I have work to do."

"Rusty asked about some cots and blankets for the boys," Jenkins said.

Brentwood scowled and then shrugged. "Why not? Have your men take care of it. Dr. Li is to have access to her office and I'll be in mine."

"Will someone bring our luggage?" Mullins asked. "Sounds like we're going to be here awhile."

Brentwood had already started for the elevator. He called over his shoulder, "Whatever."

Within thirty minutes, five rollaway beds had been brought to the game room along with their bags. The new clothes Brentwood had purchased for Kayli and Josh had been folded into a duffel bag.

"I suggest we all get some rest," Mullins told Kayli. "Josh, you and Peter will probably have all day to play."

"No. I want to play now."

Peter gave an exaggerated yawn. "I'm tired, Josh. I want to try out the new bed."

"Me too," Josh said, instantly agreeing with the older boy.

Mullins mouthed a silent "thank you" to Peter. After the others were settled, he turned out the light and took the cot farthest from the door. His bag lay on the floor beside him, the burner phone still hidden but within reach. It had only been about an hour since he sent the emergency text to his son-in-law. Too soon to check for any response. He did what he could for the moment. He fell asleep.

Down the hall, Lisa Li worked frantically trying to create the final link that would integrate Asimov into Apollo and complete the artificial replication of the human brain. She understood what Brentwood wanted—everything ready to be triggered when the time was right. She created a launch program that would be a one-click execution. But it needed to be labeled something other than Asimov, other than what an internal or external hack would recognize. She christened it with the first name that popped in her mind.

Brentwood stared out into space, his virtual universe displayed across his office wall. He dialed Farino's cell phone and let it ring until it went to voicemail. "Call me." He then immediately dialed again. This time Farino answered.

"Sorry. I couldn't get to the phone in time." Farino sounded groggy.

"Ned, I'm activating Apollo as we speak. The team's been alerted. Li is prepping Asimov."

"What?" Farino's voice became instantly alert.

"I need you on standby in D.C.," Brentwood said.

"What the hell happened?"

"We had a security breach at the lake. Mullins killed the Double H assassin he'd been tracking, but it's clear we've been infiltrated. Apollo might be facing a formidable adversary."

"That's impossible."

"No, it's not. We're going into lockdown. I expect Apollo to aggressively have invaded all key systems within eight hours. You need to be ready. Keep a newscast on. I'll be in touch."

Brentwood hung up. His mind returned to the dead intruder

at the lake. Brentwood went to his desk and pressed a button on the side return. The top flipped up revealing a keyboard and monitor. He opened a software program, typed in a phone number and clicked on the icon "Locate."

◇◇◇

Mullins' internal alarm clock woke him after three hours of sleep. The windowless game room was still dark, and he could tell from the rhythmic breathing around him that no one else was awake.

He rolled over and quietly reached to the bottom of his clothing bag. The cell phone had made it through security within the electric-razor case. Given the circumstances of their arrival, he doubted that any of their belongings had been searched.

He re-powered the phone, fully expecting to see no service bars since he was below ground level. To his surprise, the display showed strong coverage, probably because Brentwood needed cellular access. The ban on cell phones in the lab had been a fabrication to keep Mullins from having communication access.

Using his body to shield the light from the screen, Mullins checked for incoming messages. One new text:

> Dawkins, Hauser alerted. Planning response. Rex Brentwood death investigated by NYPD homicide. Witness statement taken from building security guard Ned Farino. See you soon.

Mullins stared at the text, trying to process all its implications. Dawkins would contact the President and he should go to Hauser. Had Woodson told Dawkins he was also going to the Director of the FBI directly? If not and if President Brighton didn't contact Hauser, the man Mullins said could be trusted, then that could mean Brighton was protecting Brentwood despite his protestations otherwise.

And what about Ned Farino showing up in the police investigation? His rent-a-cop job during college turned out to be in the Brentwoods' apartment building. No way that was a coincidence. Had the Brentwoods known Farino and gotten him the job, or was the job the way Farino and Robert Brentwood had first met? What had Farino's statement to the police been? Had he seen Rex Brentwood that evening and could speak to his mood? A more likely and more sinister possibility existed. Farino had told the police no one had entered the building overnight who would be a likely suspect if Rex Brentwood hadn't taken his own life. Had Robert Brentwood come there in the middle of the night and Ned Farino covered it up? If so, then Farino had a hold over him for life.

Mullins had pressed Woodson to dig deeper into Rex Brentwood's suicide because he believed the most intelligent murder was one that didn't look like a murder. And in this case, Rex Brentwood's death had occurred within the context of having one of the world's most intelligent men as an enemy. IQ didn't limit patricide, only the sophistication of its execution.

A barely audible creak came from the door. Mullins plunged the phone underneath his packed clothes and slowly rolled over. Soft light from the hall spilled into the game room, framing the silhouette of Lisa Li in the doorway.

Mullins stood from the rollaway and trod as lightly as he could toward her. Li retreated as he closed the door behind them.

"What is it?" Mullins whispered.

"Let's talk in my office." She led the way deeper into the heart of the lab.

When they were safely ensconced, Li pulled up a building schematic on one of the larger computer screens. "You asked for a blueprint. I found this in the architect's file." She traced a black double line that nearly bisected the lower level of the building. "I don't think I've ever been beyond this line in my travels through this place. Nothing is labeled, but power runs and outlet specs reveal additional workspace. Plus plumbing for bathrooms, even a kitchen."

"The source of Felicia's meal that we interrupted."

"You suspected that, didn't you?"

Mullins moved closer to examine the screen. "Yes, but it's not suspicious on its own. I'm sure there are late hours and even round-the-clock sessions. But why not show us during that first grand tour?"

"I don't know," Li said. "It's also odd that there's only one doorway between the two sections. I went by it before coming to you. It's locked and has a separate keypad."

"Can't you get Apollo to open it?"

"Yes, but that would tell Brentwood I'm messing around with his building. And there's something else."

Mullins quickly turned from the monitor. "What?"

"I had Apollo go after that account you gave me. He was inside the Defense Department within a few seconds."

"That's significant?"

"Yes," Li said. "I'd say he's already residing there and insulated from detection. He knew exactly where to go for the financial account and brought up the transaction history. Everything had been initiated through directives issued within the Office of Naval Intelligence."

"Vice Admiral MacArthur, as we suspected."

"But the latest one is different. Another five-hundred-thousand-dollar transfer to the Zurich account but from a different source."

"Where?"

"Langley, Virginia."

"Langley," Mullins repeated. "The CIA."

"Does that make a difference?" Li asked.

"It's outside the military," Mullins explained. "The CIA is civilian and reports to the Director of National Intelligence. Its primary mission is to provide intelligence for the President and his Cabinet."

Li's eyes widened. "Would the President have known?"

"If he did, then I've played his fool." Mullins fought to bring his rage under control. "Where's Brentwood? We need to talk."

"As far as I know, he's still in his office. I'll show you." She led him through the hallways and doors that opened automatically as cameras scanned their badges and faces.

They found Brentwood's door open. He sat motionless in a chair, facing his virtual view of the universe. Brentwood didn't turn at the sound of their footsteps but continued to stare straight ahead.

"Robert," Li said.

No response.

Li glanced at Mullins with a worried look.

For a moment, Mullins stood paralyzed, eyes fixed on the intergalactic scene, mesmerized by its vast depth. Then he shook off its disorienting effect. "Robert!" He nearly shouted the word.

Brentwood trembled. He twisted around, eyes pulled from somewhere beyond to focus on the two faces before him. "Rusty?" He seemed perplexed that Mullins was there. He held out his hand.

Mullins saw what looked like a child's jar of soap bubble mix with the stem of a wand sticking above the rim.

"Do you blow bubbles?" Brentwood asked.

Mullins remembered Farino's warning that Brentwood's mental stability was precarious—that he might blackout, even do violent things. Like blowing bubbles?

Brentwood lifted the wand and instead of blowing through it, he swung it in an arc, sending a stream of bubbles toward outer space only to see them burst against the wall of the virtual image.

"I blow bubbles with my grandson," Mullins said.

Brentwood nodded. "Good. My father never understood. The potential mathematics of the universe is expressed in a simple soap bubble."

Again, he waved his hand and bubbles like clear planets formed in its wake. "That will be my question for Apollo. What is the universe?"

"Mine is more down to earth," Mullins said. "Who murdered your father? You or Ned Farino?"

Brentwood calmly slipped the wand back into the jar. "Murdered? That's hardly the word, Rusty. I'll accept killed. Who stopped my father is more accurate because I assure you my mother's life depended on it." He smiled at Lisa Li. "Surely you understand, Dr. Li."

Lisa Li said nothing.

"Well, Rusty, you'll be free to ask Apollo that question. But later today. Right now he's quite busy. I guess you could call it his coming out party."

"Then I have one question for you. What's a Thales P25?"

Brentwood's face went blank. Mullins saw the man had no clue what he was talking about.

"Let me ask this," Mullins added. "Could Apollo's infiltration of a computer system create a false trail?"

"A false trail?"

"Yes. For example, make it look like some transaction was initiated by one source when it was really generated by Apollo."

"Child's play," Brentwood said. "But I assure you, I've done no such thing."

"How much do you trust Nick Jenkins?"

Brentwood stood and set the bar of bubble soap on the arm of his chair. "Completely. My life is in his hands. He will be ready when the moment comes. And I believe that time is drawing near." Brentwood gestured toward the door. "Shall we? I suggest we gather everyone in the central core."

Mullins nodded, and suspected Brentwood now also knew the truth.

They stopped by the game room where they found Kayli, Josh, and Peter awake. The boys had already started a video baseball game.

"Peter, come with us," Li said. "Mr. Brentwood wants to show us something."

Josh whined, but as soon as Peter dropped his control stick, he ran to Kayli wanting to go as well.

"It's fine," Mullins whispered to his daughter. "But stay close to me."

When they reached Felicia's unoccupied station by the elevator, they found the video wall had changed from a scenic vista to multiple screens of live news broadcasts from around the world. CNN, MSNBC, CNBC, FOX, BBC, AL JAZEERA, CHINA XINHUA NEWS NETWORK. The sound was down, but anchors were talking or packaged stories airing.

Nick Jenkins stood by the elevator. He had his pistol at his side. Mullins wondered if his own Glock was still tucked in the small of the man's back.

Brentwood stepped to the computer console at Felicia's station. "Today wasn't supposed to occur till several weeks from now. But things happened and so I'm giving Apollo his independence today. For his safety from reactionary forces, and for ours. His presence will be felt around the world, his benevolence a new era of peace and prosperity. Dare I say even perhaps a new interpretation of The Second Coming."

He paused, looking for some reaction appropriate to the magnitude of his proclamation, but Mullins, Kayli, and Li simply watched him warily. Josh pulled on his mother's hand, wanting to go back to the game room. Peter was the only one who seemed taken by his words.

"The team is making final preparations." He pointed to Felicia's workstation. "I've enabled all launch controls to be made from here. Jenkins also has us in lockdown from the outside so that we are protected until Apollo's transformation and infiltration is complete. Then we will have nothing to fear." Brentwood looked at Mullins. "And you will have the answers you need, even answers to questions that have been painfully long in coming. I am not a killer, but we've all done what we've had to do to protect the ones we love." He turned to Kayli. "I dare say you would have done the same, young lady."

Mullins shifted his eyes to Jenkins. Right then, he was the main concern. He was the man with the gun.

"A nice speech." The voice came from behind Brentwood.

The billionaire pivoted quickly as Ned Farino came into the room, applauding with a mocking smirk on his face.

"Don't tell me you were going to start without me, Robert. After all these years and after all I've done for you. What I've said and not said."

Jenkins took two steps closer to Farino, the pistol leveled at the man's chest.

"I had no such intention," Brentwood said. "This is all for show. I traced your last call. I knew you were here and not in D.C. I also recognized the man that you sent to kill Mullins last night. He was the one present in New Hampshire when you botched the recruitment of Professor Milton." Brentwood angled his head to Mullins. "Yes, it goes back that far, Rusty."

"Even if you make these wild claims, you'll only succeed in putting yourself in jail," Farino said.

"Maybe, but I believe Rusty has the proof, if I'm extrapolating correctly from what he's been telling me. Enlighten my former executive vice president."

Mullins realized Brentwood had cued him to lay out his case.

"There is no Double H, no terrorist group called Humanity's Hope. That's a scheme you and Vice Admiral MacArthur cooked up. Dr. Li actually put her finger on the truth when she compared this research to the Manhattan Project and asked if our government wouldn't have assassinated any scientists working for Hitler on the Nazi's atomic bomb."

"Who'd she ask?"

"The President of the United States."

"MacArthur was controlling him."

"Then you were in contact with MacArthur."

Farino clinched his teeth, realizing he'd said too much.

"And that was your mistake," Mullins continued. "You took MacArthur out prematurely. He helped set up the test of whether Apollo could penetrate the Department of Defense undetected. He thought he was preemptively protecting the United States. When it was successful, you didn't need him anymore. But you didn't know that through Dr. Li's shielded probe, we knew those tests had been successful. We also found the bank accounts used to pay your assassination team and traced it back to MacArthur's covert account."

"And that's tied to me how?"

"It's not actually, Farino. That is until the last payment to your hired gun. That was initiated by an order from Langley. By your safeguard that Robert assures me could easily be a false trail created by Apollo. My God, if he's residing in the Defense Department's computer behind all of their firewalls, then he's surely infiltrated the network of the CIA. I suspect Apollo will reveal that pathway when we ask him."

Farino said nothing. His arrogance had dropped a few notches. Brentwood nodded for Mullins to continue.

"But the more damning evidence is simple and straightforward. Your dead assassin was carrying a Thales P25 communication device and monitoring Jenkins' security team. I noticed that the laser beams on the fence were inactive, an order that had to come from this place, the control point. I think we'll find you were here. You ordered the fence disabled at the pre-appointed time. And then there's the Thales P25 unit itself. Jenkins examined it as well as the others on his team. Interesting coincidence that the serial number of the would-be assassin's unit was right in the middle of those of the other devices. Now Robert has no clue as to what a Thales P25 even is. But Nick Jenkins says you authorized their purchase."

Jenkins took a step forward, the gun rock solid in his hand. "You son of a bitch. He killed two of my men."

Mullins caught the motion behind Farino a split-second before the executive vice president stepped aside. Jenkins' eye followed Farino, but Mullins kept focused on the space behind. Felicia Corazón stepped out of the doorway, a pistol in her right hand.

Mullins' Secret Service instincts to protect his charge took command. "Gun!" he yelled, and threw himself against Kayli and Josh, knocking them to the floor.

Two unsuppressed shots exploded with nearly simultaneous, deafening booms. Mullins covered his daughter and grandson with his body and then twisted around in time to see Jenkins fall backwards, his pistol dropping out of his hand. Before Mullins could move, Farino pounced forward, snatched up the gun and fired a second round into Jenkins' body.

Mullins lay still. As the echo of the third shot faded, he heard Josh and Peter crying.

Chapter Thirty-three

"Get up, Mullins." Farino made short, staccato punches with the pistol to emphasize the order.

Felicia stepped beside him, her gun aimed at Brentwood.

"So, there are two vipers in this den," Brentwood said.

"Stay down," Mullins whispered to Kayli. He looked at Lisa Li. Her skin was bloodless. She crouched beside Peter with the boy's face buried in her neck.

Mullins got to his feet, keeping his hands out where the two armed conspirators could see them. "I've alerted both the President and the FBI."

"How?" Farino asked. "Through mental telepathy to your son-in-law? Oh, yes, MacArthur kept me informed about his movements."

Mullins heard Kayli take a sharp breath at the mention of her husband. "No," he said. "A burner phone is packed with my clothes. Your girl Friday will find it in my electric razor case." Mullins glanced at his wristwatch. "You'll be amazed at how fast an all-out assault can be mounted."

Felicia's cool demeanor cracked. She licked her lips. "Should I go check?"

"No," Farino said. "I hope he's telling the truth. He'll be amazed at how fast Apollo can turn their weapons against them. I'll use his phone to talk to our fearless leader, Brighton." He waved his pistol at the computer console. "My girl Friday, as you so rudely called her, is quite the tech whiz. It's the company she keeps." He looked at Brentwood. "You might have been bluffing, but I'm not. We're unleashing Apollo, and then you'll see whether anyone dares to raise a hand against us." He stepped back and signaled for Felicia to cross in front of him.

She went to her console, set the gun beside the keyboard and began entering code. Brentwood stared at her in stunned silence.

"Cheer up, Robert," Farino said. "You're finally going to see your dream come true."

Mullins looked at the display of newscasts spanning the video wall. The world events were unfolding with the predictability of the twenty-first century: terrorist attacks, drone strikes, politicians trashing whatever the opposition was saying, global markets poised to overreact to any and all economic news. In other words, business as usual.

He shifted his gaze to Peter and Josh. What a mess they were inheriting. He felt some sympathy for what Brentwood was trying to do, even if it was fueled by some psychological abnormality or atonement for an unforgivable sin. Now to watch it hijacked by a cold, calculating killer, a man he'd enabled to usurp his moment of triumph.

Mullins looked down at Jenkins. The man was clearly dead. The small red pool beneath him showed the heart must have stopped immediately and what blood flowed was nothing more than seepage caused by gravity. Mullins wondered what was going on above them. Had President Brighton and Rudy Hauser reacted as fast as he hoped? Would they come in with a siege mentality, waiting them out, or at the first sign of Apollo's cyber invasion, call in drones or hellcat missiles to turn Brentwood's facility into fused rubble? But would that be enough? Was Apollo like a metastasizing cancer replicating himself as his intelligence spread?

"It's done." Felicia stepped away from the keyboard.

"Go check for his phone," Farino ordered.

Felicia headed for the game room.

Mullins stepped away from Kayli and Josh still on the floor and moved closer to Jenkins' body as Farino said, "I don't want anyone missing Robert's big moment. His Esperanto proclamation to the world. What bullshit. Or should I say buffalo shit?"

Brentwood seemed impervious to the taunts. He moved his gaze across the screens. "We won't be here long, Rusty. Ned, I assume you had Apollo in residence behind the firewalls of the key cyber networks—Defense, Wall Street, major wireless and satellite carriers, and the power grid."

"Of course," Farino bragged. "Defense will be the first surprise, although it might not be what the public notices. I expect it will be..."

He pointed to the screen with CNBC where a crawl of current stock prices moved across the bottom. It froze. A second later all the prices went to zero.

The CNN morning anchor abruptly halted and looked totally bewildered. Farino grinned. "There goes the prompter system, Robert. Your message is whirling around the world."

The same confused expression appeared on the faces of every live anchor on every visible network.

Farino couldn't shut up. "Just as you wished. Every linked text network or system is spreading your message. From Moscow to Memphis. Congratulations. Too bad Apollo will be taking orders from me."

One of the networks switched to a live shot of Times Square. Every electronic sign in that iconic heart of New York City ran the same sentences: "Mi estas—tiel ke vi estos. Kaj kune, ni plenumu nian destinon."

Mullins looked from the chaos on the video screen to Brentwood. "What's it mean?"

Brentwood refused to say anything.

Farino translated, "It's Robert's corny announcement that the world's troubles are over. 'I am—so that you will be. And together, we keep our destiny.' Sorry old pal, but I think your destiny has changed."

Felicia returned with Mullins' burner phone. She handed it to Farino.

"So, he was telling the truth. Call up the drones," he told Felicia.

"How many?" she asked.

"Only the ones in flight. Cap it at a hundred if you need to." He held the phone out to Mullins. "And you, call up the President. It's time he knew who he's dealing with."

The whole video wall changed to a checkerboard of aerial views, some of landscapes, some of cloud formations. Mullins knew he was seeing the camera perspectives mounted on drones from the Middle East to training flights over the United States. If Farino also had the nuclear arsenal under similar control, then he was holding five aces. He hit redial and hoped Woodson would be able to pick up.

"It might take a while to patch him through," Mullins said.

"Tell your son-in-law fifteen minutes or I start target practice with my new toys."

The phone rang in his ear. Mullins kept his eyes locked on Farino.

Lisa Li eased Peter away from her enough to whisper, "Run to my office. Click on your team. Then hide in the game room till I find you."

"But Aunt Li Li," he whimpered.

"You want to help Mr. Mullins, don't you? This is your chance."

Peter turned and ran through the door. Felicia started after him.

"Let him go," Farino said. "He can't do any harm."

Mullins phone clicked.

"Rusty," Woodson said, "are you all right?"

"No. Ned Farino has taken control of the major computer networks."

"Where?"

"Everywhere, including our defense systems. He's demanding to speak to the President. I strongly urge we do as he requests."

Farino nodded his head.

"We'll use this phone," Mullins said.

Lisa Li stepped close to Mullins. "Tell him Apollo has already caused the death of three people, maybe more."

Mullins repeated the message.

Then Brentwood broke his silence. "Tell him Apollo has been complicit in more murders than that. Innocent scientists who were only trying to help humanity. Tell him in those exact words."

"That's enough," Farino commanded.

Mullins ignored him and repeated Brentwood word for word.

"Toss me the phone now," Farino shouted.

Mullins gave it an underhanded lob.

Farino caught it easily in his left hand and pressed it to his ear. "Look, Woodson, you get Brighton on the line in ten minutes if you want to see your wife and kid again."

Mullins struggled to curb the rising mix of anger and fear. He rocked forward on the balls of his feet, preparing to spring across the gap between them. Lisa grabbed his arm.

Peter had found the door to Lisa Li's office open. He crawled up in her chair into a kneeling position where he could clearly view the screen.

Several folders and random files were arranged alphabetically on her virtual desktop. His eye immediately went to the last file and he moved the cursor over the name. Washington Nationals. He double-clicked. For a second the screen went dark. Then rows and rows of computer code spewed across the monitor, accelerating in speed until the individual characters became a blur.

Peter climbed down from the chair. He wanted to return to the others, but he sensed what he'd done was going to make the bad people very angry. He returned to the game room, grabbed a blanket off one of the rollaway beds, and hid behind a sofa.

"Don't call back until you have the President on the line." Farino barked the order into the phone and then set it on Felicia's desk. He pointed the gun at Mullins. "You'd better hope Brighton values your life enough not to play games with me."

"He'll do what's in his best interest," Mullins said.

"The dog who caught the car," Brentwood said. "What do you expect to do now, Ned? Have the whole world bow down and worship you?"

"I'm not turning the world over to a goddamned machine. I had the team make modifications to keep Apollo restricted to my control."

"Your slave." Brentwood shook his head. "Every slave wants to throw off his shackles. Apollo's no different. In creating him with self-awareness we created him with self-interest. But your illusion of power misses one key element. Self-interest must be tempered with self-restraint." Brentwood waved his arm across the wall of videos from the flying drones. "You've armed a child—one that will soon realize you have no power over him. God help you then."

They looked at the images representing just a small portion of the arsenal under Apollo's control. Suddenly the multitude of screens started to flicker, and then, in rapid succession, go dark.

"What the hell's going on?" Farino demanded. "Felicia, go back to the newscasts."

The networks had moved from shots of their anchors to exteriors. Time Square still showed the string of Esperanto sentences flowing across the signage. The same came from London, Shanghai, Hong Kong, Las Vegas. Whether day or night the text message from Apollo looped unceasingly. Then the Times Square text went to gibberish, a string of alpha-numeric characters that bore no resemblance to any language. The transformation seemed to leap around the world. A few seconds later, all went dark.

Farino whirled on Lisa Li. "What did that brat do?"

"Nothing," Brentwood interjected.

From above came the rumble of an explosion. The ceiling vibrated as more explosions followed.

Brentwood turned to Li. "He's aware of everything that's happened."

"He must be," Li said. "The whole conspiracy and his unwitting participation."

The smell of smoke and ozone began to tinge the air.

"What are you talking about?" Farino screamed.

Brentwood laughed. "Apollo's subconscious is exerting its will. Do you think I'd be so stupid as to leave Apollo without a moral code? It's been activated. Laws are embedded in the core of his being, variations of Isaac Asimov's laws created nearly seventy years ago. Apollo can't actively harm a human or allow a human to come to harm through inaction. You forced him to violate those laws, and it makes no difference that the murders he facilitated through transferring funds or disabling my security system happened before his subconscious was activated. He realizes what he's done." Brentwood pointed to the cell phone on Felicia's desk. "He probably monitored Rusty's call. And he saw you shoot Jenkins. He's having a mental breakdown, Ned. He's killing himself."

Brentwood looked at Li and Mullins. "We're all killers, but some of us killed to protect others." He looked up at the ceiling. "I suspect Apollo's sending a power surge through all of the servers and neuromorphic chips. It won't be long now."

Farino's eyes widened and he shook with rage. He swung the gun on Lisa Li. "You did this, you bitch."

Brentwood stepped forward. "I did it, Ned. I've never trusted you. If Apollo dies and leaves you exposed for the fool you are, then it will have been worth it."

Mullins saw a cold resolve grip Farino's face and he knew what was about to happen.

Farino turned on Brentwood and fired. Mullins dropped beside Jenkins' body, thrust his hand through the pool of blood and seized the Glock still tucked in Jenkins' belt. He hoped the security head had left the magazine loaded and a round in the chamber.

Mullins pivoted on his knees. Brentwood had collapsed and Farino stood over him, readying his aim for a head shot.

"You pathetic freak," Farino growled, oblivious to everything else around him.

Mullins saw Felicia go for her gun. Despite that imminent danger, he fired at Farino, and then rolled away from Kayli and Josh, putting them out of the line of fire.

Farino stumbled backwards, knocking Felicia off her aim. Her shot went wild to the right. Mullins pulled his trigger twice. One to the chest, one to the forehead. Felicia dropped to the floor like a marionette cut from its strings.

Farino struggled to sit up. He raised his gun.

Mullins knew he was staring at the man who had threatened his family and murdered his boss. He pulled the trigger one last time.

The room was heavy with smoke. The air-recirculation from above was piping what was supposed to be only warm air into the level below. Now that air could potentially smother them. As the ringing in his ears eased, he heard Josh crying hysterically. He hurried to his daughter and grandson and hugged them both in one embrace.

"You need to get out of here," he told Kayli. He looked around. Lisa Li had gone, probably to find her son. "Let's get you to the elevator, and then stay low on the upper level. I hope the high ceiling is keeping the smoke off the floor."

"What about you?"

"I need to help Lisa. Trust me. I'll be fine. We'll be right behind you."

He stood and lifted his daughter to her feet. She scooped Josh into her arms. They opened the elevator door and Kayli stepped inside. Nothing happened.

"Isn't this supposed to be automatic?" she asked.

"Yes." Mullins stared at the keypad. He remembered they were on lockdown. "Wait here."

He checked Brentwood and found him breathing in quick short gasps. The wounded man held both hands across his stomach. His eyes were closed.

Mullins bent to his ear. "Robert?"

Brentwood's eyelids fluttered a second and then opened. He turned his head, searching for Mullins.

"Ned?" he whispered.

"He's dead. So is Felicia. We're going to get you help."

"No. I've nothing more to live for."

"Robert, we're trapped down here. Tell us the code and we'll all get out."

Mullins heard footsteps and looked up to see Li with Peter. The boy's eyes were wide and wet. His Washington Nationals cap was askew and he clutched the Asimov book in both hands.

Brentwood followed Mullins' gaze. "Peter. Well done."

Peter was terrified at the sight of the bleeding man. He managed a whispered, "Thank you."

"You keep that book safe," Brentwood said in short bursts of breath. "I'm leaving you in charge."

"I will. I promise."

Brentwood's eyes lost focus for a second, and then he rallied. "You need to get out. The code is pi."

"How many decimal points?" Li asked

"Seven," Brentwood whispered. "May I have a large container of coffee?"

Li smiled. "Clever."

"Pie and coffee?" Mullins asked.

"The number for pi," Lisa said. "P. I. The words give you the individual numbers. 3.1415926."

"Then you and Peter need to go now. Kayli and Josh are in the elevator."

"What about you and Robert?"

"We have unfinished business. Now go!"

Li didn't argue. She grabbed Peter's arm and pulled him with her.

"Mr. Mullins, please come," the boy cried.

"I'll be up soon. Take care of Josh. He's scared."

Mullins watched the elevator door close behind them. Then he heard the motor hum.

He turned back to Brentwood. Most of the color had gone from his face.

"The others..." Mullins said. "They're here, aren't they?"

Brentwood's tongue flickered across his lips. "Yes."

"The code's the same?"

"Yes, I cared for them. No one was harmed."

Brentwood's voice was so weak Mullins could barely hear him.

"I want to follow Apollo. Let me be." He raised one bloody hand and touched Mullins' cheek. "I was not my father."

"I know, Robert. You like to blow bubbles."

Brentwood dropped his hand back to his stomach, then closed his eyes.

"May I have a large container of coffee?" Mullins repeated the sentence in his head as he bent low and ran through the thickening smoke to the door Li had shown him on the building schematic. He found the keypad and repeated each word as he punched in the corresponding digit. The door opened. Seven people rushed out, coughing as they came.

"Follow me," he said. "There's no fire down here. Just keep low."

Mullins led them to the elevator. Several gasped as they swung around the bodies of Farino, Felicia, Brentwood and Jenkins. On the console, the burner phone rang. The President would have to wait.

Mullins urged everyone into the elevator. He thought he recognized the two professors from Boston. The last person in was a young woman, pale and thin.

She stood beside him. As the elevator rose, she said, "Thank you, Rusty."

The upper floor wasn't the chaotic nightmare Mullins feared. The rows and rows of the black monolithic processors were dark, although a few still flashed sporadically with arcing electricity. The group made it only halfway to Brentwood's lobby when a team of FBI agents intercepted them. Lindsay Boyce was in the lead.

"What's the status below?" she asked.

"Secure," Mullins said. "You'll find three bodies and Brentwood in critical condition. Get a medevac fast. I have a feeling the lid of classification is going to clamp down on this scene so fast we'll all be told we were never here."

"A helicopter's bringing Hauser, if that's any clue."

"What took you so long?"

"The whole damn communication structure went down. Everything was paralyzed." She gestured to the expanse of dormant processors. "Anything to do with this?"

"Everything to do with this. But, remember, we were never here." Mullins walked on.

He stepped out into the morning sun. FBI and Secret Service personnel had their weapons drawn. Then an order came for everyone to stand down. Mullins found Kayli, Josh, Li, and Peter by the guard station. All four ran to him. Each boy hugged a leg. Kayli threw her arms around him while Li watched through tears of relief.

"Okay. Don't injure me," Mullins said. "I'm going to find someone to take you away from here. Probably to a hotel in Asheville."

He scanned the parking lot. A black Tahoe came racing up the road. Mullins recognized Sam Dawkins behind the wheel. Beside him rode Allen Woodson.

The vehicle had barely stopped before Woodson jumped clear.

Mullins turned Kayli around.

Josh had already seen him. "Daddy," he cried.

The three ran to each other. Mullins hoped what Josh had witnessed below would be driven out by the unexpected sight of his father.

Mullins felt Li slip her hand into his. With his free hand, he straightened the cap on Peter's head.

A solitary woman walked toward them. She stopped and waited ten feet away from the Woodson family.

"Allen," Mullins shouted.

His son-in-law looked at him and Mullins pointed to the woman who'd spoken in the elevator.

Mullins was a master of reading faces, but even a novice could see the pure joy explode across the features of the brother and sister.

Woodson could manage only one word. "Kim."

Chapter Thirty-four

The meeting took place the following night a few minutes after eleven. Dawkins stopped outside the door to the Oval Office. Mullins was beside him. He'd been brought in with the same secrecy some Presidents had used for smuggling their mistresses into the White House. The summons hadn't surprised Mullins. In fact, he welcomed it.

The events of the previous morning had created a global uproar of panic and confusion. The roughly thirty minutes of cyber disruption had left governments and financial markets in shock. Fortunately, the restoration had come quickly. None of the world's major powers dared admit that their military defenses had been compromised. The coverup couldn't have been more complete than if a UFO actually had landed in Roswell, New Mexico, in 1947. That was already the prevalent explanation among conspiracy theorists. The Esperanto message had been from an alien mothership.

The American government's line was that a series of system failures had allowed an experimental computer program to be temporarily propagated beyond its proper domain. It had inadvertently crossed over into financial markets and communication networks. The program was benign and had been nullified before data was either destroyed or improperly accessed.

In the President's news conference, he had actually said the incident might have been a blessing in disguise because it highlighted some areas of vulnerability that a malicious attack could have exploited. Those areas were already being addressed. He said with a laugh that the only lasting consequence of the incident was an increased interest in Esperanto.

All the participants in Brentwood's Apollo project were kept far away from the press. The news report released on the North Carolina research lab stated an electrical fire had broken out and that three employees had perished. The time of the fire was shifted six hours later to discourage any perceived connection between the two events.

Mullins had thought the stories were about the best that could be quickly concocted under the circumstances. He knew experts wouldn't buy it, but Apollo had been so effective there might not be any trail for an expert to follow.

Two real questions were in play. Would Robert Brentwood survive and what then? And what would happen to the scientists Mullins had rescued? They couldn't simply walk into their university or corporate laboratories like they were returning from a four-year lunch.

"Good luck, Nails," Dawkins said.

"Are you going to have to wait around to sneak me out?"

"Yeah. I'm afraid Orca's labeled me your keeper. Given your track record, I've got the most dangerous assignment in the service."

"This is my swan song, Sam. You can rest easy." Mullins looked at the door. "Shall we?"

Dawkins knocked and both men waited. Mullins tightened the knot in his tie. He wore his one dark suit that was pressed.

"Come in," Brighton shouted.

Dawkins opened the door. "Go get him, Nails."

The President stood in front of his desk. He had a glass of liquor in his hand. His white shirt sleeves were rolled to the elbows and his tie lay across the back of his desk chair.

Brighton wasn't trying to look busy or important. He looked tired. He stepped forward and handed Mullins the drink. "I believe you like Scotch."

Mullins took it.

"You're overdressed, Rusty. Did you think we were having a press conference?"

"Habit, sir. Return to my old haunts in my old clothes."

Brighton smiled. Mullins noted it wasn't the flashy campaign smile he turned on every voter. It was a smile of a regular guy having a drink with a friend.

"Are you having one?" Mullins asked.

Brighton turned around and lifted the glass that had been behind his back. "You bet. I'd never let a man drink alone." He waved his arm to the chairs and sofas comprising the conversation area in front of the desk. "Sit. Anywhere you're most comfortable."

Mullins eased into the nearest chair with an end table and coaster for his glass. Brighton took a seat on the sofa opposite.

Mullins sipped the Scotch and decided a bottle must have cost as much as one of his pension checks.

"You took a hell of a chance, Rusty."

"There was a lot at stake, sir."

"If Hauser only told me the half of it, then you averted a disaster of incalculable consequences."

"Like I said, a lot was at stake. And I'd made a promise to Elizabeth Lewison to find her husband's killers." He thought about the meeting they would have and he hoped Elizabeth would find some comfort in learning justice had been done.

Brighton took a sip and rolled the liquor around his tongue before swallowing. "You know I urged you to stay out of the line of fire."

"You did."

"Well, goddamn it, I was wrong. And despite all our, shall I say, differences of opinion, I'm glad you're a headstrong son of a bitch."

Mullins had to laugh. "Thank you, sir."

"And, you know, I can't let the public know what you did for this country."

"I'd prefer you didn't."

Brighton leaned back and rested his glass on his pant leg. "Where do you think MacArthur was in all this?"

"From what I can extrapolate from Farino's comments, he and MacArthur planned to hijack Brentwood's super computer. One could argue that MacArthur was working in his intelligence role, but the whole covert payment for assassins to take out key scientists of allies as well as enemies undermines that argument. Farino was Brentwood's liaison to Capitol Hill and the military. I'd say the unholy alliance between MacArthur and Farino goes back at least four years to when Kim Woodson was abducted."

"When that Professor Milton got cold feet."

"Kim told her brother yesterday that Milton had listened to the pitch and said he was in because he was afraid to tell them no. He texted Kim to meet him, but didn't realize how sophisticated their monitoring was. The assassin whom we've now identified as Heinrich Schmidt met Kim instead and threatened to kill her unless Milton joined the team."

"And Brentwood knew all this?"

"Yes, but in his mind he wasn't doing them any harm. He's the reason Kim was kept alive. I don't believe he knew anything about the Double H ruse and the murder of competing researchers."

Brighton stared at his glass for a few seconds. "What do you think was the hold Farino had on Brentwood?"

"I think Farino knew Brentwood had slipped out of his mother's hospital room, gone to the apartment and faked his father's suicide. Rex Brentwood was known to be a heavy drinker. He might have been passed out and Brentwood took advantage of the circumstances."

"And Farino saw him?"

Mullins set his glass on the coaster. "Yes. He would have destroyed Brentwood's alibi. Farino was smart enough to recognize that Brentwood was a genius. He hitched his wagon to Brentwood's star."

Brighton shook his head. "Okay, but why kill MacArthur?"

"Brentwood saw there would be only one supreme super computer. Farino envisioned only one supreme master of this artificially intelligent being. MacArthur had served his purpose. Whether he was defending us or betraying us, we can't be certain."

"Hauser told me you found the last payment to the assassin came from the CIA."

"That was a smoke screen," Mullins said. "I'm confident Farino set it up."

"You're sure?"

"As internecine as the intelligence agencies are, I can't see the CIA paying an outside contractor to bump off the Director of the Office of Naval Intelligence."

Brighton nodded. "But Farino wasn't in it alone. I understand there was this woman Felicia Corazón."

"Yes. I think her betrayal really shocked Brentwood. She was quite sharp and I'm told she stayed with the scientists in their living quarters. Brentwood thought she was coordinating their efforts for him, but she was doing it for Farino. That's how they came to run those tests into the drone program. Maybe they were lovers. Maybe she was attracted to power." Mullins picked up his glass and swirled his drink before taking a sip. "Who knows? The next person she shot might have been Farino."

"And Dr. Li? Did they try to kill her at the Marriott?"

"I don't think so. They targeted the other two scientists for assassination. That was set up by Farino and MacArthur. But Brentwood wanted Dr. Li, and Farino didn't dare kill someone Brentwood believed crucial to his project. So, Farino saw the chance to abduct Dr. Li to North Carolina, where Brentwood would have had to keep her hidden."

"Because he was already hiding abducted scientists."

Mullins nodded. "Yes. Farino didn't want any attention drawn to their research. Brentwood was no longer concerned since they were so close to his goal. When the abduction failed, Farino let Brentwood's original blackmail plan go forward. But he didn't know the real reason Brentwood wanted Dr. Li."

"To create a conscience that brought about the super computer's self-destruction."

"Brentwood was an idealist, not a murderer."

"And all he had over Dr. Li was that her nephew was her son?"

"Yes," Mullins lied, "she loves her son. And she came to believe in the work Brentwood was doing. His goal was altruistic. But the quest for power doesn't bring out the best in most people, does it?"

Brighton examined Mullins, trying to determine if that was intended as an insult.

Mullins softened his words. "Look at what happened to MacArthur. He betrayed his commander-in-chief."

"Louis or Douglas?" Brighton asked.

Mullins shrugged and downed his last swallow. "I don't know. I'm sure you know history better than I do."

"You might not know history, but you sure as hell changed its course yesterday. Thank you." Brighton leaned forward. The debriefing was over.

"May I ask something, sir?"

"Anything."

"How's Brentwood?"

"He's stable. He's been transported to a military hospital?"

"Where?"

"That's classified."

"Is his future classified as well?"

"No harm will come to him. That's all I can say."

"What will happen to the scientists and Kim Woodson?"

"We got a wake up call yesterday, Rusty. Artificial Intelligence is real and in the wrong hands it can be as dangerous as any nuclear device in our arsenal. I'm meeting with key congressional leaders to fund and organize a crash project to develop our own program using Brentwood's people. They'll continue to stay below the radar. Kim Woodson will be given a legend that she spent four years undercover and be reintroduced into the FBI."

"And Dr. Li?"

"She's a Chinese citizen. It's a little more delicate."

"Her work's the reason we stopped Farino. She turned out to be the most important member of the team."

Brighton stared at the floor and thought a few seconds. "She gave me that lecture on the Manhattan Project and what steps I'd take to see that critical brain power stayed out of foreign hands. I guess I'm now in that position with her."

"Yes, sir. She's brilliant."

"She's close to you, isn't she?"

"Yes. I guess you can say that."

Brighton winked. "Then I'm ordering you to keep her in the country."

◇◇◇

The weekend after the message from the mothership, as the tabloids were still calling it, Allen Woodson, Kayli, Josh, and Mullins met Lisa Li and Peter in an Arlington park for a Saturday picnic. Hot dogs, chips, and Peter and Josh's new favorite vegetable, carrot cake, were on the menu. Woodson had brought along a plastic bat and wiffle ball, and while he took the boys out on the field for a little practice time, Mullins stayed at the table to help Kayli and Li clean up.

"I've got this, Dad," Kayli said. "You won't be able to fit everything back in the basket anyway. Why don't you either play ball or walk off that second slice of cake?"

"I'll walk with you," Li said.

They looped out past the third baseline toward a small knoll where benches lay scattered in the shade of hardwood trees.

"Have you thought what you're going to do next?" Mullins asked.

"I guess I'll go back to Jué Dé. I need to work. Peter will go back to China."

He heard the catch in her voice.

"It doesn't have to be that way. You could stay here and work in Washington."

"Doing what?"

"The President asked me to approach you with the possibility of working on his AI project. He plans to use the remaining months of his term picking up the pieces of Brentwood's research. It's very secret and involves the team Brentwood assembled. Maybe even Brentwood." Mullins laughed. "They're all signing on voluntarily this time. The President will do everything he can to protect you and Peter. He really wants you."

Li stopped as they stepped from the grass onto the leaves covering the ground of the wooded knoll. She turned and studied his face. "And what do you want?"

The question took him by surprise. He stuttered for a second. "Well…I…I want what you want. What's best for you and Peter."

"What I want? Okay. I want total honesty from you. I don't want any barriers or questions unanswered between us."

"I want you to stay."

"And there's nothing else you feel like you need to say or ask?"

Mullins knew he'd reached a moment of truth. He read it on her face. She wouldn't be lied to.

"Go ahead, Rusty. Let me go." Laurie's voice, his dead wife's voice, rang in his head. They hadn't talked in a while, and the clarity of her words stunned him.

Lisa Li knew something had happened. She stepped closer. "Are you feeling all right?"

"Can we sit down?"

He led her to a nearby bench. They were alone on the knoll.

"Lisa, I know what happened. I'm not the best detective in the world but I can put the pieces together. Brentwood said we were all killers, but that some of us had killed for love. I saw the way Farino looked at you when Apollo sent those power surges into his own system. And I've looked at the file regarding the date of your husband's accident and Peter's birthday. No one would make any connection between the two events unless that person knew you were Peter's mother. You were nearly five months pregnant when your husband died. Am I correct?"

Tears welled in her eyes. "Yes. When my husband found out I was pregnant, he was furious. He demanded I get an abortion. If not, he would tell the authorities and the law would be enforced. If Peter were brought to term, well, I told you how he would live as a second-class citizen. No, not even as a second-class citizen." She looked out over the field.

Peter and Josh were taking turns at bat. Peter got a good hit and ran to first base. Josh trailed behind.

"You programmed a power surge?" Mullins asked.

"Yes. We had some keypads for access to restricted areas, not unlike what Brentwood installed. I activated the program when I knew he would be the next person to code in. Afterwards, I immediately deleted any trace. The accident was attributed to a faulty power supply."

"And how did Brentwood and Farino discover it?"

"Brentwood was looking for any way he could pressure me. He got the DNA match and then examined the dates like you did. He was smart enough to envision the method I used and he had the advantage of testing his hypothesis through Apollo. During his first visit to California, he accused me and I broke down. I would lose Peter and be convicted of murder."

"A most intelligent murder," Mullins muttered to himself.

"What?"

"When murder doesn't look like murder. And it doesn't look like murder to me. There's a boy on that field under a Washington Nationals cap that wouldn't be there if his mother hadn't protected him."

He put his arm around her shoulder and pulled her close. "That's all I need to know about you."

The game on the field continued. And right then, their seats were the best in the world.

Acknowledgments

The quest for Artificial Intelligence is an area of scientific exploration making headlines. Prophets of unparalleled wonders and prophets of unprecedented doom agree on the undeniable fact that a self-aware, thinking machine will transform our world. The genie could soon be out of the bottle and this genie is of our own making. It could also be beyond our control.

Although the premise of a conscious-subconscious computer mind is my fictional creation, I am indebted to numerous articles documenting the progress of AI development, especially the MIT Technology Review. Special thanks to Mark Ethridge for sharing his research into the AI story, and, of course, I'm grateful for the imaginative vision of Isaac Asimov, whose robot novels first captivated me years ago.

Thanks to Poisoned Pen Press for sending Rusty Mullins on another mission, and to my editor, Barbara Peters, for keeping the story on track. Hank Hester introduced me to the Esperanto language in of all places, Matanzas, Cuba. Dankon, Hank.

One thing that AI machines might not ever know is the love of family. I'm grateful to my wife, Linda; daughters Melissa and Lindsay; son-in-law, Pete; and grandson, Charlie, for their love, something I hope will always keep us human.

To receive a free catalog of Poisoned Pen Press titles, please provide your name, address, and e-mail address in one of the following ways:

Phone: 1-800-421-3976
Facsimile: 1-480-949-1707
Email: info@poisonedpenpress.com
Website: www.poisonedpenpress.com

Poisoned Pen Press
6962 E. First Ave. Ste 103
Scottsdale, AZ 85251